Something Chronic

Bob Cant

All persons appearing in this work are fictitious.
Any resemblance to real persons, living or dead,
is purely coincidental.

Published by Word Power Books 2013
43 – 45 West Nicolson Street
Edinburgh EH8 9DB
www.word-power.co.uk.

Printed and bound by Martins the Printers, Berwick upon Tweed.
Designed by Leela Sooben

British Library Cataloguing in Publication Data.
A catalogue record for this book is available from the British Library.
ISBN 978-0-9566283-6-7

'And far abune the Angus straths I saw the wild geese flee,
A lang, lang skein o' beatin' wings wi their heids towards
    the sea,
And aye their cryin' voices trailed ahint them on the air --- '
'O Wind, hae mercy, haud yer whisht, for I daurna listen mair!'

Violet Jacobs, The Wild Geese

January 1999

Less than ten miles from the urban certainties of Dundee, he felt as though he were on a different planet. Nothing but hedge-less, bare ploughed fields; it was a still winter day and the only sound of life was the haunting cry of a solitary peewit. The lack of any signposts implied that travellers should be familiar with their destination before they began their journey. The professor was very relieved to turn a corner on this road with no name and find himself in sight of an imposing stone farm-house. While he wasn't exactly the bearer of bad news, he was uncertain about the kind of welcome he might receive there.

No sooner had he touched the bell on the farmhouse door than he was greeted by a chirpy wee boy with a hairstyle resem-bling the bristles of an abandoned paintbrush.

'Hello, are you the professor that's come to tell us about my Uncle Euan's illness? I'm Gregor. My mum told me to wait by the door for you.'

Before he could respond, Professor MacIntyre was ushered into an over-polished and probably under-used sitting room with a view of the Sidlaw Hills in the distance.

'You can sit down, Prof. My mum and dad will not be long but you can look at the pictures in here while you're waiting. This picture is of my dad when he won the Tractorman of the Year Award at the Forfarshire Show in 1979. That other picture is my mum when she won the competition for the Farmer's Lass at the same time. That was when they met, just after Uncle Euan became ill.'

Gregor seemed willing to chatter away but he had never met

a professor before and he wasn't altogether clear what was expected of him.

The professor didn't spend a lot of time with young children and he too was at a loss about where to steer the discussion. 'What are you planning to do when you grow up, Gregor?' he asked lamely.

'Well, I'm only ten but Miss Carnegie – she's my teacher – she thinks that I could easily...'

'Gregor, where are you? Did I no' tell you to keep an eye out for Professor MacIntyre?'

A short, dark haired woman in an apron, which she had probably not planned to show to the world, entered the room ready for a fight with her son. The Farmer's Lass had metamorphosed into the Farmer's Wife.

'Mrs Saddler, I am Professor MacIntyre. Gregor has just been showing me some of your family photos. He has been most interesting and very hospitable.'

Wilma Saddler laughed nervously and the hand that had been about to strike Gregor's head was instead proffered to welcome her guest; she attempted to use the other hand to dispense with the apron. Gregor, not bearing grudges, took the opportunity to retrieve and hide the unwanted garment behind a sofa.

'Did you have a pleasant journey out from Dundee?' She continued to laugh.

At this point, three middle-aged men of medium build in almost identical grey-brown suits came into the room; they all looked as though they would have preferred staying outside.

'This is my husband, Alistair,' said Wilma, introducing the only one who seemed to have any experience of physical labour. She laughed again.

'Aye,' said Alistair, 'I'm Euan's older brother.' He sighed as if this was just one of the many responsibilities thrust upon him by an unfair world.

The two other men introduced themselves as the family's minister and the family's bank manager. The minister's offer to say a few words of prayer was ignored by everyone.

'Anyway,' said the professor, clearing his throat, 'it's good to meet you all at last. I'm sorry that I wasn't able to be there when you visited Euan. I'm not sure how familiar everyone is with the situation regarding your brother, Mr Saddler. Perhaps it would be helpful if, for purposes of clarification, I provided some of the background to his case history. I hope that seems acceptable to everyone?'

'I think we can start,' he said, 'back in 1978, Euan had finished school and was ready to go to university but he decided to visit his sister, Irene, who was working in Kenya at the time. There were no problems while he was there but on his return, early in 1979, he complained of tiredness and headaches over a period of weeks.'

'He never liked work,' Alistair interjected.

'But nothing untoward occurred until 2nd March 1979 when he went to the polling station to cast his vote in the referendum on Home Rule,' continued the professor in a very deliberate manner.

'He was aye big on things like that,' said Alistair, obviously irritated by the whole repetition of the story of his brother's illness. 'There's no need to be meddling with things, bloody waste of money.' Wilma was frowning at him now.

'Uncle Euan went to vote with his friend, Andy Buchan,' Gregor added, 'but nobody knows what's happened to him.'

'Anyway,' said the professor, ignoring these remarks, 'he collapsed just after he'd cast his vote and had to be taken to hospital in Dundee. It took a long time to work out a diagnosis; at first, we thought it was a recurrence of the sleeping sickness epidemic of the 1920s but there were distinct differences. It also transpired that several hundred Africans in Kenya and neighbouring Tanzania had fallen ill at the same time. We are still hard put to categorise it precisely but, to all intents and purposes, we can say that it is a new form of sleeping sickness.'

'So tragic,' said the minister, 'but who are we poor mortals to question the workings of the Lord?'

Wilma drew a deep breath and shook her head.

The professor was clearly used to this kind of interruption and paused very briefly before proceeding. 'What was undoubtedly tragic was that this young man was to spend the next twenty years of his life asleep in an institution with very little contact with the outside world. Frankly, no one thought that he would ever recover. It was only due to the development of new drugs that he was able to regain consciousness and make a tentative return to the world. Which brings us to where we are today: how is Euan to be assisted to resume his life?'

'And what's to be done about this business of him mistaking folk for objects?' asked Alistair. 'When Wilma and me went to see him, he thought she was a kettle! I mean to say, a KETTLE. What's to be done about that?' He was more than irritated now.

There was a pause in the discussion. No one really had an answer.

Gregor piped up: 'Amanda's my sister and she says that if he was to mistake me for anything, it would probably be a bumble bee!'

'The confusion,' the professor explained very deliberately, 'between humans and objects, is one of the symptoms of his condition. As he recovers, we expect that he will regain his social memory and we don't yet know whether these incidences of confusion will disappear or whether he will feel more subject to the social constraints that we all experience. We don't yet understand how he perceives either himself or the world around him. The fact of the matter is that we are very unclear about his prospects for a full recovery; the drugs are very new and there could be any number of side-effects. In the short term, we will have to monitor developments very closely to establish how, if at all, he can be assisted to resume his old life.'

Everyone was sitting quietly, waiting to hear the details of the professor's plan for Euan.

'We have been fortunate enough to make contact with the Kerbit Trust which has agreed to pay the cost of his accommodation at the Wedderburn Centre, a residential care facility in Broughty Ferry, for a period of three years. They will also pay him a modest living allowance for the same period. We have no way of knowing how his intellectual capabilities will have been affected by the illness but neither is there anything to suggest that they have been damaged.

'Furthermore, they have agreed to pay for the costs of a personal psychologist who will provide daily support and monitor and review his progress thoroughly. We have been very lucky to have obtained the services of an exceptionally well-qualified psychologist, Haris Jakupovic. He has a first degree and a Masters from Edinburgh University.'

'Well, professor, I suppose you're the expert,' sighed Alistair, looking miserably out of the window. 'I'll bow to your wisdom but I don't see how you need to be getting somebody with fancy degrees when you could have got some kind of a nurse; there's loads of married women round here looking for a bit of part-time work. Wilma's cousin used to work in an old folks' home, she'd be just the ticket.' He hated discussing things where the conclusions were already obvious to anyone with any common sense.

'Euan really does require very intensive treatment and care that can only be provided by a fully trained psychologist. Haris has an enormous amount of experience working with people overcoming traumatic situations.'

'And what about the money side?' asked Alistair. 'That's why I asked our friend from the bank to come along and discuss how the finances are to be handled and bills paid and so forth.'

'Most of the finance will go directly from the Kerbit Trust to the Wedderburn Centre. Haris will support him in the management of his allowance; we are not talking about substantial sums of money, more on a par with a student grant.'

'But I've prepared an information package for him with advice about investment opportunities and so forth,' said the exasperated banker. His face turned a bright red; he muttered that he would have to go to another meeting and left the room abruptly.

'Well,' said Wilma, greatly relieved that she and her family would not be expected to have day to day responsibility for the support of Euan. 'Perhaps we could all have a cup of tea while we think over what you've been saying.' She headed off to the security of her kitchen.

'Gregor, you away and help your mother and your sister get the tea ready – make yourself useful,' barked Alistair.

'Amanda and me discussed this earlier. I made the sandwiches and she is making the tea; she'll pour out the tea and I'll hand out the sandwiches because I'm smaller than she is; I don't have obesity problems and so I'm less likely to bump into folk. It's what Miss Carnegie calls division of labour.'

'I'll gie you division of labour, you wee whippersnapper.'

A loud unfamiliar roar from the farmyard startled everyone; the roar was followed by a series of high-pitched squeals. Gregor, freeing himself from the threat of parental discipline, ran towards the window. 'It's an elephant, it looks like one of the elephants from the zoo! It's going mad and the man from the bank is running away. I don't think he knows where he's going but for a man of his age, he's running very fast.'

Pandemonium ensued as they rushed to see the banker dodging

his way between a combine harvester and a tractor. A grim-faced Alistair rushed outside, acknowledged that it really was an elephant and rushed straight back in again. 'Dial 999, somebody, there's an elephant in my farmyard! Dial 999, NOW!'

The professor and the minister were left alone in the sitting room, unsure of what to think or what to say to each other.

'Perhaps, I could say a few words of prayer,' said the minister, 'to ask the Lord to give us comfort during this unfortunate happening.'

A wide-eyed Gregor emerged from the kitchen. 'The elephants are going mad, they've started smashing up cars and...'

All thoughts of prayers were put aside as the adults, knocking aside the innocent messenger, sprinted outside to ascertain the fate of their own clearly much loved vehicles.

A newsflash could be heard coming from the kitchen radio. 'Breaking news, breaking news, this is Angelica Menmuir from Sidlaw Radio with some breaking news. We have been informed that two elephants named Jumbo and Dumbo have escaped from Dundee International Zoo, commonly known as the Diz; they are heading out to the countryside in the area around Balkerro. We are asking everyone to go indoors and make themselves as secure as possible until further notice. People should not try to speak to them or feed them. Do not approach Jumbo and Dumbo. I repeat, do not approach Jumbo and Dumbo. These elephants are very angry and distressed and their behaviour is quite unpredictable. The special armed emergency services have been called to the scene; there may well be elephant blood in the fields of Angus before the end of the day. This is Angelica Menmuir signing off your breaking news story. Please take very great care. The elephants are very angry.'

2

Euan's notebook 12th January 1999

I had a notebook in primary school and I remember writing my name and address on the cover – Euan Saddler, Balkerro, near Dundee, Angus, Scotland, Great Britain, Europe, The World, The Universe. I wonder what happened to that. I suppose I could put my new address on the cover of this notebook – Euan Saddler, Wedderburn House, Dalhousie Crescent, Broughty Ferry, Dundee.

One part of me thinks that I don't need to include all the stuff about The World; but seeing as how I have no idea where I've been for the last twenty years, maybe I should include everything, just to remind myself that I've come back to reality. I'm supposed to have had sleeping sickness but it would make just as much sense to say that I'd been kidnapped by Martians. Maybe I'll just not bother with the address. The important thing is that I'm back.

I really don't know what's going on here. I know that I'm living in some kind of residential centre and I've got my own bedroom and sitting room and bathroom. It's a big house with its own grounds. Most of it was built about a hundred years ago; there is a big new extension but I live in the older part. I don't know a lot about it but I do know that it's not a hospital. I have more space to myself here. I spend a lot of time with Haris; he's a psychologist. He has long dark hair and he's from Sarajevo. The man who cleans my room is from Somalia; he's called Sam but he says that's not his real name. There's a physiotherapist called Moira and I see her every other day. There's a receptionist called Heather who's always getting into trouble for smoking at work.

People are very kind but they all keep on and on asking questions. First thing in the morning, till last thing at night. And they always smile, whatever I say even when I just make up an answer out of politeness. They tell me that I'm on an experimental new treatment for sleeping sickness but, even though I can understand the words that they use, a lot of the time I've no idea what they're talking about. Haris says that if anything isn't clear or if I remember something that I don't understand then I should just ask him about it. He gave me this notebook to write down anything that's interesting or confusing when he's not around. He seems very kind and I think it'll be very easy to ask him about stuff.

This morning, however, I had a strange experience and I feel a bit embarrassed about asking him about this. I actually had a visitor about 5 o'clock. I had not long woken up and was thinking how quiet it was. The silence here is one of the things I like because it's very relaxing and nobody's asking questions. Then I heard a kind of rustling sound just near the curtains. It sounded like I imagine a ghost would sound; just a low 'whoosh' sort of noise. I must have spoken aloud because the next thing I heard was this voice speaking to me.

'There *are* ghosts, young man. You're quite right.' The ghost in question was a tall, elegant woman with her hair in some kind of a bun that I seem to remember has a French-sounding name. It was difficult to guess her exact age but she must have been over fifty, at least. Really old. She wore a beige dress that gave no hint of the natural shape of her body and she reminded me of black and white films that I used to watch on TV on Sunday afternoons. She was a bit like Ingrid Bergman or Barbara Stanwyck.

'You mean to say that you're dead? You're a ghost, a real ghost?' I didn't feel very subtle at that point.

'I am Edith Syme, Mrs Alexander Syme. This was my room many years ago and this was where I died. It has wonderful views, over the Tay towards Newport and out of the side windows towards Carnoustie. All those years when we were in India – my husband was with Scrymgeour's Jute in Calcutta – I dreamed of retiring to Broughty Ferry because I had grown up near here. We came back in 1947 but we had only been back two years when Alex died very suddenly. Heart attack. After he died, I used to spend a lot of time in this room. Eventually, I began to feel comfortable here and that helped me to put everything into perspective.'

'So, you became quite happy here?'

'I suppose I did. This house was far too big for two elderly people but we had got used to a certain standard of living in India and we wanted it to continue here. I was used to having lots of servants but that was just not possible in Dundee. I did have a wonderful housekeeper called Agnes Devlin, a widow from Tealing. It was the same back in India; the people from the countryside were always much more reliable than the city folk. She and I established a routine to our lives that suited us both. She had no grandchildren of her own but I had five and she helped me to enjoy spending time with them.'

I think I must have frozen at that point because I could think of nothing else to say.

'I am going to leave you now. I can see that I have startled you. Sometimes, I come here just to look at the view first thing in the morning. Sometimes, the people in the room let me in but often they don't. I am grateful that you did; you are obviously not afraid of the unknown. I don't go where I'm not welcome but I feel that I'm welcome with you. If you want to speak to me again, all you need to do is call out my name and if the atmosphere is right, I'll appear. Don't worry, I won't be bothering you every day. I just enjoy seeing the sunrise now and again. I hope that you'll soon be well and maybe the atmosphere in this room will even help you towards recovery.'

I was wide awake once she'd gone. I knew that my conversation with her was not a dream and I was debating to myself whether or not to record it in the notebook. Meeting a ghost feels like the kind of thing that you should put in a notebook but then again, it could be dangerous. I don't want anybody thinking I'm going mad and I definitely don't want to be sent back to an institution like the one I'd just left. But if I didn't write it down, it's possible I could forget all about it. And if she comes back, I might not know what to say to her if I haven't written it down. I'd nearly forgotten her name already.

No one is going to believe this. Me! Talking to a ghost. I don't know whether to tell Haris or not but first, I need to write it down. It makes no sense at all but nothing else does either.

3

There was a plethora of opinions about how to restore Euan to full health. Everyone agreed that the drug that had rescued him from the world of sleep was miraculous but that was where the agreement ended. Those of a pessimistic frame of mind predicted that its effects would soon diminish and that he was doomed to return to the life of a cabbage. 'It'll no' be lang now, oh no.' Others were drawn to more hopeful approaches and claimed that he could enjoy a long and healthy life, if only he were to base his diet on juice extracted from the bark of a tree found in the forests of Ecuador. Some believed that what was needed was a combination of tranquillisers and pain killers. Alistair and Wilma were of a traditional mindset and thought it best to leave it all to the doctors; they resisted all attempts by the minister to organise a day of prayer for Euan.

Meanwhile, Colin MacIntyre and Haris Jakupovic decided that the most secure treatment was an integrated programme of education, relaxation, exercise and gentle stimulation. Haris was to spend several hours a day in Euan's company, and he would monitor developments and change the pace of the programme as required. Euan was easily exhausted and sometimes slept for several hours a day, but as his condition improved, Haris encouraged him to be more active. It had been his idea for Euan to keep a notebook in which to record his thoughts and his memories.

It was also Haris's idea to take Euan on walks to stimulate his memory about places he had visited with his family when he was younger. One dry, clear day in February, they set off to visit the city centre where he had often gone shopping with his mother. Haris parked his car near the old dockside in Exchange Street. A graffito on a wall above the car read: **Dundee is not Stalingrad** but they were both so absorbed in wrapping themselves up for their little adventure that it went unnoticed.

As they strolled up Castle Street, Euan recalled various places from his past. He pointed out the old pie shop to Haris; the aroma of freshly roasted beans from the Quaker coffee house reminded him that coffee had been one of his mother's little treats; the bank at the top of the street had a magnificent dome that had seemed to him, as a child, to be palatial. Across the main street was the big clock outside the jeweller's shop that had been, and still was, a popular meeting place; he had always been told that if he ever became separated from his parents, he was to go there and wait until they came to fetch him; he had never had to do that but Alistair had been found there several times. Euan remembered Reform Street but the shops had changed so much that he didn't recognise any of them. He went into a building society to ask if it used to be a men's outfitters. The receptionist was startled, 'I'm a clerk, not a historian,' he uttered, before sending Euan on his way.

He recognised the grand, neo-classical building at the top of the street and drew Haris's attention to it.

'Was that your old school?' Haris asked.

'No, this is the High School, it was supposed to be a bit of a school for snobs. I went to the Harris.'

'Sorry?'

'My school was the Harris Academy – H – A – R – R – I – S – not like the way you spell your name. So, it wasn't named after you or even in advance of you. It was a funny thing about secondary schools in Dundee. Harris Academy was known as the Harris, Grove Academy was the Grove, Morgan Academy was the Morgan and the High School was just the High. Their names were all shortened in the same way.'

Haris was interested in the way that this detailed memory seemed to have appeared from nowhere. 'So, this is a special Scottish way of speaking, is it?'

'I think it's special to Dundee. You don't find it in Aberdeen or Edinburgh or anywhere else, as far as I know. It's a particular Dundee form of English.'

'I did not know that.'

'I'm glad you're able to learn something from me for a change. I like it better if it's not a one-way street.' Euan smiled to himself.

It started to rain and Haris suggested that they pop into a café for a cup of tea but that visit was curtailed when the woman behind the counter took umbrage at Euan calling her a teabag. To avoid the continuing rain, they went into a museum where they soon found themselves looking at a photographic exhibition of old Dundee. The photographs were mostly of a time before Euan had even been born but they both enjoyed looking at images of the old jute industry, trams and public holidays, all populated by short Dundonians of many ages. As they proceeded through the art galleries, Haris was delighted to discover a collection of beautifully detailed paintings of Dundee and Angus.

'These pictures remind me of Bruegel,' he remarked. He spent a long time examining them.

'These paintings are by Mackintosh Patrick,' Euan explained. 'He was a great favourite of my mum's and there was one about a farm in winter that we used to have in the living room at home. Well, it was a copy, she didn't actually have the real thing. Maybe Alistair kept it.'

'Were these paintings of places that you knew when you were growing up?' asked Haris, as he moved back into psychologist mode.

'Not exactly. The pictures had the names of real places, like Kinnordy Hill or Mains of Gray but when you went to see these places, they were not identical to what you saw in the pictures.'

'So, he used his imagination to paint them.'

'That's right. The pictures were of real places; they weren't just fantasy pictures; they were places as seen through his eye. He wasn't trying to take a photograph. It made me realise that it was important for an artist to have an imagination of his own. He wasn't just doing a carbon copy. Me and Andy used to come here sometimes when we were skipping a class. But he never painted landscapes like this; he was more interested in the human body. He read some art theory explaining that artists were in dialogue with the objects that they were painting. The art teacher was having none of it and told him that dialogue was fine and good for artists that had served their apprenticeships but that did not include us; I can still hear that typical teacher's voice saying: "Just learn your craft, Buchan, learn your craft"; he was so sarcastic.'

Haris was fascinated by this conversation, both for the memories of this Dundee artist and his friend, Andy. But before he could ask anything more, he noticed that Euan had become withdrawn. Just at that moment, two security guards appeared; one was small and fat and the other was tall and thin. Keen to avoid Euan getting involved in another case of objectification, Haris rushed him into the gents' toilet and washed his face. It might have been contrary to psychological codes of practice but it did the trick and Euan came back into the real world.

When they came out of the gents, they were both rather hungry and they went into the museum café which revelled in the name of THE SPINNER'S REST but some Dundee wise guys had succeeded in deleting some of the letters so that it read THE INNER PEST. Euan was very keen to see if they had any

Millionaires' Shortcake which was, Haris surmised, as effective a way of rotting your teeth as any he had encountered.

Having survived the INNER PEST, Euan seemed invigorated and intent on going further. They walked along Meadowside, past a building with lots of delivery vans parked outside, and then turned right up Constitution Road.

'Euan, what is a bridie?' Haris sounded puzzled.

'A bridie is a meat pie that was invented in Forfar. It contains mince and onions prepared in a special way. It also has a peculiar shape – a bit like a horseshoe. Why do you want to know that? You still feeling hungry?'

'No. You just called that man at the bus stop a bridie!'

'I wonder why I did that; he's a very ordinary-looking man. Should I go back and apologise to him?'

'I do not think that he even heard you. He was listening to music through his headphones. And he does not look at all like a bridie.' Haris was about to say that he reminded him more of a long, thin salami but he stopped himself just in time.

Haris would have been happy to turn back but Euan was having none of it; it was a gloriously crisp, clear day for walking and they headed upwards past an old graveyard and infirmary. They moved into an area of well-built streets and crescents where more prosperous Dundonians had moved to enjoy the views and the fresh air, away from the dirt and the dust that had made them rich.

Euan explained that he used to know this area very well because this was where his friend, Andy, had lived when they were both at school. Haris was frustrated by all these references to Andy Buchan; he had gone to the trouble of looking up the name in the phone book but no one was called Buchan in this part of the city. He intended to investigate this more fully but now he was concentrating on making it to the top of the Law

Hill. Euan had definitely got some kind of second wind after they left the art gallery but Haris had not been so lucky. He felt rather pathetic about being so breathless and feeling so generally unhealthy.

'Stop peching, Haris, we're nearly there.'

'Nearly where?' he gasped.

'We're near the top of the world. You can write down in your notebook that we reached the top of the world. Andy and me used to come up here a lot when we were teenagers and we wanted to get away from interfering old folk. You feel like you can see the whole world up here; the bridges over the river, the factory chimney that looks like it should be somewhere in Italy, we used to call it the Big Lum; the streets of Lochee. I always liked the sight of all those folk scurrying about, whether they were on foot, on their bikes, in buses or in their cars. They were just getting on with their lives, going to work, going home, going out to enjoy themselves. On a clear day like this, you can almost hear the buzz of their lives. I've been away but I want to get back into that buzz and be part of it again. What do I feel today, Haris? I feel that I AM ON TOP OF THE FUCKING WORLD.'

4

Euan's notebook 16th February 1999

Some days I can feel my head spinning; there's so much to learn and so much to catch up on. I feel more awake than I did a few weeks ago but that doesn't mean that things are really that much easier. What it means is that I know how difficult it is to do what I'm trying to do. I get really fed up of folk talking to me in slow, soft tones; but then when they do start to talk naturally, I sometimes don't know what they're talking about. There seem to be a lot of strange new words around. What's a laptop? Or a control freak? Or a ceedee? Or body language? And what's a neo-con? I used to be interested in politics but that's difficult too. I asked somebody one day what it was about Margaret Thatcher that seemed to rile everybody. I thought that we were having an intelligent conversation but as soon as I said that, the slow, soft tones reappeared and I was told not to worry myself about things like that. It was as if I was too young to be bothering myself with somebody like that, although she seems to have bothered everyone I've met.

I spend a lot of time every day with Haris and I enjoy that. It's very relaxed and he always makes sure that I'm doing something that's good for my health and my memory. He wants me to get used to being near real people (as opposed to doctors and nurses and psychologists!) and we often go into local cafés to have a cup of tea or something. Nobody in any of the cafés in Dundee speaks in the slow, soft tones that could drive me demented. I'm always aware that he's my psychologist but he is very friendly and sometimes we just chat about things, like old friends do. Maybe, of course, he writes about these conversations in his notebook too. I suppose that's his job.

He arranged some meetings with Alistair and Wilma and we've been out to Balkerro a few times. I enjoy going there and revisiting my old home and walking around the farm does help to remind me of wee things that used to be part of my everyday life. I think Haris is a bit disappointed that Alistair and I are not able to talk more openly with each other but then we were never very close, anyway. He was a few years older than me and he was always our father's blue-eyed boy. Definitely a bit of sibling rivalry there. It's not that Alistair's a shit but there just isn't much of a foundation to build things on. I asked him once if he knew what had happened to Andy Buchan but he just shook his head, as if my question was somehow beneath him. Conversation might be easier with my sister, Irene, and I hope that she'll soon come over from New York. Apparently, she did come when I first woke up but I don't have any memory of that.

It actually feels easier to have conversations with people that I don't know very well because I have fewer concerns about what might have gone on between us in the past. I enjoy spending time with my niece, Amanda, and my nephew, Gregor. She's fifteen and he's ten. They are both much more independent and open-minded than I would have been at their ages. Gregor has decided, or maybe he's been told, that listening to music is good for me and so he's made up some tapes of music that he thinks I might remember. The one he brought me last weekend was a real cracker – Gladys Knight and Dionne Warwick, who are on all the tapes he makes for me, as well as Kenneth McKellar, The Jam, Patti LaBelle, Van Morrison, Elton John and Tchaikovsky. He emphasised that he knew that I wasn't alive at the time of Tchaikovsky but he wanted to put some classical music on the tape. I asked him where he found all this music and he explained that he goes round to his friends' homes and borrows tapes and records from their parents. He says that they are all very helpful when they know that he's doing it for the sake of his uncle's health but sometimes they become very embarrassing when they're talking about their youth. I didn't say this to Gregor but I'm envious of the fact that they, unlike me, have youthful indiscretions to be embarrassed about.

I enjoy talking to the staff here too. Sam, the cleaner, is always very pleasant and seems to enjoy chatting about small, everyday things. The other day, he began to tell me that he comes from Somalia and that he used to be a primary school teacher. I tried to ask him some more questions but he said, very politely, that he had a lot of work to do. He was slightly distant the next day, so I obviously have to be careful not to ask him too many questions.

The other folk that are easy to talk to are the ghosts. I was sitting quietly in the garden one day, when I found myself facing a handsome, jet-black haired man wearing a collar-less shirt; he was in his early twenties and very short, probably not much more than five foot tall. Most of his teeth seemed to be rotten but the way he smiled suggested that he was not embarrassed about that in the way that I would have been. He introduced himself as Joe Devlin and he explained that he used to be the gardener at this house before the First World War.

'See, eh never realised but that wiz the best time o' meh life. Eh wiz still biding at hame but eh hid a job and pals and eh wiz courting tae. Then the war cam along and eh wiz in uniform beh October and we wiz oot in Flanders jist three weeks efter that. Eh joined up wi meh pals, ye ken; we volunteered and we jist couldnae wait tae hae a go at the gerries. It wiznae like we hated them. We aw kent that we had tae defend Belgium but, mair than onything else, we jist wanted tae hae a go. It wiznae lang, though, afore we realised jist what we let oorselves in for. A laddie that eh went tae school wi' wiz killed on the second day we were there. But the wan that really got tae me wiz Tam, ye ken. He lived just across the landing frae us; we went tae school thegither; we got oor first jobs thegither; we got pished thegither. And when eh wiz courting a lassie ca'ed Aggie, he wiz courting her pal. We were like brithers, ye ken. Eh saw him killed right in front o' meh face.'

He shook his head but he seemed to decide not to tell me any more about his friend's death. 'Nothing wiz ever the same efter that.'

I wasn't sure where to go next but he didn't go away and so I supposed that he wanted to talk a bit more; after a couple of minutes of silence, I asked him about his life before he went off to the war.

'Eh'd lived in the same hoose in Lochee aw meh life. Eh kent a-body in meh close and eh had loads o' pals; we went tae the same school thegither, ye ken, and then we went tae the fitba thegither. Eh must hae been aboot twelve when eh went tae the first game that Dundee Hibernian played at Tannadice Park. They were a grand new club and they were playing against another club ca'ed Hibernian that wiz frae Edinburgh. Efter that, eh went tae as mony of their matches as eh could. Me and Tam baith got jobs, ye ken, and so sometimes we went on the train tae see them when they were playing awa frae hame and we were aye there when they were playing in Dundee.'

He was enjoying talking about this and, even though I didn't know much about football, I enjoyed listening to him. I was getting a bit cold but I had no desire to go indoors; I was glad of the warmth of my thick woollen jacket. He changed the subject, quite suddenly, and began talking about a circus that he had once seen.

'Eh mind a braw day oot that me and Aggie hid wi Tam and his lass. There wiz a circus cam tae the Magdalen Green every summer and we went alang tae hae a look, jist a couple o' weeks afore the war began. There wiz twa boys that was ca'ed the Bellini Brothers – acrobats, ye ken – up in the air on their trapezes.

Eh could hardly believe it when wan o' them let go o' his trapeze and he seemed to be fallin doon but his brother caught him in mid air. It couldnae hae been mair than a split second but we wiz a' standin wi our mooths open like a bunch o' dafties, ye ken. Ag began tae shiver and eh took a haud o' her and made her feel fine. Eh said tae Tam efterwards that it wiz the best, the maist amazin, the maist excitin thing eh'd ever seen in meh life.'

He paused there and went into his own thoughts, perhaps about the life that he'd never had, about the exciting things that had never happened to him or maybe just about the circus. I remembered how Mrs Syme, the first ghost, had said that she felt comfortable with me and I hoped that, even though he was quiet, Joe was feeling the same way. He was the one who resumed the conversation.

'There is one wee favour ye can dae fir me, Euan. Eh wonder if ye hae ony whisky. Eh'm no able tae drink it but eh'm able tae smell it and eh jist fancy the smell o' some real whisky.'

I had to disappoint him. I'd hardly ever drunk whisky and I felt sure that I would be told that it was inappropriate and untimely for me to have alcohol in my room. But I promised Joe that I would get some for him. He told me that if I wanted to summon him again, all I needed to do was go somewhere private, close my eyes and mutter his name. As soon as I'd bought a bottle – well, it was actually a quarter bottle – I decided to summon him back in my room, where I could lock the door. He was very, very pleased. He was also pleased to hear that Dundee Hibernian had survived all those years, under a different name, and won a few cups along the way.

Both the ghosts I had encountered had been strangers. I was a bit nervous about talking to them but I wasn't scared. Maybe I was stronger than I had realised. Maybe too, it was easier to talk to folk that had no memory of me before I fell ill with no preconceptions on either side.

5

Education was a central part of Euan's recovery programme. The organisation of formal classes was fairly easy but the informal bits of education were rather more haphazard. Unpredictable stimuli popped up here, there and everywhere. Who was to say what was interesting, informal learning and what was a damaging exposure to reality? These were difficult questions and some people either assumed that they knew the answers already or they avoided discussing them; other people held endless meetings on learning strategies and the development of targeted action plans. Euan continued to learn, regardless.

Everyone agreed that Euan should be introduced to the technological world that had grown so quickly in his absence. While there were computers at the Wedderburn Centre, Haris thought that there would be additional social benefits if Euan were to enrol on a course where he would meet other students; he discovered a part-time course called New Beginnings at the Flukergate Centre. He was computer literate himself but he enrolled along with Euan so he could support him through any difficult social situations that might arise. Euan's growing curiosity was such that he asked people the sort of questions often deemed unaskable, even though everyone might want to know the answers.

Within ten minutes of starting on the course, Euan had asked one of his fellow students, a tall glamorous blonde in very tight-fitting jeans and top, why she had such large breasts.

'You dinna waste time, dae ye?' she laughed loudly. 'And ye look so quiet. Eh've aye had big boobs and three years ago, eh went for the operation tae mak them bigger. It wiz tae keep a man happy but that wiz a waste o' time; he fucked off with a sixteen year old while eh wiz still in hospital; said he wiz lonely.

But eh fairly enjoy them now. Eh used tae be called Cathy but now a'body calls me Dolly. Pleased tae meet you, Euan.'

'Pleased to meet you, Dolly.'

They soon became great friends and Dolly introduced him to the other girls. He and Haris were the only two men on this course and they had already been the object of considerable gossip. The girls knew, like everyone in Dundee, that he was the man who had suffered from sleeping sickness for twenty years and there were probably lots of questions that they wanted to ask. But they had one unspoken rule among themselves; no questions about the past. Some of these women had been abused by their husbands; some had been on hard drugs; done time in prison; others had been on the game. In fact, the no-question rule suited Euan just fine because it meant that they did not pry into his past. They just wanted everybody to relax and have a laugh together.

The girls seemed to enjoy nothing more than talking about the television programmes they watched, makeover programmes, cookery programmes, hospital dramas, late-night movies. TV was now available twenty-four hours a day and Euan wondered if the world had been taken over by voyeurs. They were all hooked on soaps; they knew that their teacher would get irritated if they left their computers and so they all just shouted at each other across the room, like their grannies in the jute mills would have done; sometimes they would have one conversation about three soaps simultaneously.

'Of course, she didna recognise her ain son at first, efter he had a face transplant...'

'Whit eh dinna understand is how come Tallon didna realise that her man wiz hae'in an affair wi his ain sister...'

'Her marriage wiz goin fine till she met that gym instructor frae Brazil...'

Euan had some vague memories of soap characters like Elsie Tanner and Hilda Ogden from *Coronation Street*; he recalled his mother talking about *The MacFlannels*. But when he heard these conversations, he wondered if he'd been ill for two hundred years; this was no memory problem, it was just another world. When he looked confused, they started to mother him and explain the storylines.

'Whit programmes dae ye like, Euan?' asked Dolly.

'No' sure, really. I've got a TV but I'm no' very bothered about watching it – I used to enjoy *Doctor Who…*'

'The doctor! Doctor Hooo! Meh god, Euan. Ye'll be telling me ye only hiv a black and white telly next. Me and the girls will help ye tae get a bit mair up tae date like.'

They brought in videos of programmes that they had recorded for him and they highlighted programmes in the local paper that they thought might interest him.

'Hiv u seen that sports quiz, Euan?' asked a short blonde woman. 'You can learn a lot aboot sport if yir trying to catch up, ken. It's a grand laugh as well. They hae wee games whaur ye hae to recognise fowk frae photographs of separate parts of their body.'

'Eh, but it's a bit oan the tame side,' said her tall dark-haired friend, 'eh mean tae say, it's aw aboot photos o' noses or ankles; there's never ony o' the mair interesting body parts.'

'Did you see that lad that wiz oan it last week?' asked the woman sitting next to her. 'Ye ken that wee jockey that had seven rides aw in one day…'

Dolly explained, through the raucous laughter, that what her friend probably meant was the jockey had won seven races on the same day.

'Eh, Dolly, that's whit eh meant, and fur aw you ken, maybe he *did* hae seven rides. Eh'm jist trying tae help Euan catch up wi the times.'

'Oh, fuckawaywiye, Euan's ower big tae be a jockey!' said a woman who spent a lot of time at the bookies.

'Aye, weel, maybe but he'll still hae time for a bit o' riding,' said the blonde.

Euan used to blush a kind of traffic-light red when he was first drawn into these conversations but, over time, he looked less and less embarrassed and he only turned a mild pink. Haris kept out of these conversations altogether and tried to look as though he was concentrating on some obscure item on the internet. This interaction between Euan and the girls was not really part of the official recovery plan but, as Haris observed in his notebook, he never mistook any of his fellow students for inanimate objects.

*****

They were driving back into Dundee one day when Euan discovered that the girls at the Flukergate Centre were not the only ones interested in soaps. They were waiting for the traffic lights at Stobswell to change when Euan spotted an enormous poster proclaiming the message: 'SCOTLAND FIRST. Born in Scotland, studying in Scotland, working in Scotland, married in Scotland, bringing up Scottish children. Put Scotland and Scottish decency into the soaps! SIGN UP FOR SCOTTISH SOAPS!' The visual image was not altogether clear but the people in it were all wearing various forms of tartan.

'I wonder what Dolly would think about that, if somebody tried to mess around with her soaps?' said Euan, pointing at the poster.

'It's a national campaign to make soap operas more Scottish,' explained Haris. 'Someone is spending a lot of money and there will soon be posters like that one everywhere. They say that people are losing their Scottish identity because they are spending all their time watching television programmes which are made elsewhere.'

'I see what they mean,' said Euan. 'There's certainly no' a soap that's made in Dundee. And the girls always talk about soaps that are made in England or Australia or America. Apparently, the Brazilian soaps are incredible.'

'Well, I never watch them.' The tone of his voice was very flat. 'The campaign is dishonest because it is about more than Scottish characters in soaps.' Haris seemed to have strong feelings about this. 'They want social conformity in the soaps and they want it in society as well. No English people, no black people, no unmarried mothers, nobody who is different from the norm. There's a radio station here in Dundee with an unpronounceable name that is obsessed with the same kind of issue. It is just the beginning of a campaign for a fundamentalist Scottish nationalism that would be completely intolerant. It is the thin start of the wedge.'

'You mean the thin end of the wedge,' corrected Euan.

'OK. But how can it be the end if it is the beginning? English is a very strange language.' Haris shook his head in bewilderment.

'You don't like nationalism very much, do you, Haris?' Several times you've said things about nationalism that I don't really understand and…'

'It does not matter. It is a long story. You would not be interested. Anyway, you have had a long day.' Haris was trying to return to professional mode and they had stopped at another set of traffic lights.

'Don't patronise me, Mister Psychologist. You're always asking me questions and I just want to know a bit more about you. I know that you have a job to do but it is strange that we spend hours and hours together and I know next to nothing about you.'

'I am supposed to be encouraging you to ask questions about

your own past, not mine. I am not really sure that it is professional.'

Euan waited. He felt sure that Haris wanted to speak but his face was completely inscrutable.

'Have you heard of Sarajevo?' asked Haris, after a long pause.

'Start of the First World War, wasn't it?'

'That is right. Well, I grew up in Sarajevo. When I was a child, it was part of Yugoslavia. My family was quite prosperous; my father was a psychiatrist and my mother was an architect; they were both members of the Communist Party, like everyone who wanted a career. I had two older brothers and two younger sisters. We were Muslims, but only in name, and I never went to a mosque. One of my sisters, Maya, married a Serb and no one thought anything about it because mixed marriages like that were very common. I left Sarajevo in 1989 to come to Edinburgh University to study for my Masters degree and while I was here, Yugoslavia began to break up. One of the breakaway states was Bosnia-Herzegovina and Sarajevo was its capital. All the conflict was not about political beliefs; it was mostly about old, long-standing hatreds.' He was talking very slowly, choosing each word with an exact precision.

'The peasants in the countryside had never liked cities like Sarajevo and they wanted to destroy it, physically and psychologically. Not only did they attack Sarajevo with shells and mortars but they tried to destroy the social fabric of the place. Suddenly, it began to matter if you were Muslim or Serb or Croat or Jewish. People seemed to begin to hate their own neighbours, people they had known all their lives, because they belonged to different groups. My sister and her husband fled to Canada because they were attacked by people in their own communities for being in a mixed marriage. The rest of my family stayed behind.'

Haris was talking more and more slowly; eventually, he stopped altogether and drove the car into a side street. Someone had written **Dundee is not Culloden** on the wall of the derelict building just next to where he parked, but they didn't notice it.

'This is very difficult to talk about and so it is better if I concentrate on it and not on the driving. Anyway, my two brothers were sent to a prison camp run by the Serb nationalists and some other members of my family fled to Austria. I was in Edinburgh and for months, I had no idea where they were but I was too scared to go back to Sarajevo to find out. The city was under attack all the time and tens of thousands of people died. But I still feel like a coward. That is why I do not like nationalism, Euan. It has taught me things about myself and about other people that are difficult to live with.'

'I'm sorry, Haris. I had no idea. But what happened to your family? Were they alright?' Euan was aghast. He really had no idea where he was going when he started the conversation.

'My brothers got out of the camps alive and, eventually, everyone went back to Sarajevo. But my second brother died shortly afterwards; he became obsessed with what he had seen and he could not escape from it, even when he was asleep. I suppose that he went mad and, finally, he hanged himself. My father could not go back to his work as a psychiatrist because he said that he had begun to believe that some people were evil. He lost the ability to believe that he could cure people of mental illness. My youngest sister became a hardline Muslim and now she wears a headscarf. She used to be a girl who liked going out to clubs and enjoying herself but now, she seems like a different person. The family that I grew up with hardly exists any more. I still see myself as a Yugo but there is no Yugoslavia.'

Euan could see that Haris was trying to control his emotions but he was still curious enough to ask another question.

'So, why Dundee? I can understand that it would be difficult to go back to Sarajevo but you have a sister in Canada. Why did you choose to stay in Dundee?'

This was easier for Haris. 'I had been a student in Edinburgh and made friends there – so I decided to stay on in Scotland. One of my best friends works in Dundee. She is called Lakshmi; she is an Indian, from Brechin.'

'An Indian, from Brechin? Is that possible?'

'It certainly is. She is lovely; you will like her. She and I were at university together. We were both outsiders – a Muslim from Bosnia who was not really a Muslim, and a Hindu from Brechin who was not really a Hindu. She was not my girlfriend; we were more like brother and sister. She got a job as editor of an alternative newspaper called the *Broughty Ferry Pilot*; her office in Terra Nova Street is not that far from the Wedderburn Centre. Not long after that, I saw this job at Ninewells Hospital and I decided to try to come here too.'

'Are you really not her boyfriend? You can tell me; your secret's safe with me.' Euan was trying to sound really sincere and supportive rather than just inquisitive.

'No, I am really not her boyfriend, Mister Detective.' Haris was relaxing again. 'You have met her boyfriend already. He is the carpenter who is working on the new entrance hall for the centre. His name is Fergus and he is from Forfar.'

'Yes, I know him. He seems very nice. He wears those bright-enough-to-knock-you-out shirts with every colour under the sun. He's usually very friendly but some days, he seems very withdrawn. I've noticed that he doesn't usually wear any of his colourful shirts on his withdrawn days. In fact, last week, he was wearing some really scruffy, old clothes and there was definitely no chat.' Euan shrugged as though he might have felt snubbed.

'Yes, you are very observant. Maybe you should become a psychologist too.'

'Ha ha! But why don't you arrange for me to meet Lakshmi and Fergus? They sound interesting and it would be good to meet some new people, as long as they're no' doctors or nurses.'

'OK. That seems like a good idea.' Haris seemed more cheerful and was getting ready to start driving again. 'Neither of them is a doctor or a nurse. They like going to pubs with music and one of their favourites is a karaoke bar on the far side of Lochee. Do you know what karaoke is?'

'I've heard of it. If I go to this pub, that'll be a chance for me to learn something different.' He nearly said that there had been no karaoke in his young day but some things are so obvious that they don't really bear saying.

6

'Good evening, Scotland, you're listening to Radio Dighty, the radio station that's owned by Scots and brings you all that's best about Scotland – the music, the news, the sport, the history, the humour. Radio Dighty is the only radio station where you can always be sure of hearing a Scots voice. Tonight you can join me, Millar Gibb, for this week's edition of 'Scottish Love Stories'. Everybody wants to know the meaning of true love. Does it have to be a minefield or can it ever be the field of dreams? This programme tries to help our listeners find out more about love in Scotland today.

'Our love story last week concerned Tosher. Now Tosher is from Alyth and he runs a successful plumbing business. He'd reached the age of 43 and he'd still never met Miss Right. He had asked several women out but he found that they were just a bunch of selfish besoms; all they were interested in was his wallet. Women's Lib has got a lot to answer for when it comes to the breakdown in traditional Scots values and decent, hard-working men are paying a heavy price. Anyway, Tosher took a bold step and he's no' the only Scotsman that has been driven to this; he advertised in a mail-order magazine for a wife from the Philippines. He got dozens of replies from women out there who understood that a man needs a wife to keep him happy. He was especially amazed that so many of them said that they had always wanted a Scots husband. They had heard that Scotland was a cold country but the hearts of its men were warm. Tosher was fair chuffed.

'He'd never been out of Scotland afore and some folk would

be feart about going all the way to the Philippines. But Tosher is one of those Scotsman who can't be held back once he gets an idea in his head – haud me back – no way. So, he bought a ticket for a package tour and set off to Manila, that's the capital of the Philippines. He took his pal, Ronnie, with him. Ronnie's already married and he was there to offer moral support and to give some tips about what to avoid and what to look out for and was that no' a really friendly thing to do? Anyway, when they got to Manila, they interviewed some o' the lassies and Ronnie made videos o' the interviews, just in case Tosher found it difficult to make up his mind. And, like Ronnie said, this was the first time they'd been abroad and so these tapes would be grand mementos for them.

'But there was no doubt about who was Tosher's favourite; a bonnie, shy, wee lassie from the hospitality industry that spoke good English. But one o' the things that really got Tosher's heart strings fair birling was the fact that she was called Heather. She had another name but she'd always wanted to go to Scotland that much that she'd changed her name to Heather. Anyway, they met on their own and that very night, Tosher asked Heather to be his wife. She accepted him and they got married with a special licence. They had to be quick for Tosher was, as I said, on a package tour. A few weeks later, Heather came back to Scotland for the first time. And what more could a lassie from a poor Third World country want than married life in a bungalow in Alyth? Lucky Heather!

'And somebody up there was looking down on them, for a few months later, she gave Tosher the son he'd always wanted, wee Callum. A couple of years later and a lassie came along as well, wee LaShona. Tosher could not believe how happy he was, a proper family man. But there was more to come. Heather was no shrinking violet (if that's no' too confusing) and she joined

the Women's Guild; it was there she got the idea of a special
re-marriage ceremony. Their marriage in Manila had been in a
registry office but Heather wanted them to have a ceremony in
church, with a new Scots version of the marriage vows. She'd
made up the vows with her new pals in the Guild and she promised to be an obedient wife at all times. So, there'll be no
arguments about the tea being late in that house! She also promised never to speak her own language again. Her language is
called Tagalog; so, you'll no' be surprised, she wanted to turn
her back on that. One of the elders at Tosher and Heather's kirk
phoned in with this story and asked that we give the listeners a
chance to decide if this should be a Radio Dighty Scottish Love
Story.

'I'd like to thank everyone who phoned into our special Love
Story phoneline. The funds raised from their calls went to a
charity which brings unemployed homeless Scots folk in London
back to their homeland. It's called ROOT, which stands for Rescue
Our Overseas Tramps and you can get more details about how
to give donations from the Radio Dighty website. Some of our
callers were worried that Heather might be a bit on the dark
side but a caller from Letham pointed out that she's no' from
somewhere like Africa and you'll probably no' be able to tell that
her kiddies are half-caste at all. A 93-year-old caller from
Monifieth said that Heather fair reminded him o' his young days
when lassies did as they were bidden. In the end, I am happy to
say that 76% of you decided that the story of Tosher and Heather
should be counted as one of our Scottish Love Stories.

'There's lots of folks that accuse Radio Dighty and organisations like Scotland First of being racist. That's just an excuse to
try to get us closed down in these politically correct times. But
this result shows that's no' true. If folk come to Scotland and
accept our way of life, and if women know their proper place,

then there's no doubt they are welcome here. But they have to
stick to the rules. And her pals at the Women's Guild said Heather
fits in so well, that you can almost forget she's coloured. To
Tosher and Heather, we send you the blessings of Radio Dighty
listeners. The special Radio Dighty Scottish Love Story plaque
will soon be on its way and I have no doubt it will enjoy pride
of place on your mantelpiece. God bless you both and wee Callum
and wee LaShona.

'Now we end tonight's programme with Bonnie Swankie
singing *Jon Anderson, My Jo* by the greatest of all love poets,
Scotland's very own Rabbie Burns.'

7

Euan's notebook 18th April 1999

I was pleased once we'd agreed a date for the trip to the karaoke pub but I was also nervous about it. I was spending far too much time with doctors and nurses but at least I had some idea about what they were supposed to be doing. As Haris would say, I knew where the boundaries were. This trip was going to be more difficult. I didn't know where the boundaries would be and I was afraid that I might fall off a cliff, metaphorically speaking. I also knew that if I didn't put myself into more of these challenging situations then I'd spend the next twenty years trapped, not in a coma, but in a residential care centre. Anyway, everyone said that karaoke was a great laugh, as well as a great leveller, and so I wanted to approach the evening in that frame of mind.

But before I went there, I decided to summon the ghost of Mrs Syme once more. It might seem strange to want to talk to a ghost rather than a real living person but the trouble was that lots of the real, living people whom I knew had a formal relationship with me; you could say that they were paid to talk nicely to me. I wanted a different kind of conversation. I remembered that the first time we'd spoken, she'd told me about returning to Dundee after many years in India; maybe she would have some tips about what to do when you've been away from a place for a long time. She was a bit older than me and so I felt obliged to call her Mrs Syme rather than Edith. She seemed pleased to be summoned and once she started talking about India, there was no stopping her.

'We lived in India for the whole of our married life up until 1947. Our life in Calcutta was really very comfortable. It was a kind of Little Scotland and we had no contact at all with Indians unless they were servants or employees at the mills. We belonged to the Caledonian Society and every year, we celebrated New Year and Burns' Night and St Andrew's Day with our Scots friends. My husband had gone to the Morgan and there was even a Morgan Academy Former Pupils' Club. Alex was very successful in his job and, for the last few years there, we were really the top dogs. If the Viceroy came to Calcutta on a visit, we were always asked to meet him. Latterly, I was the *burra memsahib*.'

'What does that mean, Mrs Syme? I've never heard of that.' She was going too fast for me.

'No, I am so sorry. These phrases have really disappeared with that way of life. The expatriate community was very hierarchical and people were known according to the job held by the man in the family. Alex was the manager of one of Scrymgeour's biggest mills and so, in that locality, he was known as the *burra sahib*; as his wife, I was known as the *burra memsahib*.'

'Are these Indian words?' They were completely new to me.

'That's right. Originally, they were Hindustani words but they were used so extensively by the British in India that they became part of our language, in time. I suppose it all seems strange to an outsider but it was rather a strange way of life. Although we were quite well to do, we never owned our own house. We moved around, depending on where Alex's job was and we lived in the married quarters wherever we went. You inherited the furniture of the previous inhabitants and you learned about their habits from the condition of the furniture.'

'It does sound very claustrophobic.' I was thinking that, perhaps, it wasn't all that different from living in a residential centre, like I did.

'Yes, it could be. Alex used to say it reminded him of village life in Scotland,' she explained. 'Everyone helped everyone else out but everyone knew everyone else's business.'

'And did you ever go to other places in India? Or were you stuck there altogether, all year round?' I was becoming more curious about this vanished way of life.

She sighed. 'It was terribly hot in Bengal, especially in October time. At first, we just had to put up with it and we were young and we managed. But, as we moved up the social scale, we used to go up into the hills to cooler places like Simla or Darjeeling every year.

'When we came back to Broughty Ferry, I think we assumed that it would be rather like going up country during the hot season, a bit of a break from our routine. But, of course, it wasn't like that at all; my assumptions could not have been more wrong. When we moved into our house, where you are living now, we made contact with all our old friends and relatives. At first, that was fine; we were some sort of novelty. But we soon stopped being a novelty and we had to get on with life as best we could. There were some old India hands who never really accepted that they had moved away and they couldn't talk about anything else except their old life. I didn't want to do that. I tried very hard to fit in but the more I tried to integrate, the more people seemed to notice the parts that were different. When they talked about the war, they had a set of shared memories, whether that was about bombing raids or shortages or fear of the Nazis. I had memories of the war too; we lived in fear of the Japanese invading Bengal; we heard stories about the camps set up by the Japanese for people who'd not been able to get away from Singapore. People here were polite when I told them about that but they wanted to get back to the conversations and the memories that they were familiar with; my memories just didn't fit. I'm quite a conventional person and I felt that sense of exclusion rather badly.'

This wasn't really what I had wanted to hear but I understood that feeling quite well. I knew about being a novelty and I knew that, after just three months, some of it was wearing off; I was concerned about what the next stage might be.

She looked out of the window; she seemed a bit upset and I hoped that she wasn't going to cry, but she pulled herself together. 'Eventually, things did improve but when they did, I was surprised by where the improvement came from. It wasn't from my friends or my relatives; it was actually from Agnes Devlin, my house-keeper. She had never known anyone who had lived in India; she wasn't from that sort of class. I had assumed that she would only be interested in talking about her life in Tealing but she, more than anyone else, was curious about the details of my daily life. How did I deal with the heat? What kind of food did we eat? Where did the children go to school? How did we travel from one place to another? Those were the sort of ordinary things that had preoccupied me all the years when I'd been there and she was much more interested in that than my tales of a visit from the Viceroy. I began to enjoy talking with her and I began to relax.

'She also helped me to relax with my grandchildren when they came to stay; she persuaded me that they might like to eat some of the sort of things that I'd talked about eating in India; it was difficult, of course, to get ingredients in the Ferry but we tried and the children seemed to enjoy their visits to me. When I began to have a life of my own, I found that it was much easier to relate to old friends and new acquaintances as well. We still had different assumptions about lots of things but they didn't seem to matter so much. I eventually found that I felt at home here and it was really all due to Agnes. I never told her that, of course, because if you become too close to servants, they can take liber-ties. But I did leave her my Singer sewing machine in my will and I'm sure that she was happy with that. She was with me right up until the end and I didn't have to go into a hospital ward to end my days.'

I sensed that she felt that she might have said enough for one day and we bade each other farewell. There were lots of things for me to think about but one word that struck a particular chord with me was 'assumptions'; she'd made assumptions about what other people might or might not do and she'd had to revise them to help her face up to reality. There wasn't a lot in common between expatriate life in India in the 1940s and my trip to a karaoke bar but I was resolved not to make too many assumptions about what I might find there.

8

The taxi was taking its time wandering around the maze of Dundee's back streets. It was the night of the visit to the karaoke pub and Euan was trying to stay calm; he was trying to keep all his assumptions under control and he had been doing a lot of deep breathing. This was the first time he had met Fergus and Lakshmi and although they were very friendly and welcoming, he still felt like the new boy in the class. They were Haris's closest friends and they had lots of things in common which Euan could not begin to understand. However, what united all four of them that night was a desire to have a good time. Haris and Lakshmi were both dressed entirely in black and they could, with their strong handsome features and their long jet-black hair, be taken for brother and sister; but while he was still and calm, she was a proper fidget. Fergus had (apparently) washed his hair especially for the occasion and he was wearing an alarmingly brilliant sunset-red shirt. The conversation jumped around from football to films to music. Fergus was busy explaining that karaoke was a very democratic form of music making and Euan could deduce from the way the other two were shuffling around that this might be one of his hobby horses. One part of him wondered if this was really the way he wanted to spend an evening but the part of him that was curious about different experiences won this internal battle.

Euan had never seen this particular pub before. It was called the Muckle Shovel but, apparently, that was a fairly recent name. For many years, Fergus explained, it had been known as the Last Chance Saloon but when the previous landlord had been drowned on a publicans' outing to Lunan Bay, it was felt that it was time for a name change. By popular demand, it became the Muckle Shovel. The licensing authorities seemed unaware that this was in honour of a Dundee granny called Big Mags McGinty, who had threatened to murder a poll tax inspector with a muckle shovel.

When Euan finally saw the pub, he realised how difficult it must have been to give it any name at all. It looked like an unloved building; its walls were coated entirely in traditional Scots harling and none of the windows was less than twelve feet from the ground. Just as they were getting out of the taxi, he could make out, through the drizzle, another SCOTLAND FIRST poster. This one encouraged all Scots to listen to indigenous music, past or present, in preference to anything foreign or unnatural. The words on the poster warned against the rape of Scots culture and the image showed a small, young, white, tartan-clad woman being threatened by an older, dark skinned man with an unidentifiable musical instrument in his hand. It was so close to the pub that it looked as though it might be advertising a forthcoming attraction. Fergus went off to examine the poster while the others went inside to find a table.

A tall, muscle-bound man, wearing a tasselled waistcoat and a Stetson, was welcoming new arrivals into his crowded pub. 'Eh see ye've brought me another customer the night, Lakshmi. Ye'll be wanting a discount at this rate. Eh'm pleased to meet you, Euan, and eh hope you'll hae a braw night here. Maybe ye'll gie the karaoke a try in a wee while. Lakshmi's a bit backward in coming forward but Haris and Fergus are mair likely to hae a go when they've had a pint or twa.'

Euan smiled and said nothing but the idea of Haris singing in public was right off the scale of his assumptions. It was somewhat of a shock to realise that his nice, friendly-but-professional psychologist really might have another side to his personality; part of him wasn't sure if he was ready for the shock of seeing Haris getting pissed enough to take to the stage in a karaoke bar. But it was something to look forward to; it should be a laugh.

As Euan looked around the pub, which was designed to look like a bar straight from a Hollywood Western, he realised that there were people of all ages, teenagers, grannies, middle-aged people with children as well as young men and women exchanging suspicious glances. Lakshmi explained to Euan, once they'd got settled at their table, that since the man at the door had taken over the pub, it had become a great magnet for lovers of Country and Western. He'd been a junkie but since becoming clean, he'd become addicted to the gym culture; his muscles were legendary – hence, his nickname, Arnie.

'Anyway, Euan,' she said, 'you haven't asked me any questions yet. I was told to expect a barrage of questions; so barrage away.'

'Well,' said Euan, 'your friend, Haris, is trying to train me to be more restrained with my curiosity and we've introduced the ten-minute rule; that means that I try not to ask a new person a question of a personal nature until ten minutes after I've met them. And, as it happens, I think it's over ten minutes now since we met; I think my time for restraint must be nearly up. So, my first question is: How come you're Asian if you're from Brechin?'

'That's straightforward enough,' Lakshmi laughed. 'My grand-parents are really the ones that brought me up. They're white Scots, just like you and Fergus, and I can see by the look on your face that you've never heard these two words, white Scots, together. Is that right?'

'Yeah, that's right. When I was growing up in the Seventies, I think we just assumed that Scots were white; you never even discussed it; it was just, well, natural. I only ever saw Asians on

TV, although I mind that the first shop I ever knew to stay open until midnight was called Akbar's stores. We called it Aki Paki – just for a joke, like – never to his face; he was an awful nice man.' Euan was beginning to feel that he might be skating on thin ice here. 'Me and my pals all talked about apartheid and we thought that was terrible. So it wasn't like we were racists but stuff like Aki Paki was different, just a wee joke. But you don't think it's very funny, do you? Sorry, Lakshmi, really.'

'You're dead right I don't think it's funny,' she replied. 'But your apologies are accepted. There's so much more that I can say about the whole business of wee jokes but this is no' really the best place to be doing that. We're supposed to be having a night out and getting to know each other.' At that point, someone who appeared to be a longstanding customer of this bar began to bellow out the words of *Sweet Dreams*. 'And I don't really want to be competing with Patsy Cline. I don't know about you?'

'I can hardly hear myself think, let alone have a discussion about anything serious.'

'So, why don't you come round the *Pilot* offices next Tuesday to carry on our discussion? It'll be at a quiet point in our production cycle and there'll be time to have a proper chat in peace and I can show you the way that a modern-day paper is produced.' She was still friendly but also rather business-like in the way that she fitted him into her schedule.

'That'll be great.' He meant it but he looked a bit crestfallen.

Lakshmi put her hand on his arm. 'Euan, it's complicated, and that's a fact. I'm pleased that you're making time to learn all about racism and humour in Scotland rather than just assume you know all that there is to know.'

It was just as well that 'Patsy Cline' was so loud; all they could do was smile at each other. Euan felt he could easily have made matters a whole load worse if he'd opened his mouth again. The singer reached a crescendo and both her friends applauded loudly. Fergus joined them at this point, looking slightly flushed and rather pleased with himself. 'Arnie's just going to make an announcement,' he said.

'Ladies and gentlemen, if eh could just hae your attention for a wee moment. It has come to meh attention that a tin of meh best gloss paint has been stolen, but eh'm happy to say that thanks to meh good friend, Fergus Nicol, eh've discovered where it's gone.' He paused and held up his arm for effect. 'It's aw ower that SCOTLAND FIRST poster that wiz stuck up outside meh front door, without so much as a bye your leave and eh'm happy to say that the message is now unreadable. Finally, eh want to say that, proud as eh am tae be Scottish, the Muckle Shovel welcomes everybody, wherever they come from, whether it's Iceland or Greenland or Blueland. And it's jist the same if you're normal or gay or a dinnae ken, you're welcome here, just so long as you buy a drink and enjoy yourselves and let other folk get on wi' enjoying themselves.'

A great cheer went up. 'Arnie for Provost!' cried an excitable looking youth with a fake leather holster.

*****

Later, when Euan went to the bar to buy his round, he soon found himself in conversation with three drinkers in checked shirts who looked permanently attached to their bar stools. It was difficult to tell their ages but they were probably somewhere between forty and sixty. And they were friendly.

'Eh've no seen ye afore, son. Is this yer first time here?' asked a man with a Dundee accent.

'It is,' said Euan, unsure about what to say next. They immediately introduced themselves and hands were shaken.

'Welcome tae the Muckle Shovel,' said one of them. 'Aroond here, fowk ca' me Babe.'

'Babe?' Euan stuttered.

'Benefits and bugger all else!' He laughed with as much enjoyment as he obviously had done a thousand times before.

'So, you must be the laddie that had sleeping sickness,' piped up the third one.

Euan laughed, amused at the idea of meeting someone as nosey as himself. His fear of falling off a cliff, socially, was disappearing.

'Ye've missed a lot,' said Babe. 'Maggie Thatcher's come and gone...'

'And ta'en the poll tax wi' her,' said the Dundonian.

The nosey one explained a bit more about himself and his pals. 'And then there wiz the Falklands War, the war tae get the auld sow re-elected. But that's whaur me and the boys met up. Ah'm originally frae Kirrie but when the war cam tae an end, ah decided tae emigrate doon here tae Dundee.'

Babe looked knowingly at him, 'As if there wiznae enough sheep molesting inbreeds doon here already!'

'That's rich coming frae an Arbroath lad like yersel, you fish-fingering git!' The Dundonian was quick as a flash.

'The only fish he ever caught, Euan, wiz the crabs,' explained the nosey one.

They all laughed at their banter, more than Euan did, in fact. He realised that he was just the latest actor with a walk-on role in a long-running, alcohol-fuelled saga.

'Ye'll maybe mind the Berlin Wall,' said the Dundonian. 'Nae mair. Noo it's jist like bloody Disneyland, ye ken. A' thae years we wiz telt tae worry aboot the red Menace and it's jist disappeared, like the mist on the tap o' the Law Hull.'

The nosey one decided to up the tempo a bit. 'There's some

boy high up in the Russian government that cam tae work at the berries in the Carse. He used tae be in the KGB but he wanted tae lie low a bit – hae a kind o' a career break – afore he becam Prime Minister.'

'So, he put the berries on his CV, like?' asked Babe.

The nosey one continued: 'When he wiz in Blair he was incognito, ye ken, but somebody must of foond oot aboot him cuz there's a song aboot him.'

'Ye're jokin?' said the Dundonian.

'No, and it's a song that ye a ken, it goes Ra-Ra-Rasputin. Fowk thought it was aboot an auld mad monk but I can reveal to you that it wiz aboot this politician boy – Rasp-Putin…'

'Fuckwaywiye, ye're jist a havering bugger.'

Just at that point, Euan's drinks arrived. The nosey one recommended he try the pear cider the next time and Euan headed back to his table with the tray of drinks.

'We thought you'd been kidnapped,' said Fergus, clearly pleased to see his pint.

Before Euan got a chance to respond, a 'shoosh' went round the room and he could hear the beginnings of the sound of another Patsy Cline number, *Walking After Midnight*. He was pleased when he realised that the singer was none other than his fellow student, Dolly Fullerton, shimmering in a sequinned top that she seemed to have been poured into. Her singing voice was quite wonderful and the audience was rapt. Not even the sound of a crisp packet being opened.

Afterwards, she came over to speak to them and everyone seemed to know her already. Euan was pleased that these new friends of his seemed to be on good terms with one another. She was telling them about the fun run that she was organising in Bannockbrae, the housing scheme where she lived. Euan quite fancied the idea; it would be another chance to visit somewhere different and meet some more new people. He was looking around for Haris to put the idea to him when he realised that he and Fergus had already taken to the stage to give their own interpretation of *From a Distance,* with what can only be called laldy.

'Switch aff yir hearing aid,' an octogenarian bellowed to his wife.

9

Familiarity can be confusing as well as comforting. Lakshmi's office on Terra Nova Street was not far away from the Wedderburn Centre but Euan managed to get lost on his first visit there. He thought that he remembered the quickest route but many of the well-known landmarks had changed their appearance or been demolished; pedestrianised streets and one-way traffic added to the complexity of his journey. He recalled that there had been a cinema in the vicinity but it was now derelict. There had also been a pub called The Whalebone just across the road from the cinema but the full-length glass windows and the tables on the pavement suggested that it had been transformed into something more like a bistro than a traditional Scots watering hole.

He was looking forward to meeting Lakshmi properly. His previous meeting with her had ended awkwardly but he was determined not to let that put him off getting to know her. The office where she edited the *Broughty Ferry Pilot* was much smaller than Euan had expected and there was definitely no room for printing presses; it was on the ground floor of a tenement building and it had the hallmarks of having been a shop in its day; now its walls were covered with community posters and memorable front pages. Clad in workaday denim jeans and shirt, Lakshmi was pleased to see him but she wasted no time on pleasantries before launching into an explanation of the paper.

'The name, *Broughty Ferry Pilot*, comes from the name of a paper that was around about a hundred years ago. We were a completely new paper but, by choosing the name we did, we wanted to show a bit of respect for the history of the community where we were based. We do loads of local reports on things like school sports days and flower shows and the gigs at The Whalebone. Anything that happens approximately within three miles of Broughty Ferry is liable to be covered by us. When your new wing at the Wedderburn Centre was opened, we carried a story with pictures all about that. We do stuff about healthy living, like exercise and diet. We have a regular local history column that is based on interviews that we carry out with some of the old folk here. Some of our readers are from Bangladesh and West Africa and we carry stories from there too. We're always ready to do some investigative journalism too, about things like dodgy property development.'

'And you do some national stuff as well, don't you?' asked Euan.

'Aye,' said Lakshmi, really in her stride now, 'we have covered a lot about the democratic deficit and the new parliament fits into that theme very well. We've got some voxpop stuff from folk on the streets about what they expect of it and I'm also planning to do an interview with the local MSPs, once they're elected. Dundee often gets ignored by the media and politicians from the Central Belt and we're very good at making a real stooshie if there's any sign of Dundee being sidelined. You may have heard that there are to be elections later on this year for the new Lord Provost. Currently, he's just a guy that opens exhibitions and stuff but after this new law kicks in, it will be a powerful executive post. In this case, Dundee is no' to be ignored; we're to be the guinea pigs. The first elections will happen here in November and if they work out all right, then they'll maybe try them out in the other cities. Craig Baxter, the trade unionist, is supposed to be planning to stand for the post. Maybe, you've met him?' she asked.

'I don't know him that well but we used to travel into Dundee on the same school bus.' Euan sat down next to a photocopier.

'They're no' wrong when they say Scotland's a village!' Lakshmi laughed and groaned at the same time.

'Talking of villages,' Euan said, veering off topic, 'I was just thinking when I came here that me and my pal, Andy, once went to the cinema across the road to see *Brigadoon*. But we didn't tell anybody that we were going to see it in case we were told off for laughing at Scotland.'

'Told off by folk who said that the storyline made a mockery of the dynamism of Scotland, perhaps? Its stereotypical portrayal of Scotland as a country stuck in a mythical past, blah blah blah?'

Euan laughed in agreement.

'Aye, I know them well, folk that have got nothing better to do than worry about daft Hollywood movies! Anyway, I like Cyd Charisse and Gene Kelly. The dancing is great, especially that sequence that looks like a reel, apart from the fact that all the dancers are facing the camera rather than each other.' She paused for about a second before she got back to what proved to be a more political direction.

'Anyway, we promised to continue the conversation that we were having in the Shovel last week. Are you up for that?'

'Definitely,' said Euan, pleased that the ice had been broken.

'Ok,' said Lakshmi. 'I was telling you about my grandparents. My granddad was a postie and my gran was a school cleaner. Their daughter, my mum, went to university, became involved with an Indian medical student and got pregnant. I mean, I like to think that she got involved with him but it might have been a one-night stand, for all I know. My grandparents agreed to look after me for a year or two until she finished her degree but, in the end, I never moved out. They were brilliant and they made me feel more like a bonus than a burden to them. They probably spoiled me and they've always been really good to me, even when they didn't understand what I was doing. My granddad is a bit of an autodidact, like Fergus, really, and as soon as he discovered that he was going to have an Indian granddaughter, he started reading up everything he could about India and turned it into a really magical story for me. It was his idea too to make Lakshmi my middle name; she's a Hindu goddess who's supposed to bring money and luck. My first name is Aileen and until I was about 13, I was just plain Aileen Forsyth.'

She was pacing round the office as she spoke, watering plants, checking email messages and tidying any stray pieces of paper that were distracting her; a woman with a vision, for sure but also a woman with a domestic sense of order. Her mind never seemed to be still, always observing, always analysing, always explaining.

'Did something happen to you when you were 13, then?' asked Euan, really absorbed by the whole story.

'It certainly did. It was a horrible experience at the time but it really shaped my view of the world from there on. We lived in Brechin and, while I don't want to give you the impression that it was the multiracial capital of Scotland, it was a lot better for kids from minority ethnic backgrounds than most other wee towns in Scotland. There were always black folk around from the US air base and so I grew up not feeling strange because I wasn't white; nobody ever stared at me just because of the way I looked.

'When I was 13, my class went on some sort of day trip to Aberdeen and that was something else altogether. It had this reputation as the oil capital of Scotland, a really go-getting place, but people there were giggling and laughing and pointing at me like they were in a zoo. A couple of girls, complete strangers, came over and touched me, just to see what my skin was like, I suppose. Never spoke, never asked me anything, they just touched me and ran away back to their pals. It looked as if they'd done it for a bet. I was really upset and spent the whole journey on the bus home crying. When I got home, I told Gran and Granddad that from then on, I was going to be Lakshmi. They didn't argue but they told me later that they thought it would be a passing phase. Twenty years later, the phase still hasn't passed.'

Euan could feel that this was a story that she had told many times but repetition had not blunted its edge. He realised that he had never really thought that racism was something that could happen in Scotland; he had rather assumed that it was something to be found in distant places. Assumptions causing bother again.

She went on to explain how this experience had shaped so much of her politics. Romantic nationalism was never on the cards for her and that was one of the things that she found she had in common with Haris. Her awareness of what had happened to Bosnia a few years earlier had made her even more critical of anything that looked like narrow-minded nationalism.

'I'm proud of being Scottish and I would have no problems if Scotland did become an independent republic but that really is not one of my priorities. Absolutely not! Scotland needs to make friends and allies if it's going to improve the lives of people here and, for me, interdependence is more of a priority than going it alone. Fantasising about independence and nationalist nonsense is a waste of good brain power, as far as I'm concerned.' She was quite fiery and Euan was pleased that she was on his side, so to speak; he suspected that she would be a terrifying enemy.

Euan decided to move the discussion a bit nearer home and asked her what she thought about Scotland First and the posters like the one they'd put up outside the Muckel Shovel.

'They're very dangerous, them and Radio Dighty. What's

particularly insidious about them is the way that they tap into things that folk feel comfortable talking about. If you ask folk for their views on, say, sustainable development or economic self-sufficiency, you'll shut lots of them up because these are such complicated concepts. But if you ask them to talk about Scottish heroes or soap operas, they are likely to feel more comfortable expressing their views about that. These kinds of discussions draw folk into their nasty world, almost without realising what's going on. They had a programme recently about refugees and instead of saying, Send Them Back, which is what they think, they called it Bide A Wee; their whole anti-asylum-seeker policy disguised in some old couthy Scots saying.' She paused again, for a second. 'Hang on a minute, I never even offered you a cup of tea or coffee. Would you like one?'

Euan had no sooner nodded his head than she went off to fill a kettle. He looked out of the window to see that a real thick mist had come down and he couldn't even see the old pub on the other side of the street.

Lakshmi returned with the kettle. 'You must think I'm really rude, no' even offering you a cup until you've listened to me putting the world to rights.' They both laughed but Euan really was feeling thirsty.

'Anyway,' said Lakshmi, 'where was I?' She continued with her analysis of what she called the real problems of poverty, poor housing, unemployment and environmental neglect but it wasn't long before she moved on to the problems that Scots generate for themselves through their consumption of alcohol and hard drugs, as well as other self-destructive tendencies.

'And I'm no' just being moralistic about folk that don't know any better,' she explained. 'Fergus and I have been together for about seven years now and one of the main reasons why we don't actually live together is because I can't handle it when he goes into one of his drinking phases. It's no' as if he's violent or anything but he does become someone else and he hates the world; worst of all, he hates himself. I do love him more than anyone else I've ever known but I canna take that on. You can't love someone out of a drink problem.'

They were both silent for a moment but that was interrupted by the ringing of her mobile phone; she'd ignored calls on the landline but she answered this one. It was brief and she was taking in information rather than saying very much herself.

'I'd completely forgotten,' she said to Euan, 'that there's some music on across the road in The Whalebone this evening. It was taken over last year by a couple of women and they were just reminding me about tonight's gig; they want a write up in the *Pilot*. They're trying to turn it into a more women-friendly space and they've got this women's band down from Orkney. It'll be a good night. Maybe you want to come along?'

'Are men allowed in?' he asked nervously.

'It's not women only; it's more of a women-friendly ambience. In most pubs, the ambience is set by men but in The Whalebone, they're trying to make a space where a woman, any woman, will feel comfortable.'

Euan was rather puzzled. 'I'm no' sure if we had ambiences back in the 70s.'

'Oh, you did,' she smiled. 'Think about all these pubs full of men just before or after a football match; you couldn't say that places like that have a women-friendly ambience? Everyone just used to take places like that for granted but now we try to understand them better and analyse the way that a particular ambience works. In The Whalebone, one of the things you'll find is that the TV never has football on; if men complain about that they are just invited to go to another pub. But it's more complicated...' Her mobile rang again.

Euan had plenty of time to think more about assumptions and ambiences while she took this, much longer, call. He thought that it might be a good idea to write down a list of ambiences in his notebook as a way of helping him to make more sense of it. He even wrote the word 'AMBIENCE' in block capitals at the top of a new page. His mind was racing, and he was thinking about how he used to take so much for granted, and not just ambiences. Since he had come back from the Big Sleep, it seemed quite the reverse and nobody seemed to be able to take anything for granted at all; everything seemed to be up for discussion.

His reverie was cut short by Lakshmi finishing her phone call. 'I need to go, Euan. I'm sorry, we'll get to The Whalebone another time. It's just that there's a news story that I have to attend to. You know about all these animals breaking free from places where they were supposed to be confined?'

'Like the bulls from the Perth Bull Sale?'

'Aye, and the elephants from the zoo. Well, this time it's horses. There were some horse trailers going up to Aberdeenshire for the Worldwide Clydesdale Jamboree and they seem to have been held up by the fog at Claypotts Castle. About twenty horses broke out of the trailers and they're charging down the road towards Stobswell. I'll need to get my camera and go up the town. Do you want to come along, or are you ready for home?'

Words weren't really necessary in reply and they were out the door together, as soon as blink. Runaway horses on the streets of Dundee definitely could not be taken for granted.

10

Euan's notebook 22nd April 1999

I'd arranged to meet Fergus on Thursday. There was something I really liked about him, only five foot six, wiry, always on the go, an archetypal wee Dundee man. We were heading west, along the Perth Road, when it started to rain and we went to shelter in the shopping mall in the Flukergate Centre. It soon turned to sleet and lots of folk, especially pensioners in anoraks and homeless teenagers in sleeping bags, had had the same idea; they were fairly enjoying a good girn about the unseasonal weather.

Fergus was not going to be put off his stride by the weather. 'Flukergate is one of these medieval names that seem to tickle the fancy of town planners. It goes back to the 12th century when it was the heart of the city but the planners overlooked the ability of Dundonians to put their own handle on things. Before it had even opened, it was nicknamed the Fuckergate; no' exactly the image that had been intended, but there you go.'

I went there three days a week for my IT course but I didn't know anything about its history and I'd never even gone shopping there. Fergus, it turned out, was an enthusiastic shopper.

'There's a wee shop here,' he explained, 'that's really good for shirts and they sell five for the price of three. That's where I got this. Lakshmi thinks that orange doesn't really suit me but I like it. Maybe, we could just pop in here for a wee minute to see if there's anything that takes your fancy?'

I didn't really need five shirts but they were good value and we made sure that we didn't come away with any that were identical. I didn't have enough money on me to pay for them all but Fergus, the shirt evangelist, lent me some so that I could pay for my chosen five. He was a fast shopper and after about only ten minutes, we came out with several bags advertising the name of the shop, Breeks and Semmits, for all the world to see.

After this, I was feeling a bit peckish and, now that the sleet had stopped, we headed off to a restaurant called Ashet near the Blackness Library. Fergus had been at school with Murray Chan, the owner, but he said that wasn't the only reason for going there. It turned out to have a really different atmosphere from the restaurants that I remembered from the 1970s; I suppose you could call it an ambience. One whole wall was all reinforced glass and there was a fantastic view of the River Tay. We sat down at some fashionable steel tables with uncomfortable steel chairs but before I had even got my coat off, Fergus was telling me all about what he'd thought when he first heard about me.

'When I first read about you in the papers, the focus was on the power of these wonder drugs but I began to wonder what it would all be like for you. How would you cope with returning to a world that had changed so much since you were last here? How would you cope with having to take drugs all the time, especially knowing that they might stop being effective? And now that I know you and I can see that you're coping really well, I've written down stuff about that in my diary.'

I probably blushed at that point and I was pleased to concentrate on the menu, to change the topic as much as anything else. There were lots of different types of food, almost too many for me to choose from, but choice is the name of today's game. Murray, the owner, came from a Chinese family and, when he decided to open a restaurant, he didn't want it to be a traditional Chinese restaurant like you get all over Scotland. So, there were different sections on the menu – Chinese, Scottish, American and Spanish; every day, there were four special dishes, with one from each section. I opted for the lemon chicken, which was that day's

Chinese special, and Fergus ordered a couple of tapas. We both ordered a bottle of lager. Not that eating stopped him from talking; he liked to talk about history and ideas and politics and literature and football and anything that stimulated his mind. He mentioned a science-fiction film called *The Matrix* and he was really frustrated that its Scottish release date was so much later than the American one. I was really more curious about him; I wanted to know what made Fergus Fergus.

He'd just popped some *patatas bravas* into his mouth when I took my chance.

'So, Fergus, what about you? Tell me a bit about your life story. What have you been doing with your life so far? What is it that makes you tick?'

'Where would you like me to start?' He reached for his lager.

'How about the beginning? Where were you born? That sort of stuff.'

'Well, I was born in Forfar thirty-two years ago,' he said. 'It's no' changed all that much in all those years. It's still a wee market town with about ten thousand inhabitants; some folk call it peaceful, other folk call it boring. My dad was great but jobwise you could say that he did not have a brilliant career. His first job was at Forfar Railway Station but as soon as he was beginning to enjoy that, Mr Beeching closed down that line; then he went to Dundee to work in the docks and they closed down his yard almost immediately; then he got a job driving a Co-op van but after a year or two, they cut back the rural service; he worked in one of the textile mills for a while but the same thing happened again. He was a walking case-study of the changing economic history of Scotland.'

'My god! How did he take all that?' My head was spinning with all this but, at the same time, I was trying to enjoy my lemon chicken.

'No' very well. He had a long nervous breakdown when I was in primary school and he never went back to full-time work again. He got an allotment and I think that looking after that, looking after me and the house was what kept him sane or, at least, sort of sane. His experience made us all very wary of medication that's supposed to treat mental health problems. He had a couple of experiences where he was dulled into a zombie-like condition; my mum decided that this was no life for him and she began to wean him off these medications until he was back in the real world. It's made me very suspicious of medicine and what it can do to folk; it's also made me very suspicious of the way that doctors label their patients and once you get a particular label, it's very difficult to get away from that. I don't know whether it's inherited or not but I've had some mental health problems too. I think that medication can be helpful for some folk, in some circumstances, but I try to avoid it as much as possible. Anyway, going back to my dad and mum. She was always the main breadwinner. We had no money and the only holiday I ever had was going out to the allotment. We had no TV but I had a fantastic childhood; we were always discussing things and I was encouraged to use the library as soon as I could read.'

'And that,' I asked, 'must be one of the reasons why you always have a book with you nowadays?'

'I suppose so. Being an only child in a house without a TV meant that I had plenty of time for reading. I loved being able to transport myself away into another world. Murray was a big reader as well. His family was Chinese and they all had a strong work ethic and so he really wanted to do well at school. We became friends on our first day at secondary school.' It reminded me of the way I met Andy on my first day at secondary school. 'In lots of ways, we were very different. He focused very strongly on what he needed to do to get to where he next wanted to be; so it was important to him to be the school dux. Whereas I liked studying things if they interested me and sometimes, I would go off at a tangent from what we were supposed to be learning but I was still learning. Other folk thought we were a right pair of swots. We stuck together too because we both got bullied quite a bit; him, because he was Chinese and me, because my dad stayed at home trying no' to have another nervous breakdown. But at least we learned to stand up for ourselves and for each other.'

'But surely,' I asked, 'everybody didn't bully you?' I was looking around to see if there was any sign of Murray but he must have been somewhere else.

'No, but lots of folk just kept out of the way. There was one gang that liked to pick on us when we were on our own, especially at going home time. You'll maybe know one of them; if you ever listen to Radio Dighty, there's a presenter called Millar Gibb. He was one of the bullies back then and he uses his programmes on the radio to bully folk now.'

'Lakshmi mentioned it to me but I don't think I've ever really listened to it.' I thought that my brother liked it but I decided not to mention that.

I could see that Fergus was getting irritated, just at the thought of Miller Gibb and Radio Dighty. 'I think he's venomous but he's also very clever. He's very good at packaging his message up in a whole load of Scottish music or some other sentimental palaver so that the audience just loves him.'

What with me never having listened to this radio station, that was a bit of a dead end for a conversation and so I changed the subject to Fergus's work as a joiner. I knew that he liked talking about that and it was definitely un-controversial.

'I became a joiner because I wanted to do something with my

hands but what I hadn't realised was just how scarce real joiners are in Scotland. So, I was able to make a lot of money and then go travelling. I also discovered that you can get work as a joiner anywhere in the world. Like when I got to New Zealand a few years ago, I was soon skint but there was no problem getting decent work. I knew other travellers that had to wash dishes and clean out lavvies to make ends meet but joinery was good to me and my wallet. Some folk say that God smiles on the righteous but I say that if you believe that, you'll believe anything!'

'And I think Haris said that you met Lakshmi while you were off travelling. Is that right?' I asked.

'Aye, that's right. We met in India, in an amazing city called Hampi. It used to be the capital of a Hindu empire but it's no' on the tourist trail and hardly anybody's heard of it, unless they're an obsessive, like me!'

'You go all that way and you meet somebody from Brechin!'

'Another obsessive!'

'Just think how much you could have saved if you'd both stayed at home and gone on a bus trip around Angus instead!'

We both laughed at this very sensible East of Scotland pound-saving idea.

I did enjoy being with Fergus. It wouldn't be true to say that he was relaxing company but he did have an energy about him that I enjoyed. No danger of a hushed tone here. I hoped I'd be able to spend more time with him.

11

Bannockbrae had not featured on Euan's rediscovery agenda. It had a reputation as one of the worst housing schemes in Dundee; someone had even written a song called *The Badlands of Bannockbrae*. It was the product of a particularly miserable style of 1970s municipal planning and it was the kind of place that no municipal planner would consider living in, not even for a second. The folk who did live there, the Bannocks, had developed all sorts of ways of coping with their situation. They organised activities that some of their mainstream funders thought were 'un-necessary' – like fireworks on Midsummer's Day or the Condom Culture disco on St Valentine's Day – because they knew, better than anyone else, that raising a wee bit of a smile could make all the difference between despair and hope.

Bannockbrae was where Dolly lived and she had asked Euan and Haris to join in the annual fun run to raise some funds for the community Christmas club. It was a dreich morning. Just a short bus ride from the Wedderburn Centre, it felt like they were entering a different time zone. The multis looked neglected and empty; the shops and half of the ground-level houses were boarded up like fortresses. The planners had imagined that the residents would all have cars but this assumption had only resulted in the scheme's roads becoming a rat run for bad tempered drivers seeking to avoid the ever-changing complexities of the one-way system. The overall design had also resulted in the whole place being a wind trap, a breeze trap, a gale trap; whatever the weather in other parts of Dundee, Bannockbrae was always blustery and never calm.

When they stepped off the bus, both Euan and Haris felt very tall. The Bannocks were, generally speaking, on the short side. Dolly emerged from the prefabricated building that was the hub of the Community Association. There was a graffito on the side of the building that read **Dundee is not Port Stanley** but no one mentioned it.

'Welcome to Bannockbrae. It's grand to see you both here. Come inside, eh'll mak you a cup o' tea.'

'Some paracetamol would be nice,' whispered a hoarse, rather worse for wear Haris.

'Oh, eh, nae bother. Eh tak it you were oot on the toon, Haris.'

'Something like that,' he whispered back.

'The run'll do ye good, then, put some fresh air in your lungs.'

Haris grunted something indecipherable.

'Haris doesn't usually work on Sunday mornings,' explained Euan, more cheerfully than might have been necessary. 'But I'm looking forward to the run. I do quite a lot of jogging and that's how come I have this tracksuit.'

Haris looked as though he wanted to slap him but concentrated on his tea.

They were joined at this point by a tall handsome balding man, who looked as if he had more money to spend on his clothes than the average Bannock. He also gave the impression that he might spend some time at the gym.

'Euan, this is a friend o' mine, Craig Baxter, he's been on and on at me about meeting you.'

'Actually, Euan, you probably don't remember me but we used to know each other. I was the year ahead of you at the Harris and we used to travel into Dundee on the same bus.'

Euan nodded his head. 'Were you one of the guys that was always talking about football? Was it you that spent one whole journey discussing all the moves and passes made by Celtic when they won some big match in Lisbon? I was amazed that you'd never been to the match.'

'Well, being an avid Arab, I only ever went to Dundee United matches but the European Cup was different.' He smiled as though he was always happy to talk about this famous match. 'I was never normally interested in West Coast teams like Celtic but the Lions of Lisbon were something else. Their victory was in 1967 when I was about seven but I could never know too much about that match.'

'He's no' changed then,' muttered Dolly, as she left the room.

'And these conversations must have been about ten years later. I seem to remember you played a lot of football. Did you become a professional footballer?' asked Euan.

'No chance,' he laughed. 'I left school as soon as I did my Highers. I would have gone sooner but my folks kept on at me to get some qualifications first. I went travelling in Europe, grape picking in France and bar work in Spain. Eventually I came back to Scotland and I got work on the oil rigs. I'd got used to earning money and university just seemed like bairns' stuff to me. The rigs were good for earning money fast but it had its drawbacks. When you're young you'll put up with a lot as long as you're earning good money and able to have a good time. But the thing that got me involved in union work was the lack of proper safety. There were one or two terrible disasters with dozens of men killed and nobody was accountable. That's when I really became a trade unionist and when I'd had enough of the rigs, I got work here as an official with the Jute and General Workers' Union.'

His voice had begun in a chatty tone but had moved more and more into political mode; he paused, almost as if he was giving his audience time to reflect on his message.

'But I thought that there was hardly any jute produced in Dundee now?' said Euan.

'That's right but trade unions can be really sentimental and because the Jute Workers' Union had been a good union, nobody wanted to let the name go. Most of our members now work in places where people never used to be unionised, like catering and casinos and supermarkets.'

The question Euan really wanted to ask Craig was if he and Dolly were an item, even though he knew that was out of kilter with the political tone of the conversation. But before he could make up his mind what to do, he was interrupted by the return of Dolly herself.

'Eh've just left Haris lying doon in meh flat. He said he wanted to go tae a quiet, dark place. There's no much chance o' that in Bannockbrae but maybe he'll get a chance tae sleep aff last night while we're running oot here.'

'So, are we ready for off?' asked Craig. 'What's the route this year?'

'Well, it's a round trip. We go along Peploe Way, turn right down Cadell Crescent, go right along past Kesson House and then we're into the Gee Gees…'

'The Gee Gees,' said Euan. 'Does Bannockbrae have a race course?'

'No,' laughed Dolly. 'There is a betting shop but nae race-course. The Gee Gees is Grassic Gibbon Gardens – three Gs. Ye ken?'

'Ok,' said Euan. 'It's no' really a very long run.'

'Three miles, but there's still some fowk will need a smoking break!'

By this time, there were several hundred people of all ages and shapes and conditions gathered outside the prefabricated huts that were home to the Community Association. There were some younger folk and one or two ex-druggies who intended to run the whole three miles seriously and establish new personal bests for themselves but most folk looked ready for ambling rather than running. It was just as well that there was no preliminary medical examination because some of the amblers would have been disallowed from doing even that. Everybody who wanted to take part was allowed to do so, however many chronic diseases they had in their possession. An older woman was struggling to get the good natured crowd to stand in a line for the beginning of the race. It was made more complicated by the fact that her young grandson kept waving the starting flag and blowing a whistle as if the race really was beginning; eventually she took the flag and the whistle off him and skelped him round the head for good measure. The race was ten minutes late in starting.

Euan decided to amble along with Dolly rather than run; Craig had gone off to do what he called networking. Dolly was pointing out the landmarks of Bannockbrae to Euan when he asked her if she and Craig were a couple.

'Weel, he sniffs around a bit now and then. We got tae ken each other during the Timex strike a few years back. We've had some good times thegither but we're no what ye would ca' a couple and that's fine by me,' she explained without drawing breath. Euan wanted to ask a bit more but they were joined by a couple of youths; one of whom looked like a typical, wee, under-nourished Bannock; the other was taller and seemed altogether more confident. They stood so close together that they almost seemed bound to each other but the differences in their upbringing had left distinctions in their height, their physiques and the way that they looked at the rest of the world.

'Euan, this is my cousin, Kyle, and his pal, Kenny Horsburgh.'

Kyle grunted and looked down; Kenny looked Euan straight in the eye.

'So, how are you finding life in the New Scotland, Euan?' he asked.

'Very good so far, everybody's very friendly to me.'

'That's good. That's as it should be. Scotland has been famous the world over for its hospitality. We need to be resolved to make sure that these historical values are the basis of our society today. Anyway, sorry not to be able to chat longer but me and Kyle have to go to do some work at the radio station. I'll try and speak to you properly some other time, Euan, about what you think of Scotland today.' He had a very direct, no nonsense way of speaking. 'We'll invite you to come along to the William Wallace Youth League to talk about your experiences as a Scottish hero.'

'Me? I'm no hero.' Euan was rather taken aback by this suggestion.

'That's where you're wrong, Euan.' He was polite but he was behaving like someone who was used to getting his own way. 'To come back from the dead after twenty years, as you have done, is a heroic act that does your Scottish upbringing proud. We try to encourage our members to learn about heroic Scots of the past and present. You could be an inspiration to them.'

Euan felt embarrassed and smiled a rather weak and definitely unheroic smile.

Kenny shook hands with Euan and Dolly while Kyle slouched off without having said a single word.

'Kenny seems an interesting guy,' said Euan. 'Seems to have a few strong opinions about Scotland.'

'He's no' short o' opinions, that's for sure. Ye'd never guess he's only 19. Him and Kyle met at a Runrig concert a few months back and they spend aw their time thegither now.'

'Are they gay?'

Dolly laughed. 'Eh don't think so and Kenny would not thank you for saying that. He told me one time that homosexuality was un-Scottish but then he widnae be the first man tae say one thing and dae the opposite when it comes tae sex. Eh think they're just pals but they are right close. And Kyle certainly needs pals. His mum was meh cousin and we worked together at Timex for a while. But she had a bloody terrible time wi' the men in her life, wi' a' kinds o' abuse. Kyle's dad walked oot on her when Kyle wiz jist six months auld.'

'You're talking about her in the past tense as though she was dead.'

'Eh, she's deid a' right, never even saw thirty.' Dolly drew breath. 'One o' her boyfriends wiz into hard drugs and they used to share needles wi' their pals when they were injecting themselves wi' heroin and ither stuff that wiz even worse. That whole group were infected wi' HIV and eh don't think there's ony o' them left now. This wiz before the treatments cam in and a lot o' them would not even go tae tak the test tae see if they'd been infected. They did not want to know. Kyle's mum lost weight something awfae; she must have been tae aboot four stone when she died. It was Kyle that found her, the poor laddie. He lives wi' his grannie but it's hard for her looking after a seventeen year old. She gets by wi' her Prozac.'

They walked along in silence for a bit. Some boys were throwing stones at a wall. There was some shouting in the distance that suggested some runners had crossed the finishing line.

'Eh promised Kyle's mum that eh'd keep an eye on him and so eh try tae get him involved in some o' the community things that are going on in the scheme. But, tae be truthful, he hates Bannockbrae; thinks it's responsible for what happened tae his mum. He's absolutely deid set against drugs and eh know that he wants tae get away from the scheme as soon as he can. Eh know that Kenny's a bit fu' o' himsel but he is a pal for him and he never touches drugs. He's a big noise in the William Wallace Youth League but ehm no sure if many ither young fowk are interested in their politics; they ca' them the Wully Wallies and somehow eh don't think Kenny would think that wiz funny. But Kyle and Kenny do lots o' stuff thegither. They seem to go to the library in the Flukergate a lot and there's this radio stuff that he mentioned.'

'What do you mean, Dolly? Some kind of youth radio?'

'No, it's more like a radio for old bampots. Eh don't know if ye've heard it at all – Radio Dighty?' Dolly did not look like she was a fan of this particular station.

Euan nodded. He noticed that the windows of the entire ground floor of Kesson House were boarded up; hopefully, nobody was living in these flats.

'Ye ken that one o' the reasons for choosing the name is that it's hard for folk who're no Scots to pronounce it!'

Euan looked puzzled.

'It's named after the Dighty Burn. But the main attraction in the name is that English folk can't pronounce it right; some make it rhyme with eighty and some say Dickty because they have difficulty with the ch-sound. Like we didn't have enough tae worry aboot without a load of bampot shite like that.'

'Who pays for that? Radio stations must cost money. Kenny looks fairly prosperous. Is it his money that pays for it?'

'No, Kenny's family, the Horsburghs, are well to do, right enough. They own a construction company that built some of these damp houses we're stuck in.' She pointed her hand towards the nearest building. 'Eh think their main interest is money, big money, and they're no' bothered about where it comes frae. Eh'm no' sure what they think o' Kenny's ideas, if they even ken aboot them. The money for Radio Dighty seems tae come from a multimillionaire in Texas who goes by the name of Logan J. Tree. Apparently, his mither wiz frae Arbroath. Eh'm a wee bit worried about Kyle getting mixed up wi' that lot but eh hav nae real alternative tae offer him. Eh jist hope that Kyle gets a bit o' confidence frae having a good time wi' his pal.' She didn't sound very convinced.

'I'm always being told that young folk grow out of their daft ideas and maybe that's what will happen with Kyle. I mean to say, he's only into ideas rather than drugs.'

'Eh hope ye're right, Euan. Eh hope ye're right. No lang now till we get oor peh and chips.'

Euan sounded as though he was looking forward to this. 'We'll see if Haris is ready to come back into the land of the living.'

Dolly grunted. 'Eh, but will his hangover be mair painful than meh blisters? Tae be truthful, thae trainers are useless as shite.'

12

Euan's notebook 3rd May 1999

My early life had been spent on the farm, but there hadn't been much chance to talk, or even think, about farming since I'd come back. I remember that there were clear, well-established patterns to the year – ploughing, sowing, planting, putting the cattle out, clatting neeps, bringing in the hay, picking berries, the grain harvest, the potato harvest, bringing the cattle in, the threshing machines and then, the still of winter. I remember too that there were endless opportunities for chat, whether we were stooking or picking berries or feeding cattle. There was also solitary work like howking neeps on frosty mornings or removing stones from the fields before the ploughing could begin, and if you wanted to have a moan about that there were always other folk who'd done those same jobs. The cycles of farming life seemed unchanging and everyone seemed to accept the sense of them without question. There was little or no choice about life on the farm; you just had to adjust to whatever the seasons decided to throw your way. But farming has changed; the whole process of mechanisation and the de-population of the countryside were things which I would never have predicted. Gregor is growing up in the same place as I did but it feels light years away from the world I remember.

I decided it would be a good idea to talk to someone who could remember those days; someone who would remember me too from those days. Peem Duthie had come to work on our farm when I was two; he must have been in his thirties at the time. Swack was the word that my parents used to describe his agility. My memories are of someone who had settled into a measured relationship with the ups and downs of country life. Peem had become the rock on which farm life rested and he never appeared to be thrown by events. As my father became more involved in the National Farmers' Union, the Kirk Session, the cattle market and the clutter of committees that surrounded all that, Peem was left to manage the farm. As the grieve, Peem was the one who, in reality, hired the other farmworkers; he was the one who offered them regular support and caution. Every evening, he and my father would have interminable conversations about the state of the day's work or the state of the next harvest or the state of agriculture. Their discussions were a bit like some ancient ritual where ideas were thrown up in the air and tested until such time as they both agreed which one was strongest.

It could possibly have been the closest relationship that my father had with anyone. But it was strange that they never set foot in each other's houses. Haris would have called that a boundary issue but, at the time, it was probably some kind of thing about the fact that they belonged to different classes. There was a thing about names; Peem never used any name to address my father and my father never called him anything other than Peem. There was a formality too about the way that they referred to each other's wives; always Mrs Saddler and Mrs Duthie. The two women waited every night in their own houses for the return of their men, sometimes at seven o'clock, sometimes at eight, sometimes later. They always waited and always separately.

Peem would never have assumed any informality or closeness with my mother. 'Looks like we're due some more rain, Mrs Saddler.' He was, however, prepared to take on a much closer, more involved role with me and my brother. He introduced us gently to all the skills of the farming trade and spent time with us when we made the mistakes that wee boys make when learning to stook or milk cows. Far more than an employee, he took on the role of a father outdoors. Both his sons were several years older than me and I wondered if he had been more of a father to me than he had been to them.

I remember the way that he had encouraged me to hear the sounds of the countryside. He used to enjoy listening to birdsong and he had told me that his favourites were the lark and the chaffinch. But most of all, I remember him explaining to my six-year-old self how to distinguish a blackbird from a crow by the colour of its beak. I was very proud of this nugget of information and made sure that everyone else in my class at school became aware of it as well. Peem never expressed any political views to me except when he told me about how the Chinese Communist government had tried to wipe out the sparrow. I felt quite protective towards the wee spuggies after that.

When I got around to summoning him, he did look pretty much like I would have predicted. He was a short, broad-chested man in his mid-fifties with brylcreemed hair and a V-necked woollen pullover; he had a broken nose too but he never told us how he had acquired it. I remembered him as being tall but my clearest memories of him dated from the time when I was a wee boy looking up to him and now he was looking up to me. He had always been a courteous man and so our conversation started gradually and politely; it took us some time to get into our stride.

'Aye, you and your brother were a grand pair o' lads. I often telt your father how proud he should be o' the pair o' you. You were mair one for the book learning than Alistair but we need both types of folk to mak the world go round, the practical men and the brainy men. I mind how pleased I was when I heard you were to be goin' to university. It's only them with a top quality brain that can do that. Your sister was brainy as well; she made the most o' her chances and good luck to her; there's no' many lassies that could get as far on in the world as she has done. I can tell you that your father was real proud o' the pair o' you.'

I shook my head. 'I wish that he'd made time to tell us that. He made it really difficult for Irene to study what she wanted to study and he never seemed interested in what I wanted to do either.'

'Aye, men like your father often don't say much about what makes them proud. I think if there's a reason for it, it's because they don't want to make you big headed.'

He seemed eager to talk about my father. 'Ye know, I was right lucky to work for your father. Right from the time that I started to work here, I knew that I was expected to be in charge o' the day to day business o' running the farm. I made the decisions about when work started; about the cattle that we bought; about the men that we hired. And I made sure that I talked to him about every single thing; I never got above myself. No' many men in my position got the chances that I did here at Balkerro. I realised that if I played my cards right by him, he would play his cards right by me. Of course, he could get real nasty from time to time and there were times when I thought of lookin' for another fee. But I knew full well that I'd never get a chance to build up an Aberdeen Angus herd like I did here. It wizna the money that kept me here so much as the chance to do something worthwhile.' He nodded his head.

He was well respected by everyone else who worked on the farm. When we were clatting, he liked to make sure that everyone felt comfortable with the conversation. I remember one day Tam Mudie dropped a jeely piece on the ground and we spent the next few hours till lousing time arguing the toss over whether to say, 'You'll eat a peck o' dirt afore ye dee' or, alternatively, 'You'll eat a speck o' dirt afore ye dee'. A peck, I had discovered that day, is an old form of measuring liquid that amounts to about sixteen pints and that seems like a lot of dirt. But back and forward the conversation went, history, geography, the Bible, weighing systems, public health, women's place in the home; there seemed to be no area of human life that was not touched by this topic. It was a good natured discussion about something that didn't really matter very much in the scheme of things but Peem made sure that it lasted as long as it kept our spirits up; I can't remember what topic we moved on to next but I left the field at the end of the day with a feeling of having enjoyed myself as well as having worked hard. And the next day, I had been happy to go out clatting again, curious about what that day's conversation would be. There were times too when Peem would draw things to a close when he thought a limit has been reached. When some of the lads started to boast about their successes with women, there would come a point when Peem would draw the conversation back to something that he considered more respectable. And the way that he did it caused no offence; it was understood and accepted that Peem set the rules of the day.

It was different with the folk that came out from Dundee, particularly for the berries or the potato harvest. They seemed to have different rules altogether and they didn't accept Peem's role as master of the conversation. In fact, they didn't accept his authority at all and behaved just exactly as they wanted.

'Some o' the lads frae Dundee were a bit on the coarse side. I'm no' saying that they were all the same but some o' them were up to no good, and that's a fact. It could be the way that they grew up; I hear they do things differently there. I only ever went to Dundee myself three or four times. The first time was when I was 18; I was going on National Service down South and I had to catch the train from Dundee.'

'But it was so near. Did you never fancy going there for a night out?'

'No' really, no. I'm a countryman and I made my enjoyment in the country. I was the same with Edinburgh; every year we would go down to Ingliston for the Highland Show and I never bothered to go into the town. Some o' the other lads wanted to make a night o' it when they had a chance to enjoy themselves; they wanted to behave like single men but that didn't interest me. I would offer to keep an eye on their beasts so that they could go off and enjoy themselves. I was always happiest here. When I was a lad I would cycle to dances in other villages and I had a braw time that way. In fact, that's how I met the wife. When we were courting, I would cycle seven miles to see her and then seven miles back home at the end o' the night. That's the way things were and the world was no worse for that. When the laddies were growing up, we would go up to my sister's place at Killin for our holidays and there was a chance to go fishing there. I always thought that I was lucky to be able to enjoy the country like I did. We used to go down to Carnoustie when the laddies were wee because they liked the sea and building sand castles and all that kind o' thing. We had some grand times there but, to be honest, I would far rather have been up in a glen. And that's a fact.'

'What did your sons do when they grew up? Did they work on the land as well?' They could only have been a few years older than me but when you're a child even two or three years difference in age can seem like a generation. I really didn't remember very much about them at all.

'Chance would have been a fine thing!' He sounded almost angry; I had obviously upset him. 'There was less and less work on the land for them. They have all kinds of machines nowadays to do jobs that would have been done by farm workers before. My older laddie, Jim, went off to the Black Watch and eventually became a sergeant major; he did really well for himself. Scott had a harder time finding work that suited him and he had a harder time finding a wife that suited him as well. He went down South and drifted for a while. The last I heard he was working in a bar on the Isle of Man.' He shook his head in disappointment. 'There's only so much you can do wi' your bairns and then it's up to them to make the most of what's there for them. But life for Scott was much much harder than ever it was for me. There was no place for him here.'

This expression of disappointment was more personal than I expected from Peem. He had hardly ever discussed his family life with me and why would he? He was a private man and I'm sure that he thought it was for the best if people kept their feelings to themselves. I had touched this dignified man in a damaged place. I had reminded him that the countryside had no need for men like him or his sons any more. I never even mentioned the birdsong.

13

'Good evening, Scotland, you are listening to Radio Dighty, the radio station that's owned by Scots and brings you all the best in Scotland – the music, the news, the history, the sport, the humour. Radio Dighty is the only radio station where you can always be sure of hearing an honest to god Scottish accent and nae doubt about it. Tonight, you can join me, Miller Gibb, for a discussion on Scottish heroes.

'You'll mind that last week I asked you to send in your thoughts about who should be included in the shortlist for our forthcoming competition on Scottish heroes. And, my word, there was no hauding ye back. The phonelines and the email were near fit to bursting with your responses. So, thanks very much to all those o' you that took part. We'll read out extracts from some o' the messages.

'A caller from Lintrathan nominated William Wallace, the greatest Scottish freedom fighter o' all time. Our caller pointed out that he had heard very little about William Wallace when he was at school except that he was defeated by the English. It was only when he saw the film *Braveheart* that he began to realise just how much popular support he had throughout Scotland. He was more than just a brave man, he was a great leader. He was defeated, for sure, but it was only because of the bullying power of a thieving nation that was ten times bigger than Scotland itself. That's as true today as it was then. But our caller is no' interested in excuses and he makes a plea for Scots education to make more space in the curriculum for William Wallace. At a time when more power is being devolved to this great country of ours, Wallace provides a great role model for all Scots who are proud of the country that they call home.

'William Wallace was also nominated by a caller from Ardler who reminded us that he was a real man, unlike Edward the Second who was king of England at that time. Because this is a family programme, I am no' able to use the words that the caller used. There might be young children listening and so let's just say that Edward the Second was a bit of a pushover. In the end, the red hot poker that finished him off was a bit more than he'd bargained for but it would be true to say that he'd been asking for it. Thankfully, no such suggestions can ever be made about Wallace or any of our other great Scottish heroes, past or present.

'Most of the heroes that folk have nominated have been men, and that's no surprise. We're thinking about maybe having a competition soon on great Scottish housewives and that'll be a chance for the womenfolk to come forward. But one woman that has been nominated in the heroes section is Mary Slessor. I didn't know much about Mary but a caller from Newtyle filled me in on some of her details. She was a millworker in Dundee. She never got herself a man and so, she spent a lot o' time in the kirk and was well known for being religious. Eventually in 1876 she decided to go off to Calabar in West Africa as a missionary. West Africa was in an awful state at the time and the folk there must have been fair chuffed that this lassie from Dundee bothered to go all that distance to convert them. In the end, she stayed there for forty years and you can see her face on the back o' some Scottish pound notes. When you look at the state of Africa now, you think maybe they could be doing with another Mary Slessor to go over there and help them out. The thing was that Mary did not bring loads o' Africans back here but she took Scottish values out to them. There's a lot about Mary Slessor to inspire young women today.

'A caller from Padanarm reminded us of a film called Geordie that he saw when he was just a loon back in the 50s. The film was a bit before my time but it was about a wee laddie that decides to build himself up into a man with muscles. Apparently, he was a right wee nyaff but, after exercise and self-discipline, he went on to become a champion hammer thrower at the Olympic Games. It's no' a true story but it's the kind of thing that we could be doing to show to our young folk to encourage them to build themselves up into strong young men and, of course, women too. If Scotland is to become the great country that it should be then it needs to be full of healthy, confident young folk. I don't know if any listeners tonight are involved with organising the Thrums Show. Hammer throwing is a grand Scottish sport and that's the kind of thing they could be putting into next year's programme. Thanks to our caller for bringing that to our attention.

'A caller from Oathlaw mentioned the name of Robert Louis Stevenson and he wondered how come it was that a great author like Stevenson had never had a monument built for him. Walter Scott has the Scott Monument, but there are no plans for a Stevenson Monument. Our friend from Oathlaw is right that Stevenson was a great author. I remember how much I used to enjoy reading *Kidnapped* and *Treasure Island* when I was a wee boy; they are grand stories, right enough. But the thing is, you see, I'm no' sure if you can say that Stevenson was a Scottish hero. His grandfather and other folk in his family built famous lighthouses but he did nothing like that. In fact, he spent a lot of his life trying to get away from Scotland. He went to Bournemouth and then he ended up on some primitive island in the middle o' the Pacific. After he died, the folk there were in an awful state about him and they built a monument for him. A great writer but what did he ever do for the country of his birth?

I am sure folk will want to say more about that. This is a discussion programme, so get back to me with your thoughts.

'Some of you wanted to nominate the great Celtic team that went all the way to Portugal and won the first ever European Cup in 1967. They are known to football fans the world over as the Lions of Lisbon. One of the best known facts about this team is that all the players were born within thirty miles of the centre of Glasgow. There are, of course, folk that would say that Celtic is a team that owes more loyalty to the Bishop of Rome but we say that kind of opinion is nonsense. These boys were Scots, through and through, they were playing for their native land and they made their countrymen proud of them. Whatever church they went to, they were Scots heroes, make no mistake.

'Rabbie Burns was one of your favourite nominees and his poetry is read and admired all over the world. Who needs Shakespeare when you can listen to the fine words of the great Ayrshire poet? We have had an unprecedented number of calls about Burns and I am going to throw open the discussion to any questions and comments that you might have about the Immortal Rabbie. But before that discussion begins, let's just spend a few minutes listening to *My Love Is Like A Red Red Rose*, sung by our very own Bonnie Swankie.'

14

Euan's notebook 7th May 1999

I feel much healthier and much stronger than I did even a few weeks ago. I notice that I've got more staying power than I used to do, whether we're at the gym or out walking. I also seem to have much more staying power than Haris. I think of 39 as being my biological age and 19 as being my conscious age. According to my biological age, I am older than Haris but, according to my conscious age, I am younger than him. It's no wonder if he doesn't know whether to feel pleased or irritated about my rude health.

He's definitely pleased about my memory and the way that it seems to be improving. It's funny the way that wee things can just set off a whole load of bigger memories. The other day, Amanda gave me a packet of begonia bulbs. She knew that I was trying to brighten up my room and she thought that I might enjoy trying to grow something. It was kind of her and I'm going to give it a try, though I won't place any bets on the survival chances of the begonias. But it got me thinking about how my mother always had a few plants on the go. She always seemed to grow the same things, hyacinths, daffodils, geraniums and they were always flowering plants. For some reason, she wasn't so keen on plants like aspidistras which had no flowers. I remember too that she used to be quite envious of one of her friends who had a greenhouse and she enjoyed going over there to admire the latest blooms. These thoughts just triggered off memories of the smell of the rooms when I was growing up, as well as the colours. I didn't pay much attention to my mother's plants at the time, but the memory of them reminded me of what my home felt like more than words were able to do.

A few weeks previously, I had another set of memories triggered off about the British Linen Bank. I was on the point of opening my own bank account and I remembered that I'd always liked that name. I wanted to have a cheque book that said British Linen Bank on it, just like the boy in *Kidnapped* did. I couldn't find out where there was a branch in Dundee and Haris had never heard of it. I went to Heather, the receptionist, and she told me that it had been swallowed up by one of the bigger banks a few years back. So, that was that. It was difficult to understand just why I had liked the name; maybe just because it was unusual, or it was a bit comic, or maybe because I liked the feel of linen.

After my conversation with Peem, I found myself thinking more and more about my father. I hadn't thought about him very much when I returned to the world but as I became more aware of my own emotions, I realised that I was remembering all sorts of feelings about him and they were difficult feelings. He never beat me up or anything like that but I couldn't remember any good times that we had had together. I have lots of memories of times spent with my mother and Alistair and Irene but he does not figure in these at all. It was almost as though he wasn't there. He certainly never taught me anything and I had no sense of comfort about him. There was just a big cloud of uncertainty.

It had to be done; I would have to summon his ghost; I couldn't avoid him. In fact, that's not true. He is dead and I could easily avoid his ghost. What I mean is that since I have these ghost-summoning powers, I could use them to make contact with him and maybe understand him a bit better. Sometimes my medication can make me feel a bit woozy and, since meeting ghosts can be tiring, I decided that I would only contact him on a day when I was feeling fresh and strong.

He had been in his seventies when he died but the ghost looked about 50. He wasn't as tall as I remembered him being and, in fact, we were about the same height. He looked prosperous and he had a slightly restless, slightly irritable air about him. He was wearing the sort of sensible suit that he might have worn to go to his beloved Perth Bull Sales. Or he might have been on his way to a meeting of the Kirk Session. He had been very proud of being a Church elder even though his Christian beliefs might have been a bit difficult for Jesus to recognise. He was never one for loving his neighbour, as far as I can recall. There was a gleam of self-satisfaction about him. Joe Devlin had told me that ghosts appeared as they were when they were at their happiest and he probably was at his happiest as a public figure.

One of his great bugbears was the moral inadequacy of the people of Dundee and once he realised that I was living in Dundee, he wasted no time in repeating some of his views about them. 'I've always said Dundee folk are awful coarse. You'll mind that I used to have a lot of trouble with some of these tinks coming out to Balkerro and demanding to use what they called their rights of way, walking through my fields, stealing tatties and disturbing the cattle. Said they wanted to enjoy the beauty of the countryside and some of them wanted to fish as well. They told me that the law was on their side and maybe it was because the law's certainly never on the side of the farmer. Oh, no! But I used to find that a bit of barbed wire fencing, some extra ploughing and the sight of me with a shotgun would scare off most of them. They wanted to relax in the countryside but I could fairly spoil that for them, the bloody tinks.'

I guess some folk never change. My father had always been one to carry on conversations about whatever was on his mind regardless of who he was talking to. Not only that, he was able to convince himself that whatever was on his mind was the most important thing in the world. Clearly even death had not separated him from his fixation about Dundonians. Maybe I was being selfish but since I had been in a coma at the time of his death and now I wasn't, I thought he might have found the time to ask me how I was. But, in his way, he went on to talk about me, at me.

'We tried our best for you, your mother and me, but then you got this illness. I always knew that it wasn't a good idea going to Africa but you and your mother knew better. She should never have been allowed to give you all that money for the airfare. She told me it was her savings and she could do what she wanted with it; that's fair enough. But it should have gone into the farmhouse and I wouldn't have minded if she'd spent it on a cooker or something else like that. And after you got ill, I told her as much; I just told her to think about where her fancy ideas had got us. Anyway, you've paid the price for what you did but it's fine to see you back in the land of the living and that's a fact.

'Oh aye, your mother and me, we wanted to give you, and your brother and sister, the chances that we never had. Of course, it wasn't easy with the world being the way it is and folk no' wanting to work. Nowadays they just expect to collect their salaries with no thought for their responsibilities. We tried, your mother and me, to instil in you the proper way to live...'

He went on like this for about an hour and so it was difficult to find out about the things that I wanted to know about. He mentioned my mother a lot and he seemed especially proud of the fact that she did not spend a lot of time away from home like the wives of some other men. But it was all general stuff and he never really gave me any recent information about her. I gathered that she was ill but he never mentioned that. He did talk about how he had always tried to make sure that she was able to have outings with us when we were children.

'I mind taking you and your mother to the zoo or the Diz, as folk in Dundee called it. You were that excited, we could hardly keep you sitting down in the back of the car. You had this list of animals that you wanted to see, lions, elephants, giraffes and so on. Your mother was worried that you would be disappointed but, apparently, they'd just got two young elephants that fairly took your fancy. They'd got daft names that bairns like yourself would mind but I can't, for the life of me, remember what they were.'

'Dumbo and Jumbo.' It's funny how my memory managed to recapture these names from nowhere.

'That's it. Daft names. Aye, it was a shame that I couldn't come in with you but I had some business to attend to.'

I had forgotten that it had been his way to drive us to the door of some place or other and then leave us to enjoy ourselves as he went off to attend to his business. Being dumped like that made me feel that I was just a scunner but I was amazed that he had remembered about those elephants. As we separated, he said that it had been fine to see me and I believed him but his monologue reminded me of how difficult it had always been to talk to him.

He was just about to go when he said something that truly amazed me. 'It was an awful shame about Andy Buchan. Terrible for his mother and father, a terrible business. He could have been a grand lad too but he just got in with the wrong company. But he was a pal for you. I often thought he was a bit big for his boots but he was always polite to your mother and he was a pal for you. We all need a pal, just somebody to keep an eye on things, somebody that knows what you're talking about. You'll need to find yourself another pal.' And then he was gone.

There were all kinds of questions buzzing around in my head after this encounter. I had hardly said a word during the whole hour. Maybe meeting up with ghosts of familiar people was more

draining than meeting up with the ghosts of strangers just because
of all the emotions they triggered. His remarks about Andy left
me speechless because I had a very strong memory of his disap-
proval of our friendship; but I was touched by his concern about
my need for a pal. Even more than that, I was curious to find
out just what had happened to Andy. Why did no one want to
talk about him? The way people spoke about him made me think
he was dead, although no one had actually said that. Maybe he
was in prison or living some kind of disgraceful life. But I had
a gut feeling that he was dead. If that was the case, I would be
able to summon his ghost and talk to him. Somehow, that seemed
a risk too far. I needed to know more about his life in the years
when I had been asleep before I could take that step.

15

Memories are complicated and unpredictable enough even for folk that haven't had sleeping sickness. Sometimes they'll do as they're bidden but you can never rely on that; sometimes memories intermingle and become confused so that what had been a clear memory at one time can appear incoherent the next; clarity is no guarantee of their accuracy; memories can be manipulated; memories really are something of a minefield.

Despite all this, it was the shared opinion of Euan's care team that the stimulation of his memories had been a successful exercise. They appeared to have helped him to grow in confidence and he seemed more able to relate to the demands of the everyday world; those embarrassing incidents when he called people a frog or a teapot were becoming less frequent. A decision was made to expose him to larger, less controlled group settings and Alistair and Wilma agreed to ask a few family members and friends from his past to meet him. There was a risk that he might be overwhelmed by the numbers but it was agreed that Haris could take him off somewhere quiet if that were to happen.

The countryside, on the day of the visit, was green and lush, just on the cusp of spring and summer. When they were nearly at the farmhouse, Euan persuaded Haris to drive to the ruins of an old flax mill; it was situated in wet, unploughable land which had always acted as a magnet for birds and other wildlife. He and Andy often used to go there when they wanted to be somewhere where they knew they would not be disturbed; this was where they had gone when they had their first smoke. He and Haris sat without speaking for a few minutes; it was a neglected, wild place, unlike any of the carefully manicured fields around it; soon they were rewarded by the sight of a hawk hovering over the old pond.

By the time they arrived at Balkerro, there was no sign of any hawks but there appeared to be dozens of cars parked in and around the farm steading.

'It looks as though Alistair and Wilma have gone over the top with the invitations,' said Euan, almost reading Haris's mind.

'We do not have to stay,' said Haris. 'If you do not feel comfortable, we shall leave immediately. I thought that we agreed that there would just be a few old friends and relatives.' He shook his head.

'Let's give it a go, Haris. I'm a bit nervous but I do want to give it a go. And, you're right, if it's too much, we just leave.'

As they stood at the front door, they could see that the lounge and the dining room were so full of people that the space felt claustrophobic. Although it was a clear day outside, these rooms dated from the time when windows had been small and there was very little natural light. Euan stood quietly, weighing up his options.

'Hello, Uncle Euan. Hello, Uncle Haris,' cried a cheerful young voice. 'I counted all the folk coming in and there's sixty-six here. It's very exciting. Mum's worried that she's gonna run out of food. There's no sausage rolls left.'

'You're looking very smart in that kilt, Gregor,' said Euan.

Gregor blushed. 'Mum says we all have to make an effort for you. Dad says it's no' necessary to be making a fuss but I wanted to do my best.'

'Are you having a good time?' asked Haris.

'It's very nice, but there's no' other boys or girls here apart from me and Amanda. My friend, Adam, wanted to come but his mum wouldn't let him because she said that you might be a bit scarey, Uncle Euan. She was worried that you would start having fits or something. I told her that was silly and then Mum told me I had to say sorry to her.' He blushed again.

'So, Gregor, do you know who all these people are?' asked Haris.

'Well,' said Gregor proudly, 'I made name badges for them all when they came in, to make it easier for Uncle Euan. All the men in suits over there are Dad's pals and most of them are farmers; he's speaking to his lawyer just now and he's got a different colour of suit from all the others. All the women over there with Mum at the food table are her chums; most of them are farmers' wives and some of them belong to her curling club. The really old folk near the window are your uncles and aunties; some of them are over seventy and a lot of the ladies have been crying because they're worried about seeing you. That's the minister and his wife with them. The men and women, near the old folk, were in your class at school but they all look much older than you.'

'Are you flattering me, Gregor?' asked Euan.

'No, really, you're the youngest looking old person I know.' There wasn't even a glimmer of a smile on Gregor's face.

Haris laughed. 'And who are those young men standing near the farmers?' he asked.

'They're the Latvians. I'm quite good at spelling but their names were really difficult when I was writing their badges. They work on some of the farms round here at harvest time and berry time. Some of them stay all the year round until they've saved enough money to go back to Latvia and start their own businesses. Dad says that they're much better workers than folk from Dundee and they don't answer back when he tells them what to do. They're very good at drinking and so when they heard that there was a party today, they came along to join in. They brought their own beer with them and Dad says that folk from Dundee would never do that.'

Haris had been worried that perhaps everyone would have gone silent or started staring at Euan when he came in. But Wilma and Alistair had asked them to behave normally and they all carried on with their own conversations. Euan just stood there, absorbing the atmosphere and, after a few minutes, he began chatting with Gregor and Haris; he was still rather nervous. But he decided to stay and make the best of the situation.

An elderly woman in a crushed silk frock that she last wore at a wedding in Montrose rushed over to Euan. In tears, she threw her arms round him and cried out: 'Oh, Euan, Euan, what a miracle to see you here! Your father would have been so proud, if only he had been spared, Euan. You're just the spitting image of him, the spitting image. And your poor mother – aye, well.' She dried her eyes and noticed Gregor. Patting his head, she enquired, 'And how's the wee man the day?' She was about to continue but an involuntary sob slowed her down.

'Gregor's just been telling us that he's started learning to play the double bass for the Forfarshire Youth Orchestra,' explained Euan.

'Oh, my goodness, that's clever of you. But how do you reach round it? Are you no' a bit on the wee side or do they put you on a box like they did with Alan Ladd?'

Gregor was puzzled. 'Does he play the double bass?'

'Oh, no, he was an actor, but he was a bit on the wee side, like yourself. He made some grand films about farming folk. You'll maybe have seen *Shane*? It's often on TV on Sunday after-noons and your Uncle George and me fairly enjoy it. Anyway, what was I saying? Because he was wee, like yourself, he used to have to stand on a box when he was kissing his girlfriend. Uncle George will mind better than me but I think he used to kiss that Veronica lassie. Aye, he stood on a box.'

Gregor began to assure this strange auntie that kissing was

not allowed at the Forfarshire Youth Orchestra, when Euan changed the tempo in the conversation by telling her she looked like a turnip. Gregor gasped in amazement. This was the first time he had heard such name calling; if only Adam had been here to hear it. Haris looked worried and put his hand on Euan's elbow, ready to steer him away. The auntie, however, continued talking as if nothing had happened.

'I'm sure it was Veronica, and her other name was something to do with water, I think. Veronica Poole or something like that. Oh, my memory's fairly going. Still, I shouldn't complain. At least I haven't had to be put away like your poor mother, Euan. Oh aye, things could be much, much worse. I just try to count my blessings. What else can you do?'

Haris was trying to move Euan away gracefully when Gregor pointed out Uncle George to his absent-minded auntie.

'He'll mind the name o' that Veronica lassie. George, George!' She headed off towards her husband.

The mood that had led to Euan mistaking his auntie for a turnip seemed to have passed. He and Haris went on a foray for sandwiches when they came across Alistair and Amanda with a bevy of besuited farmers and the solitary lawyer.

'Oh, you're the spitting image of your father, Euan. There's nae doubt about that,' said a man whose name badge was upside down. Grunts of agreement ensued.

An older man joined in, 'I can hardly credit how much you're like your father. If I hadna been a pall bearer at his funeral, I would swear blind that you were him, I would that.' Another murmur of agreement was followed by silence.

The man with the upside-down badge took on a leadership role in the conversation. 'Aye, Euan, ye'll maybe be thinking about finding a lassie to settle down wi'; you'll have a bit of lost time to catch up on. Still, I hope you're as lucky in love as your brother and Wilma.' He began to tell a story which the expressions on the faces of the others showed they had heard it many times before.

'He was a right lad was your brother, fairly one for sowing his wild oats. Anyway, when the time came for him and Wilma to settle down, they came back from their honeymoon and he told her that he wanted to lay down some rules. What they'd call ground rules nowadays. He told her that they would be fine as long as she made sure that he was happy and she'd need to keep the house clean, and keep his bed warm. I'll no' go into the details seeing as how we have a young lady here. She'd have to have his meals ready on the table, whatever time he came in. And he warned her no' to start any nagging. If he was late back frae Forfar or anywhere else, she should still have his tea on the table, and if he was so pished that he couldn't drive back then he would expect her to come and fetch him. And, he said, if she did all that, they would be fine and happy.' The speaker had got the attention of everyone around him. 'And, apparently, Wilma told him that she only had one ground rule: there would be sex in the house every night at eight o'clock, whether he was there or not.' Amanda went bright red but all the others laughed heartily. 'So, Euan, take my advice – find a woman like Wilma and you'll no' want for anything!'

Marriage had not been in Euan's thoughts and he was not sure what to say next. Everyone had stopped talking and it seemed like they were waiting for some kind of response.

'I see you've had a grand lambing this year, Alistair?' said the pall bearer, moving on to safer ground.

'Aye, we have that,' said Alistair. 'I've never been a great believer in winter lambing. Mind, I've had a grand assistant this year.'

There were murmurs of interest.

'Aye, Amanda's been helping me out this year. She was on and on at me to let her have a go but I must say, she's a natural, there's nae doubt about that. It's more like me that's helping her now.'

Amanda went an even deeper red than previously as her father's farming friends all turned towards her. 'I'd like to train as a vet, if I can get enough Highers, and that will give me the choice of working anywhere in the world or coming back to Balkerro.' She was amazed at her own confidence in stating this. It was what she'd thought for a long time but she'd never really said it out loud. Everyone usually treated her as a big, fat, daft lassie but she had other ideas.

The farmers murmured in a chorus of something that sounded like approval and her dad seemed a bit surprised too. She'd never said this to him either. And then the conversation moved on again.

'That was a terrible carry on at the Perth Sales,' said the man with the upside-down badge, 'wi' the bulls escaping from the market. Apparently, they made their way right through Tay Street and into the park at North Inch. I heard the police were no use, they were complaining that bull catching wasn't part of their job description!'

'I don't know what things are coming to,' said a man in a suit that he had outgrown. 'First the elephants from the Diz and then the Perth Sales, no' to mention the Clydesdales at Stobswell. There's something no' right.'

'I dinna ken if you'll mind Jockie Henderson's horse, a grand big Clydesdale that went by the name o' Clyde,' said the pall bearer. 'Oh, he was a grand horse. He never had to be tethered up because he kent where he had to be at any particular time in the day. Mair sense than some o' Jockie's bairns. Aye, he kent fine where his ain stall was. A grand working horse wi' plenty o' discipline. You never got horses like him just running away on a whim.'

'He came to a sad end, though.'

'What happened to him?' asked Amanda, who, like Euan and Haris, had never heard the story before.

'Weel,' explained the pall bearer, 'it was a Saturday afternoon and the Hendersons had aw gone into Dundee. The men had gone to Dens Park, for they were aw Dundee supporters and Jessie, that's Mrs Henderson, and the lassies – I cannae mind now how mony there were o' them – the womenfolk were shopping and then they aw went and had their tea in the Deep Sea. The young lads stayed on in the toon but Jockie and Jessie and the lassies cam back on the 7 o'clock bus. Weel, by the time they got back hame, the place was up in flames. They were never sure what had started the fire but there was naebody there and it soon got a grip on the whole place. It's the worst thing that can happen tae ony farmer. The hoose was a' right but the steading was burned doon. Some neighbour had called the fire brigade but ye ken whit they lads frae Dundee are like, they didna ken where to get the water. Whole place burned tae a cinder and Jessie's hair went white on the spot.'

'And the horse,' asked Amanda. 'What happened to the horse?'

'Aye, he died in his stall. Stood there and took the flames, like a real hero.'

'But I thought you said that he wasn't tied up. Surely, he could have run away?' she asked.

'He kent whit time he was supposed to be in his stall and whit time he was supposed to come oot and the time o' the fire was no' the right time for him to be moving. Aye, Clyde, a grand horse.' The pall bearer looked suitably solemn to mark the death of this much loved animal.

Amanda burst into tears. 'He burned to death! A grand horse! More like a brainwashed horse!'

'Amanda, calm down, now,' said Alistair. 'No need to be upsetting yourself about something that happened forty years ago.'

She rushed off in floods of tears.

'Aye, I suppose she's at a sensitive age,' said the pall bearer. 'Still, Alistair, it's grand that you've got her to help you wi' the lambs.'

But the story of the fire, familiar though it was, had distressed them all and they made off in pursuit of the comfort they expected from their wives and daughters. Alistair wondered whether he should do the same but he still had the lawyer to entertain. Haris and Gregor went off to see if there was any food left while Euan parked himself on a sofa.

'Euan! Euan!' A voice cried out as if the sleeping sickness might have rendered him deaf. 'Euan, Euan. It's Pam, your own Pammy! I wasn't sure how much you would remember of me so I brought some old photos with me to help your memory.' The woman bearing the photographs was about the same age as Euan and she was wearing fawn slacks and a multi-coloured top with leaping fish on it. 'So make some room for me on the sofa and we'll start at the beginning. I hope you'll remember me. My name is Pam Hosie – well, I used to be Pam Syme – but this is so exciting I'm just all over the place. But before we start looking at the piccies, can I just say that you're the spitting image of your father. It's all in the genes, as they say. Anyway, the piccies that I want you to look at first are the ones that we took when we all went on that trip to Holland. We must have been about fifteen at the time and it was the first time most of us had been out of the country or even away from our parents. We all had such fun, if you remember, but, looking back, we must have been a nightmare for the teachers, an absolute nightmare. I could never be a teacher, just couldn't handle the discipline at all. So, to get back to the business in hand. Your psychologist, Haris...'

'Just like the school.'

'Oh, goodness me, yes,' giggled Pam, 'I never thought of that

– makes it easy to remember – he said that it would be nice if you could be reminded of good times that you had with your school friends. He said not to bring too many pictures and so, I thought I would just concentrate on the trip to Holland. Here's the picture of us standing waiting to go on the bus that took us down to London. That's you and me there, looking all shy and young.'

Then Euan spotted a photo of a pretty, dark haired girl. 'And is that Deirdre Buchan? She was Andy's sister, wasn't she?'

'Oh, yes, poor Andy, so tragic, so, so tragic but let's not dwell on that today. This is a good memories day. Actually, talking about memories, it's such a coincidence that the home where you're staying used to be my grandmother's house. I haven't been back there since I was about five or six, just after she died. We had some lovely times there with her. I think she was better able to relax with her grandchildren than she did with her own children in India. I have some wonderful memories of that house. She was very, very nice.'

Euan wondered if he should mention his recent encounters with Pam's granny but thought better of it.

'We'd really love you to come and see us sometime,' said Pam. 'I could invite along the whole gang from your schooldays and get my husband to do a Barbie; some men will do anything if there's a gadget involved and my husband's one of them! Don't think I'm being silly but the sleeping sickness has been really good for your looks. We're all middle-aged fuddy duddies, solicitors, social work managers, accountants and so on and we look like old wrecks beside you. Of course, there are some unattached ladies too. My sister in law is always on the lookout for Mr Right and my next door neighbour is divorced – with your looks, they could pass you off as a toy boy.' She laughed, almost as if she didn't quite believe that anyone would enjoy her sense of humour.

'What's a toy boy?'

'Oh, dear, there's me making assumptions when so much has changed since we were both young. Time flies, as they say.' She couldn't stop laughing.

Euan did not get the chance to learn about toy boys because at that moment, he told Pam she looked like an aspidistra. She became a bit flushed and tearful as she looked around, desperately, for Haris. She was concerned that she might have tired Euan out and she had been looking forward to seeing him so much. It was really quite nerve-racking. She didn't know how his family could cope. She didn't want to leave him alone while she went off to look for Haris when he was looking so withdrawn. She wondered why he had called her an aspidistra; maybe it was because she had been talking about fuddy duddies? It must be terribly challenging for Haris to work with someone as unpredictable as Euan but he seemed so calm and professional. Maybe he could explain if there was a link between the aspidistra and something she had done.

'Attention, please, ladies and gentlemen.' It was the man with the upside-down badge taking on a leadership role again. 'We all know why we're here today, to welcome Euan Saddler back into the bosom of the community that he left so suddenly twenty years ago. And we are all very pleased to see you here today, Euan, even though you are better looking than aw the rest of us. What we'd like to do now is remind you of some of the dancing that we used to do in this part of the world when you were growing up. By that I mean dances like Broon's Reel, Strip the Willow, Dashing White Sergeant, favourites for dancers of all ages. There was a time when this kind of dancing seemed to be going out of fashion but I'm glad to say that it's making a comeback. I notice that one of the younger guests today has gone to the trouble to wear a kilt. Well done, Gregor. You've certainly put us older lads to shame. You're a bit on the wee side to take part in the dancing today but you can help the DJ with the music; that's the great thing about country dancing, there's something for everybody to do.' He looked around to check that he had the attention of his audience.

'Now, the first dance is going to be Broon's Reel and because there's no' a lot of room in here, it's only the first six couples on the floor that get to dance. And the other thing is that we're going to start with a ladies' choice, because we're getting ready for the twenty-first century here when men and women will be equal. I keep telling the wife about this but she'll no believe me; she just tells me to shut up or she'll gie me a skelp! Anyway, it's a ladies' choice. And could I ask you all to help move back the furniture a bit to make more room. Take care no' to scratch anything or you'll have Wilma to answer to!'

Haris was making his way across the room to Euan with a plate of sandwiches. He knew it was a stereotype but country dancing, or peasant dancing, as he called it to himself, often involved throwing women into the air. Maybe, Brown's Reel was different but he didn't want to take a chance. Throwing women in the air was not part of Euan's recovery programme. When he reached them, he could see that Pam seemed very agitated. She seemed upset that Euan had called her an aspidistra but he couldn't help her, since he didn't know what an aspidistra was. He explained that he needed to find somewhere quiet for Euan to rest before they went back to Dundee. He guessed that Gregor, now that he had been publicly forbidden from dancing, would be able to suggest somewhere.

Gregor looked pleased to be asked to do something. 'He can go into my room, Uncle Haris. Nobody will be up there. I tidied it up this morning and he can listen to some music on my CD player. I've got the latest Whitney Houston CD but maybe Cher would be better for a man of his age.'

They made their way up the stair and Gregor's room was as tidy as promised. On the walls there were posters of Kylie, David Beckham and the Dundee United team. Euan looked really tired and fell asleep on the bed as soon as he lay down. Haris and Gregor attacked the sandwiches.

'I'll stand guard outside, Uncle Haris, just to make sure that no one comes in.'

Two minutes later, Gregor heard an elderly voice cry out. 'Gregor, have you seen your Uncle Euan?' It was the elderly auntie in the crushed silk frock.

'He's having a rest, for medical reasons,' explained Gregor, standing at the top of the stairs, as if preparing for a siege.

'Oh, well, maybe that's for the best. It's maybe been too much for him today, what with him no' being well a' that time. I suppose he has his nurse wi' him, does he?'

Gregor wasn't really sure about how much detail to disclose and just stood firmly where he was.

'Anyway, Gregor, you tell him when he wakes up that I minded the name o' that lassie that used to kiss Alan Ladd when he was standing on a box. I knew it was something to do with water and it was Veronica Lochhead. It just came back to me when I was having some of the sponge cake that your mother made. So, you'll mind and tell him when he wakes up; I would have been worried silly if I hadn't remembered it. And mind, Gregor, don't you worry if lassies don't want to kiss you if you're still wee when you're bigger, if you ken what I mean; just think of Alan Ladd and if he can do it, so can you. I can stop worrying about my memory now that I've told you and you'll no' forget to tell Euan, will you?'

'I won't forget,' said Gregor to his departing auntie's back, 'even if I am wee.'

16

Euan's notebook 15th June 1999

When it comes to sex, it seems completely different from what it used to be; certainly, talking about it seems different. Folk seem to talk about sex all the time and there's advice about condoms on every street corner. Gregor showed me a book that his mum had given him called *A Beginner's Guide To Puberty*. Women are allowed to talk about sex too as though it's something they might enjoy. In the middle of all this, I began to realise that I needed to do something about my own sexual feelings. I was well enough versed in the theory but now I needed some practice. And there was an urgency to it, twenty years of missed sexual opportunity fairly sharpened my mind. The thing is that I have gradually come to realise it's men I want to have sex with. Sometimes I see a guy and I just get that draw-in-your-breath sort of feeling that makes me know that I would happily talk to him for hours about cricket in Albania, just so that I could be near him and smell the whiff of sex coming off him. Sometimes I'll see a guy sitting somewhere and my eye goes towards his crotch and the fold in his jeans and the hint of the shape of what's inside takes me somewhere else completely different and completely wonderful. And it's no' that I get an erection when I see these guys (though sometimes I do) it's just that I know something has to happen sometime. I have to get to know some of these crotches better, I have to get my hands on a cock. These vague fantasies that I was having about Fergus will go nowhere; he's not interested in men, sexually.

And so I dithered away, unsure about what to do with my sexual desires. I knew that I did not feel entirely confident talking about my feelings, either with my new living friends or my old ghostly friends. Grab the bull by the horns, that's what I had to do. I saw an advert in a magazine for some kind of gay community helpline in London and I decided to phone there for a chat. There was one in Dundee but I was scared in case the phone was answered by someone I knew. That makes no sense, of course, because if they were answering the phone then they would probably be gay themselves or what they call gay-friendly. But it was anonymity that I wanted more than anything else and I thought I could get that better from the London helpline. It took ages to get through but when I did, I spoke to a really friendly man who said he came from Yorkshire. He'd never been to Dundee but his main advice was to head for the bus station; he told me that if you're in a small city and you're looking for a gay bar, you should head for the bus station or the rail station and you'll always find one in spitting distance. He also told me, or even instructed me, to be sure to have some condoms with me; just like a boy scout, I should be prepared. Anyway, I followed his advice and headed for the bus station and there it was, Dundee's most prominent gay bar and it was lime green. All it said above the door was kps'. Apparently, the original plan had been to name it in honour of a famous Canadian lesbian but the decorator got confused and wrote a 'p' by mistake.

I trembled my way into the bar. It was buzzing with all the expectations of a Saturday night. There was a segregated air about the place; one side was given over to women playing pool and the other to men consuming alcohol, as if it was the last day before Prohibition. I was hardly in the door when a man in a red leather jacket hiccupped into my ear. 'Hello there, big boy,' he lisped as he staggered towards the gents. Maybe these condoms would come in handy after all, but the sound of vomiting implied that they were unlikely to be used with Red Leather Jacket. When he emerged, he was preoccupied with wiping a soft, greenish substance off his jacket and walked right past me, without a glance.

I told myself that I didn't really fancy him anyway and stood near one end of the bar, hoping that somebody else might find me interesting. There were all shapes and sizes of guys in here. Some of them were in what looked like impenetrable groups; they seemed to take it in turns to tell stories which were all followed by gales of laughter. Some guys were looking round to see what they could see; sometimes one moved towards another and asked for a light for a cigarette, just to make a connection. Some guys were incapable of standing up unaided. Some looked like they didn't want to be there at all.

'It's a helluva dump in here and the state of some of these guys makes me wonder why I bother,' said a man into my left ear.

'It's my first time in here,' I trembled back.

'If you've any sense, you'll make it your last,' uttered the John Knox of the gay scene.

This was not the way I wanted to spend the evening; I smiled nervously and moved away.

After a few minutes, a man with bleach blond hair, who seemed less pissed than everyone else in the bar, sidled up to me with a big cheesy grin on his face.

'Hi,' he said. 'I saw you standing there on your own. I've never been one to stand on ceremony, so I thought I'd come over and say hi. Some people tell me I'm just too on but what's the point in waiting? Life's just too short.'

I went back into whispering mode again, 'I'm Euan.'

'Don't think I've seen you in here before. You must be a first timer, if you'll excuse my French.'

I was really inaudible now. 'Yes, it's my first time.'

'Probably in more ways than one,' he laughed and tossed his head back. 'Well, I suppose kps' is as good a place to start feeling your way around as any. I always say that life is a buffet, well, for some of us, it's a finger buffet.' His laugh became even louder.

I think he must have sensed that I was going to be harder work than he anticipated and it was then that he asked me over to join his friends. A tough looking man with no hair and a US marines' jacket was holding forth about his most recent sexual experiences. I stood there, soaking up the atmosphere rather than the words until I heard him mention the word, Bosnia.

'... hung like a fucking donkey, eh'm telling ye, eh could hardly get meh mooth roond it. And he says aw the guys are like that whaur he comes frae. So, eh asks him whaur that it is because ye can get flights tae aw kinds of places nowadays and then he tells me it's fuckin Bosnia - jist meh fucking luck, fuckin Bosnia - fuckawaywiye. See eh like a big knob as much as the next guy but eh'm no going awa there tae get ma ba's blown tae fuckin buggery by some fuckin Serb nationalist cunt. Eh'll jist stick wi' Ibiza but eh dinnae think he kent whit eh wiz talking aboot.'

I was stunned. I only knew one Bosnian. Could it be him? Surely not. A smile must have come across my face as I thought about the steps I might take to find out if Haris's cock was the same mega-cock that my new friend was talking about. But it puzzled me at the same time and the puzzlement must have shown on my face.

'Don't look so worried,' a dark haired handsome man said to me. He was a fit, masculine-looking, rugby-player type. He had the kind of good looks that my mother used to call chocolate box, over six feet tall with deep dark eyes and jet black hair. He looked altogether easier to be with than any of the other guys, Red Leather Jacket or John Knox or Bleach Blond or Shaved Head. He quickly introduced himself as Chris and after just a few minutes, he suggested we could go back to his place. I recognised the name because it was only a couple of streets away from the Wedderburn Centre. He had his car and said he couldn't drink any more safely. It was all a bit rushed but what the hell?

As we made our way towards the door, Bleach Blond caught my arm. 'I hope you know what you're doing, Euan.'

'I've got condoms, if that's what you mean,' I replied, with a minimum of politeness.

'OK, OK, you know what they say, "Shop till you drop, fuck till you flop". And you can tell me all about it next time you see me. Promise!'

'I promise,' I said, as I pulled my hand away from him and made for the door. This was a very important experience and I didn't want to keep Chris waiting.

I was no good at recognising makes of cars but I was impressed by this one, whatever it was. Comfortable seats as well as God knows how many buttons and gadgets. Best of all, it moved through the streets smoothly and soundlessly. We didn't say much on the way there but it wasn't long before we drew into the drive of his detached house. It seemed impressively large for a single man and I guessed he must be rich and successful to afford something on this scale. Maybe, I could become what Pam had called a toy boy. I had my life with him mapped out before we'd even got in the front door. He poured himself a large whisky but, remembering my medication, I stuck with something less powerful. My levels of excitement were so high I could have happily drunk cauld tea with sand in it.

When he took me upstairs, I began to get very nervous and wished that I'd maybe had a wee gin to calm those nerves. We went into a room with an enormous double bed which really did not look very well-used, more like a room in a hotel than his personal bedroom. I didn't know exactly what his intentions had been but he seemed surprised when I produced the condoms.

He didn't waste time on what we used to call foreplay; maybe that was one of those 70s things that had gone out of fashion? I knew that there was a range of things that guys could do with each other but before I knew what was happening, he had me squatting like a dog and he was pumping away inside me like – well, I don't know what it was like except a man fucking another man for the first time. I had expected it to be painful but he seemed to be pretty skilful with the lubricating oil. I was just starting to moan away when he finished, after one hundred and seven seconds! That was the great thing about these new watches; you could time any experience to the last second.

'I'd have taken it a bit easier if I'd known that it was your first time,' he said with a grin as he rolled over and headed for sleep.

It was only then I noticed that he hadn't used a condom. I'd been too excited to think about it and probably he had been as well. I'd have to remind him the next time. In fact, I decided to remind him there and then.

'Oy, Chris, wake up, wake up. Are you ready for a second round?'

'You're a horny young bugger,' he replied. As I moved closer to him, I could feel that he was becoming interested again.

'Shall I put the condom on this time?'

'No need for all that. I'm clean and I guess you must be too, you wee virgin.'

I could see that he was really hard by now.

'No condom, no sex.' I declared, much to his surprise.

'OK, OK, blackmailer!'

He was a bit slower this time. Four minutes and twelve seconds was much more enjoyable. I could get used to this. I thought I'd like to fuck him the next time but he really was asleep by the time I started to make a move in that direction. I told myself to be patient.

I suddenly remembered a cruel phrase that the lads used to say about women who had sex with men before they were married. 'She'll no die wondering.' There were lots of things I had to learn about sex yet but it was now the case that I wouldn't die wondering what it was like. I now knew what it was like and I wanted more of it. And, if the worse came to the worst and my sleeping sickness reappeared, I wouldn't die wondering either. It must have been with that thought that I fell asleep.

17

'Well, lads and lasses of all ages, you're tuned into Radio Dighty, the radio station that's owned by Scots and brings you all that's best about Scotland – the music, the news, the sport, the history, the humour. Radio Dighty is the only station where you can always be sure of hearing a Scots voice. In a few minutes time, we'll be taking you over to the Inverbervie sheepdog trials but first we're joined by Millar Gibb who is bringing you the latest profile in his series of Scots Heroes.'

'Thank you, this is Millar Gibb. This series aims to bring to the attention of the public important Scots who have often been overlooked or forgotten, men and women who have played their part in making this nation great. There are all kinds of lessons that we can learn from their lives as well as from their exclusion from our history books. Tonight's hero is James Adair, an authentic Scotsman, a man who, shamefully, has been written out of our history books. He was a man of the 1950s with an eternal message that is as true for our time as it was then.

'The London government of the day set up a Royal Commission to examine the sexual problems that were plaguing them in England, particularly the problem of homosexuality. The Scottish member on the commission was a Church of Scotland elder called James Adair. Lots of folk would not have wanted to give up two years of their life to look at something as sordid as this but Adair was a Scotsman who never flinched in defence of his moral values. He was prepared to devote that time to making sure that Scotland remained unpolluted by the scourge of homo-sexuality. The rest of the commissioners went along with the idea that homosexuality should be made legal. They said that they didn't approve of it but, like the spineless English liberals that they were, they recommended that there was no need for any law against the activities of these unfortunate misfits, as long as they were doing what they were doing in private. God help us! Adair took a much clearer, more moral, more Scottish position and he argued that legalising homosexuality would only encourage folk that didn't know better. As he said in his minority report: 'The presence of adult male lovers living openly and notoriously under the approval of the law is bound to have a regrettable and pernicious effect on the young people of the community.' He was successful with his argument, to a certain extent, and he ensured that Scotland remained free of sodomy for over a decade. Sadly, his battle was lost in 1980 when the law was changed in line with the law down South.

'Most of us recognise, of course, that homosexuality is un-Scottish, as un-Scottish as vegetarian haggis. And when we look at our great heroes over the ages whether it's Robert Bruce, Adam Smith, David Livingstone, as well as the great footballing legends of our own times, no one has ever been able to point the finger at them and say 'poof.' It's a different matter altogether when it comes to England, the place is just hoaching with them. Since the last election of 1997, a whole number of MPs and ministers from what used to be called the Labour Party have, as they say themselves, 'come out' but I am happy to say that not a single Scots MP has sullied the name of his country in this way. I am not one for Westminster party politics but, fair dues to them, there are no homosexual MPs from Scotland and that is testament to the brave struggle of James Adair all those years ago. There will be some of the politically correct lobby that tell me it is homophobic to speak in this way but I have to say no to that charge. For, while I have many disagreements with the

Pope, when His Holiness tells us to love the sinner but hate the
sin, I could not agree more. Many of these people cannot help
themselves any more than somebody can help being left-handed
or diabetic. It's a condition that deserves all our sympathy and
our compassion and our prayers. But it is a disorder and, thanks
to the influence of Adair, there are no open homosexuals in
public life in Scotland. There is no place for them to disrupt the
life of the nation with their shrill, unrepresentative demands.
They are, in Scotland, well and truly out of sight.

'An even bigger problem than the real homosexuals are the
folk who, for want of a better term, I might call bogus homosexuals. In these difficult times, many men are turning to
homosexuality because women are breaking away from their
traditional roles as housekeepers and child nurturers; many
women are not fulfilling their marriage contracts. And such men,
betrayed by the women in their lives, are turning towards homosexuality because homosexual sex is sex without commitment
and sex without responsibility. These men, hurt by the betrayal
of their women, are being lured away from the path of Scots
love; all around them, they can see homosexuals satisfying their
every lust or whim without any thought of the consequences.
Many of us believe that Adair was right in his fears about homosexuality becoming too easy. For why else would the good Lord
have invented the disease of AIDS? AIDS acts as a warning to
women to resume their traditional role of protecting men from
their basest desires; it also acts as a warning to men to put aside
their sinful behaviour and save their lives with the love of a good
woman. Adair, of course, could not predict the terrible menace
of AIDS but he was right to point out that society needed to be
protected from unnatural homosexual life-threatening
practices.

'Adair was far-sighted in his views and his memory is being

celebrated by campaigns all over Scotland inviting people to become Adair Aware. Particularly important in these campaigns will be the William Wallace Youth Leagues which are, I am happy to say, springing up all over the country and helping young Scots to put some meaning into their lives. We have Kenny Horsburgh, a representative of the William Wallace Youth League with us in the studio today and he is going to tell us about some of the campaigns that they are organising to promote Adair Aware.

'Kenny, thanks for being with us tonight. Can you tell us about what it was that led to the establishment of these campaigns.'

'Well, Millar, we were worried about the way in which homosexuality is being glamourised these days. All kinds of celebrities are popping up and saying that it's cool to be homosexual or bisexual and some of the more vulnerable young people in our society are going along with that notion. They were going along to these clubs and discos and having sex with strangers and all kinds of folk. They were missing out on all kinds of life chances and they were giving the cities of Scotland a bad name. We all know what happened to Sodom and Gomorrah and we did not want the same to happen to Dundee and Edinburgh.'

'I can understand that and I'm sure that many of our listeners will feel the same. But why did you choose a name like Adair Aware? It's a bit on the obscure side, is it no'?'

'That's a good question, Millar, and that's partly why we chose it. Because it's obscure, folk will wonder what it means. It's a bit like advertising where the best adverts nowadays don't just tell you the name of the product that they want you to buy; they make you wonder what the advert is all about; they make you use your imagination. That's the same principle as Adair Aware. Some of our members wanted to call it Down with Poofs. But that's so obvious that folk are not going to ask us questions about it, because they'll think they know what it's about. With

Adair Aware, we get lots of questions. We wear badges and stickers and put up posters in our meeting places and we do get lots of intelligent young folk coming up to us and asking what it's all about.'

'Ok, so questions are fine but that is hardly going to change the world, is it?'

'No, Millar, you're right. Questions alone are not enough but we are beginning to organise local campaigns and get coverage in the local press. We have some successful campaigns under way to challenge the right of homosexual people to meet in public places like schools. Will the bairns be safe? Do you want your bairns to be sitting on toilet seats that might have been used by homosexuals the night before? You can never be too careful. We are also putting pressure on schools, especially secondary schools, to take steps to prevent young people leaving school with the idea that homosexuality is ok. We plan to ask the Scots Parliament, once it's up and running, to monitor the influx of unnecessary homosexual foreigners into this beautiful country of ours, especially during the Edinburgh Festival. That might do some damage to the economy but what's the point in having a successful economy if you have lost your sense of morality. In time, we would like to go on to have re-entry services in churches for homosexuals who have decided to turn their backs on their lives of sin and re-enter the world of normality. We are hoping that some of our friends in the Kirk will agree to carry out baptism services for these repentant folk.'

'And are you getting much support?'

'Yes, Millar, we certainly are that. Sometimes we get that much support we hardly know what to do with it. One thing that we are clear about is that we are a disciplined campaign. Some folk think that we want folk to go to homosexual meeting places and areas where these poor souls go looking for sex and beat up the people they find there. Nothing could be further from the truth. We are interested in winning folk over to our ideas rather than breaking their legs or kicking their heads in or mutilating the private parts of their bodies. We are not thugs. You will remember the bomber that went to a homosexual bar in London a few months ago; a bar, by the way, that was named after a famous Dundonian without a by your leave; but one of the worst things that happened was that one of the dead was not even a homosexual; so, we instruct all our followers to be very cautious and disciplined and patient.'

'Well, Kenny, many thanks for that. It looks like it will be a long haul. I'm sure that all our listeners will wish you all the very best in your campaigns. People often criticise our young folk and say that they are apathetic and self-centred; the activities of the William Wallace Youth League show that this is just not true. There is a whole generation of authentic young Scots growing up who are keen to ensure, as James Adair was, that Scotland remains free of alien cultural influences such as visible, shameless homosexuality. We should be proud of the efforts of the William Wallace Youth League to keep alive the spirit of James Adair. I ask you all to join in their campaign to be Adair Aware and help to keep homosexuals and homosexuality out of sight.'

18

Euan's notebook 24th June 1999

It was over a week since I'd seen Chris. At first, I convinced myself that because he had more experience of the gay world, he should call me to arrange a date to meet again. But as I felt randier and randier, I soon convinced myself that because I was less experienced, he might not want to be pushy and so he might be waiting for me to make the first move. My self-persuasive powers could work wonders, especially when there was a possibility of having sex. I kept on telling myself that I'd already missed out on twenty years of my life and I could not afford to miss out on any more. Chris and Euan, the names sounded good together, Euan and Chris, Chris and Euan. I might get a bracelet made just with our initials on it; in time, I might even move on to a tattoo. I was planning some kind of future together for us, after we'd had sex. He had given me one of those long mobile numbers and I must have missed out a digit because I never even got the ringing tone.

It seemed like time to grab the bull by the horns again. So I decided I'd go directly to his house and, after we'd had sex, we could plan our future together and then, maybe, we could have sex again. Sex was only one step on the way but it was a badly wanted step. I put on one of the new shirts that I'd bought with Fergus. I also had a quick wank before I set out so that I didn't behave too desperately; I checked that there were no stains on the shirt.

I recognised Chris's car in the drive and rang the doorbell in a spirit of hope. I was surprised when a child came to the door but I was shocked when she ran off to get her daddy. Daddy was clearly even more shocked when he saw me.

'What the hell are you doing here?' he barked.

'I, ehm, I was just passing because, ehm, of course, I live very near here, just over in Dalhousie Crescent, ehm, and it's so near as to be almost spitting distance and, ehm, I thought I'd just drop in to say hello!' I was going through a very rapid learning curve here but I had a lot of recent experience of learning curves. I was not going to be daunted, even if I was havering away pathetically. The mood was, to say the least, very tense but our little standoff was interrupted by the screech of car brakes.

'Mummy, Mummy,' a child cried, running towards the car.

Before I got a chance to meet Mummy, I was pushed into a small utility room just beside the front door. It all happened so quickly that I didn't resist. Once I was in there, I heard the door being locked from the outside. Now I'd been kidnapped and was stuck in a room with a washing machine and a tumble dryer for company. I was in a state of some shock and sat down on an old stool while I collected my thoughts. After about twenty minutes, I'd had enough. I started calling out and banging on the door. When there was no response, I looked around for a sharp object to help me force my way out but, just as I was picking up a claw hammer, the key turned and there was Chris before me. I couldn't understand why he looked quite so terrified but, in retrospect, the sight of me clutching a serious-looking weapon might have been just a bit disconcerting. We stared at each other for a moment or maybe a fraction of a moment.

'Who's this man, Daddy?' piped up a child's voice, totally unaware of her father's previous history with me.

'I've just been inside your utility room, repairing your mummy's washing machine,' I heard myself saying. 'But it's alright now and I don't think there should be any more problems with it.' All the time, I had my eye on the front door and was trying to calculate how to reach it without bumping into Chris or knocking

over the wee curly-haired Shirley Temple. I even attempted to
smile in the way I imagined a washing machine repair man might
smile at a young child.

'You don't look like a washing machine man,' Shirley asserted.
'The last one who came to see Mummy had on a uniform and
he let us play with his car keys while he and Mummy went
upstairs…'

Mummy appeared at this point, laughing, it has to be said,
rather hysterically. 'Oh, don't pay attention to Tabitha, she's such
a one for stories.'

'Stories are very important for identity formation; it's been
well recognised in all kinds of research, all over the world.'
Memories of things that Haris had said made their way to the
front of my memory. I was anxious about what might next make
its way out of my mouth but all my concentration was really
focused on the front door. There seemed to be only a Yale lock
and it should be easy to run down the drive, if only I could make
it to the door.

'Where's your car?' asked the ever curious Tabitha-Shirley.

'Oh, we travel by bus. We're a very environmentally-friendly
company; our slogan is "If It's Green, It's Clean".'

'You're being *silly*,' laughed Tabitha-Shirley, as if this was the
funniest thing she had heard all week. 'If it's clean it should be
white, not green.' She thought this was hilarious and rushed off
to find another child to share the story about the funny washing
machine man.

'Anyway,' I said, 'I'd love to stay and chat but I must be off
– to catch my bus.' I was within reach of the door now.

Mummy was reaching for her handbag, perhaps for a cheque
book. 'How much do we owe you, for your time?'

'Oh, not to worry,' I could feel myself forming a new different
lie-for-mothers, as opposed to the recently told lie-for-children,

'this was just a preliminary visit to diagnose the situation. I'll be back tomorrow to carry out the actual repair.'

Mummy seemed to fall for that one and followed Tabitha-Shirley into the safety of the kitchen. 'I'll look forward to that,' she trilled.

Chris, meanwhile, had begun to resemble a volcano – just before the moment of explosion. Any intelligence he had had evaporated and, rather than assisting me out of his house, he seemed intent on grabbing hold of me. I skipped past him with a previously unrecognised athleticism, put my hand on the Yale and opened the door. Against all his obvious best interests, he seized my jacket sleeve. It was strange to remember how I'd thought Chris had chocolate box good looks when I met him; now he'd turned into one of Frankenstein's mistakes.

'Don't you ever turn up here again,' he shouted into my face. 'Do you hear me? Useless wee prick.'

There were all kinds of witty remarks I wish I'd made in response to that but I was focused on making my getaway; I reckoned that the last thing he'd want would be a scene on the doorstep. Eventually, I resorted to the oldest trick in the book and kneed him in the groin. 'Something to remember me by!' I shouted, as I pulled free. All kinds of oaths followed me down the drive. Today was providing endless learning opportunities for Tabitha-Shirley.

It was only when I reached the bus stop that I realised the hammer was still in my hand. I seemed to remember that the bus company had a rule about passengers not being allowed to travel if they were carrying unsheathed weapons. So I offered the hammer to a couple of passing pensioners and they went off home, chuckling at their unexpected good fortune. Once I got on the bus, I had to decide where to go. It was a bit early in the day for gay bars but I realised that I wanted to be in kps' more than anywhere else. I wanted to be somewhere comfortable to get over my romantic loss – never mind my chance to have some regular sex. At least, I hadn't ended up with a tattoo!

The happy hour was in full swing when I arrived there. The pub looked rather shabbier than I remembered from my first visit. Bleached Blond greeted me with an operatic gesture and held out his cheek for me to kiss.

'Do tell! Your face has a story just bursting its way out. Don't say you've been let down by Mr Slime?'

I was surprised that he remembered me at all but I recalled his words of warning as I had run out of the bar into the arms of Chris, just a week previously. So, I told him everything about the Great Seduction and the Great Escape. He was very sympathetic and it felt good to get it off my chest.

'Why don't you come and join us and I'll introduce you to some of my pals.' He seemed to have so many and this lot looked completely different from the ones he'd been with a week ago. Apart from anything else, the experience with Chris had taught me that I needed a few more friends of my own. After all the introductions, I was persuaded to tell the story of my troubles with Chris all over again and I began to realise that my little escapade was really not the end of the world. My new friends all seemed to think it was a hoot and I began to realise that it did have a comical side.

I was on my way to the loo when, out of the side of my eye, I thought I caught sight of Dolly's cousin, Kyle Fullerton, but I couldn't really be sure and by the time I was returning to my seat, he had vanished, if he'd been there at all.

A guy with curly red hair and blue eyes introduced himself; he was called Stephen and he was collecting signatures on a petition for Planet Scotland. It was in favour of Scottish multiculturalism and it reminded me of Rock Against Racism; it wanted to break down barriers between social groups that, traditionally, did not get along with each other. It was opposed to the messages that were being pumped out by Scotland First and Radio Dighty but it was a more complex message than the one they were promoting and I noticed that most people who signed the petition did so only after some discussion with Stephen or one of his friends. I'd been very wary of Scotland First for some time and I knew that my new friends, Haris, Lakshmi and Fergus, were the kind of people that Scotland First didn't like. I used to be politically aware but since I'd woken up, I'd been concentrating on my own personal stuff rather than getting involved in more collective things.

Stephen was a teacher in his mid-thirties and he came across as very genuine. He began to tell me about a big multicultural festival that they were hoping to organise; he asked me if I'd like to take part and, just in case I misunderstood his intentions, he mentioned that he had a long-term boyfriend in Spain called Jose Mateo. Stephen was rather tall for my taste but I could easily have misunderstood his intentions, given half a chance; having put aside my desire, I did realise that he would be a good friend to have. He gave me a mobile number with the correct number of digits and we promised to meet up later in the week. I sensed that he knew about my history but it was nice to have an initial conversation with someone that wasn't entirely about sleeping sickness.

Later on that evening, I got off with a Spaniard called Gorka, who was visiting Dundee for a medical conference and staying in rather a posh hotel on the Perth Road. He said he never had sex without condoms and that was fine by me. I promised to look him up if ever I went to Bilbao and we parted on good terms.

It's funny the way a day can turn out.

19

Haris had got to know Euan very well in the seven or eight months that they had been working together but he was surprised when Euan announced that he would like to visit his mother. It was something that he had hoped would happen in the course of time but this came right out of the blue.

A conversation with Sam had triggered it off for Euan. They liked chatting away together but their conversations were about things that were of no great importance, the weather, football and programmes they'd seen on TV. Sam was normally an outwardly cheerful, friendly guy but one day, he was looking really miserable and, while he was hoovering Euan's room, he began to talk about a recent tragedy in his family. When they had fled from the civil war in Somalia, he had come to Scotland but other members of his family had scattered all over Europe. His nephew, who was a refugee in Denmark, had committed suicide and Sam was unable to go the funeral, because his visa did not allow him to leave the country. He had wanted to pay his respects to the young man, who had only been 19, but he was also very anxious to spend time with his sister. He felt that one of the worst things in the world for a parent must be to outlive a child and he believed that his presence would have been a source of comfort to her. Sam clearly found it painful to talk about this; he did not switch off the hoover so that it was difficult for Euan to pick up all the detail. There was prob-ably nothing really meaningful that he could have said but the noise made it impossible for him even to grunt in sympathy. He stood still and listened and hoped that it was obvious that he was listening. As soon as he finished hoovering, Sam left the room.

It prompted Euan to think about how his mother might have felt when she lost him to sleeping sickness. One of the frustrating things about his conversation with his father's ghost was that he had been unable to get any sense of his mother's life; there had been lots of his father's self-righteous indignation but no real sense of what his mother had been feeling. Perhaps his father had never known what she was feeling? He knew that a visit would be difficult because she suffered from some kind of dementia; Alistair and Wilma felt it was a waste of their time to sit in a room with someone who had no notion of who they were.

'I had a good relationship with my mother,' he explained to Haris. 'She was very supportive of me, and of Irene, when we talked about going to university. No one in our family had ever done that and she encouraged us to believe that we could do it. She herself had left school when she was 14 or 15; her family didn't think that it was worthwhile educating a girl. My father had got the son and heir that he wanted in Alistair and so he wasn't too bothered about what I did, as long as I didn't disgrace the family name. When I said that I wanted to study history, she enjoyed discussing different historical periods with me; we talked about the periods that interested me and I'm afraid that I never found out if they really interested her.'

Haris suggested that if there were things that Euan felt guilty about in relation to his mother, her illness meant that there would be no possibility of apologising to her or appeasing his guilt. If there was to be a visit, he should be realistic about the woman he was likely to meet. There might be no conversation at all; it might be quite a distressing experience. Euan agreed to sleep on the idea but the next day, he was as determined as ever and they set out after lunch.

Haris drove through Carnoustie and out into the countryside, well away from the beaches and the golf courses. The last mile was along a wooded road beside a field where a combine harvester was surging its way through a crop of rich, heavy barley; the nursing home had been an old church manse and it seemed to be trying to offer the securities and the atmosphere of fifty years ago to its elderly residents. The manager greeted them with a brisk old-fashioned courtesy and escorted them through to the reception lounge.

'I think I should warn you, Mr Saddler, that she might not know who you are. She's been very preoccupied today with something about *The Mikado*. She might be talking about something else now but it has been *The Mikado* all morning.'

When they entered the room, they could hardly see her at first; age had shrunk her to the size of a child. White haired, tiny, clasping her arthritic hands together, she was seated in an armchair that seemed much too big for her.

'Helen, Helen, we've got a visitor for you today,' said the manager, seemingly unaware of the fact that no one had ever called her Helen, although that was the name on her birth certificate. 'It's Euan. Do you remember him? Say hello to Euan.'

The look that 'Helen' gave Euan was one of non-recognition. It was as though she was seeing nothing at all. When Euan reached out to touch her, she flinched but it was unclear whether it was fear or something akin to an animal reflex. Euan blew his nose very vigorously. He had brought some photographs with him from the days of his childhood; people from a different time were grooming horses, picking berries, building sandcastles or just standing around for the benefit of the photographer. It was hard for Euan because he was not able to recognise many of these people himself but he thought it was worth persisting, partly because he couldn't think of anything else to do. All they had in common was a shared past but it seemed to be beyond their reach to share it in the present.

He pondered on the fact that he had seemed to be nothing more than a shell for many years. He had been told that people, including his mother and Andy, had visited him when they could and had tried to communicate with him. Knowing this did not make the task of talking to his mother any easier. He looked at the face that had once been so familiar for any signs that she even recognised him. Without a conversation, without any dialogue, it seemed hopeless. All he could do was recall the fact that she had once been one of the most important people in his life, but there was no way that memory could overcome the obviously enormous physical barriers.

A tiny breakthrough came when 'Helen' seemed to recognise a cat in one of the photographs. 'Ginger,' she said warmly. Euan remembered that they had had a cat called Ginger but it was hard to build a conversation around that and he made no headway at all.

He decided that he was trying too hard. Perhaps, the best way was just to sit with her and hold her hand; perhaps, the physical contact would generate some other response. She didn't flinch when he took her hand and so, possibly, that represented some form of progress. He stroked her hand occasionally but for the most part, they simply sat in silence. A long time passed. Haris had gone out of the room and so they were on their own. It was certainly peaceful.

After about an hour, he decided to make a move. He didn't see any signs of any responsiveness on her part but he told himself that this first visit was only a start. He could come back again another day and take it from there. But, just as he was getting up, he recalled that the manager saying she had been talking about *The Mikado* all morning. She had once told him that, not long after she was married, she had been asked to take the part of Katisha in a local amateur production but his father had objected. Euan always felt that the musical genes had missed his generation; his mother had been musical and both Amanda and Gregor were too; he was hopeless and he knew it. He had not seen *The Mikado* since he was a boy but something possessed him to sing aloud a fragment of Katisha's song.

Bow, bow to his daughter in law elect.

He couldn't explain why he did it and at first he could see no response. Just as he was standing up to go, he heard his mother say: "You're still tone deaf, then." He jumped in surprise that she had made this connection. He wished that he knew some more of the lines of this long forgotten song but he didn't; there seemed no point in running out into the corridor to see if anyone was a Gilbert and Sullivan fan. So, he stayed where he was to see if she recalled anything more. He hummed the song a few more times but nothing happened. He kissed her on the forehead one last time and promised that he would come back to see her. He told himself that before the next visit he would find out the words of Katisha's song. He turned back at the door to see if there were any more signs of life but she had shrunk back into her secret world again.

He promised Haris, as they were driving back to Dundee, that he would return to visit her again very soon.

The combine harvester had finished its work in the field outside the nursing home and the disgorged straw was lying lifeless, untended and unlovely.

20

Euan's notebook remained untouched over the next few weeks. He was very very busy, busier than he had ever been since he woke from the long sleep.

Sex was taking up quite a lot of his time and that is probably not a surprise. Now that he had found the sex he liked, he was pursuing it with vigour; clichés like practice making perfect come to mind. It was pointed out to him that the Dundee scene liked fresh meat and he seemed to be making the most of that before he went stale, so to speak. Euan also found that there was quite a bit of choice when it came to his sexual repertoire. He had no regrets about the four-minute fuck with Mister Married but he soon learned that there were lots of other things that he could enjoy instead of, or as well as, fucking. He discovered, in this order, blow jobs and 69s and, his current favourite, frottage; and, of course, there was always good old-fashioned wanking. He also noticed that he didn't have to write their names down to remember what they were; it was rather like what they used to say about riding a bike. So the notebook gathered dust for these few weeks. He was glad too that he had his own key to the Wedderburn Centre so that he didn't have to wake anyone up when he came in at 4am. He wasn't quite gallus enough to walk past reception without a second thought on the days when he came in after 9am but at least he was able to share a cheeky smile with whoever was around at that time.

He had told Stephen all the details of the unprotected fuck and they went along to the clinic together so that he could be tested for HIV. The nurse must have got his number because he came away from there with enough condoms to last a decade or two. Stephen and the nurse were both completely matter of fact about it; they didn't avoid the sexual health issues but there was no big drama about them either. Stephen was always very easy to talk to. His boyfriend from Spain was around quite a lot too. When he saw the two of them together, Euan sometimes envied them being a couple but other times when he was cruising the bars, he wasn't so sure if coupledom was what he wanted.

He was definitely not seeing Haris as much as he used to. The one-to-one professional contact had come to an end and they did not seem to be going out to pubs together as much as they used to. He still hadn't told Haris the story about the man in kps' boasting about the well-hung Bosnian pick-up. He was learning not to be embarrassed about cock talk but there was something that inhibited him from discussing the legend of this particular cock with Haris. He wasn't sure if it was some kind of taboo but he didn't make the time to think through the reasons for his reticence. He really did not know how to explain it at all and he didn't write any of this down in the notebook.

It wasn't just the notebook that was neglected. He was making less and less contact with the ghosts these days. It wasn't so much a conscious decision as the fact that he felt that he was in an altogether different place from them. There could be no way forward for them together; he had a chance of a future and they did not.

The new Scots parliament had been opened and that brought back all kinds of memories for him of the 1979 referendum. Lakshmi had gone down to Edinburgh to cover it for the *Pilot* and he had thought about going with her but decided against it. He watched it alone on TV in his room. It was a grand ceremony but the part he liked best was the rendition of *A Man's A Man For A' That* by Sheena Wellington; Lakshmi said she came from

Dundee. He couldn't help but think about what might have been if the referendum in 1979 had gone the other way and if he hadn't become ill. But he knew that kind of thinking was a waste of time. There was an atmosphere of hope all over Scotland now and he felt lucky to be a part of that.

The Planet Scotland Festival was what really took up most of his time when he wasn't having sex. He was in their office everyday; he got to know the other Planet volunteers; they were of all shapes and sizes and came from every walk of Dundee life. He discovered that Stephen was involved with a gay campaigning group called Outwith and they distributed their leaflets about the festival on the gay scene. During the day, if he wasn't in the office, he was often to be found handing out leaflets to shoppers in the Flukergate or persuading shopkeepers and publicans to display posters for the festival.

He bumped into his old schoolmate, Craig Baxter, several times because his union, the Jute and General Workers' Union, was supporting the festival and they were providing the office space. He was rumoured to be planning to run as Lord Provost and he wanted to mention the elections in his speech on the day of the festival. Stephen welcomed his support but persuaded him not to mention his electoral plans in case it overshadowed the media coverage of the day. The event was not anti-political but Stephen didn't want it to be dominated by any one political faction. Euan was impressed by Stephen's assertiveness; Craig did not make his pre-election speech but neither did he get the hump about being put in his place. Radio Dighty was loud in its denunciations of the festival, dubbing the organisers 'muddled misfits'. Craig didn't rise to their bait; he knew the value of nurturing his likely supporters and biding his time.

On the day of the festival, Euan's job was to welcome the performers and get them settled into the Caird Hall dressing rooms before their appearances in the adjoining square, if it was fine, or in the hall, if it was raining. The Forfarshire Youth Orchestra arrived early in their coach; this was Gregor's first public performance with them and he was very excited. Three elderly ladies in their seventies arrived by taxi from Monifieth; they were known as the Brierley Sisters and had been very popular in wartime Dundee with local lads, GIs and POWs alike. Next came a minibus with the Glen Clova Fiddlers Band and, on their tail, another minibus containing a local women's drumming group, the Bolshie Bettys. The Uhuru Choir was expected too but they got caught up on the one-way system and arrived really late. It was all rather chaotic but very good hearted and Euan enjoyed rushing about doing odd jobs for them all.

He spotted Kyle Fullerton hovering around, on his own, on the edge of the square. He never saw him talking to anyone, not even his more self-confident pal, Kenny.

The biggest attraction of the event was a group called Endriggs. They seemed to bring out particular venom from Radio Dighty. Euan had never heard of them but he was sure that Gregor would have done and he was correct.

'They play lots of Scottish traditional music with pipes and fiddles and accordions but they also mix it with Asian music as well. One of the group plays a drum that they call a tabla; there's a lady who plays something that looks like a funny guitar and it's called a sitar. The lead singer is called Ludo; his real name is Darren McGillvray but he changed his name to Ludo because that's the Latin word for play and he likes to play with different kinds of music. I thought that Ludo was just a game like Snakes and Ladders but he says it was a Latin word and Miss Carnegie says that's right. After listening to Endriggs, I've decided to learn to play the fiddle; I mean, the double bass is alright but it can get a wee bit boring and so, I've started going to fiddle classes.'

It turned out to be a fine day. The City Square was soon packed full of folk celebrating the Planet Scotland Festival and they behaved as though all their dreams and hopes had been satisfied when Endriggs arrived on stage. The lead singer was a skinny wee thing, clearly bursting with confidence and imagination; he was dressed like a traditional ploughman with a waistcoat, a collarless shirt, braces holding up his trousers and big tackety boots; but, unlike the men in the fields, he had applied kohl to his eyebrows and eyelids. He introduced the members of this unique Asian-Scots band. The noisy crowd soon became enthralled when they heard the traditional airs of *Ae Fond Kiss*; before they became too comfortable with the familiarity of the song, the tabla and the sitar took centre stage and the melody shifted into a raag whose sheer audacity transported everyone to what felt like a more beautiful and harmonious planet.

Endriggs were so all absorbing that no one heard the announcement from an unattended radio backstage.

'Breaking news, breaking news. This is Angelica Menmuir from Sidlaw Radio with some news just in from the Dundee International Zoo. We are reliably informed that there has been a breakout from the large birds section of the zoo's aviary. We are told that a wheen of birds including their golden eagles and their macaws and their parrots and their swans have escaped and are flying along the Nethergate towards the City Square. The police have already called on the services of the Wild Life Protection Team and they are working to bring these beautiful creatures back to the zoo. Our reporter on the scene says the birds have been spotted around the Caird Hall, almost as if they're listening to the music being played at today's festival for Planet Scotland. It's also rumoured, but I cannot confirm this, that they've been joined by a flock of geese having a wee rehearsal for their winter passage south. I would urge you all not to do anything at all to scare or disturb these beautiful creatures. Please do not try to capture them yourselves. This is Angelica Menmuir signing off for Sidlaw Radio.'

The festival went on well into the evening when there was an enormous display of fireworks over the Tay. A large graffito adorned a building at the edge of the square, **Dundee is not Srebrenica.** Some folk thought it was one of the slogans of Planet Scotland, and maybe it was, but no one knew for certain.

21

Euan's notebook 31st August 1999

I hadn't used my notebook for ages but when I saw the letter with the unfamiliar handwriting, it seemed like it might be an occasion to write something down. I never used to understand it when my mother would look at the postmark on an envelope and speculate about the writer rather than just opening it. It had always just seemed like a waste of time to my youthful self and yet here I was doing the same thing. It was quite a big brown envelope that looked as if there was another one inside it. The postmark appeared to be somewhere in North London. The writing was a complete mystery to me.

When I opened it, I saw that there was a covering note from Andy's sister, Deirdre. I have very little memory of what she said but she was trying to explain something about why she had to send me the letter rather than give it to me personally, as she would have preferred to do. I did recognise the writing on this letter, it was Andy's. All those years and I knew it was him straightaway. I ripped open this one without another thought.

The first thing I saw was the date, 1995. I knew what that implied but I didn't pause to reflect on it.

Dear Euan,
I don't know if you'll ever see this but I know for sure that you'll never see me and so I wanted to leave you a message – a welcome-back-to-earth message. I always had great faith in you and I still have great faith that you'll recover from that accursed sleeping sickness. The last time I visited you, you certainly looked a lot younger than you should have done. You bastard!

I've asked Deirdre to give this to you and I'm sure she can give you more details about what has happened to me. I was diagnosed HIV Positive six years ago now, so that sorted out my thirtieth birthday plans – gin, gin and more gin! For a while it was touch and go as to whether I'd die of HIV or liver disease but I decided to give pride of place to the HIV. I gave up alcohol and though that's not going to save my life, it does mean that I won't waste any of the time that's left to me getting over hangovers.

I've lost lots of friends, as well as two ex-boyfriends, so I kind of know what to expect. It seems at the moment that I've not got long but you can never tell; I've had pneumonia twice and I've recovered twice. I've learned lots of things about myself as well. I've certainly learned to be assertive, particularly with doctors. At first, they behaved as though my health was nothing to do with me but since I have become more assertive with them they've changed their tune and we seem to get on much better than we used to. I don't think we had assertiveness when we were growing up but it really is all the thing nowadays; you may have learned as much by the time you read this.

I'm writing this in London where I've lived for about ten years now. If you do decide eventually that you are gay, and please make up your mind before you're too old, then get on that train down to London at once. You'll have a fab, fab time and even if I never get to shag you, there's lots of others who'll jump at the chance – believe me, they will! I sometimes wonder if it was the lack of assertiveness in our lives that was the reason why we never did get around to having sex, too polite, just waiting for the other one to ask.

What is important is that I remember loads of wonderful times with you like having our first secret smoke at the old mill, listening to Stevie Wonder, going camping in the rain in Glen

Doll, *trying to buy a drink in Glasgow when we were still sixteen.*
And how many hours of our lives did we waste hanging around
in DeMarco's coffee bar? A lot of the things that I remember
about you were wee things, wee incidents, but I thank my lucky
stars that I met you. It was with you that I first learned that I
could relate to another person. I learned that you could be close
to someone and we didn't always have to be talking or doing
something exciting; you and me could just be together without
a word passing between us. I always had faith in you, right from
the time when I met you in our first week at the Harris. And I
have faith now that you'll come out of your coma.

I've had a good life since we were last together and I hope
that you'll get the chance for some of the good life too. I didn't
spend all those years thinking about you, it would be a lie to
say that I did. There was so much that I wanted to do, so much
that I wanted to find out. Sometimes when I did think of you,
I wished you were there with me; other times, it was just too
painful to allow myself to think about you; sometimes I was
just too selfish to be thinking about anything else other than
what I had on my mind at that moment. But I am thinking about
you now; I'm pretty much housebound at the moment and so I
have a lot of time for thinking. Thinking about you is generally
pretty good. I have no regrets about how we were together and
that's more than I can say about some of the other relationships
I've been involved in. Actually, relationship is not really the right
word; sometimes I just followed my cock without a thought.
However, there is nothing I regret. What I regret is stuff like the
years that you and I could have spent getting to know each other
better.

Anyway, I've got this fucking virus. Folk will tell you that I
got it because I was a slut. I got it because it was an illness that
was widespread at the time when I was sleeping around; it's no

one's fault, it's just a matter of circumstance. As for you, my only advice is to use condoms. I made lots of mistakes; you'll make lots of mistakes; using condoms makes it possible to get over some of the mistakes. And it's not all been mistakes; I've had lots of laughs and you will too. If you want to meet up with any of my London mates, Deirdre can put you in touch. They've all heard all about you. Some of them even call you Sleeping Beauty and I'm sure you can live up to that!

No more to say, everything to say. Don't bother about missing me. I don't want you to forget about me but memories are just memories. Above all, just get on with the business of living your life now.

Loads of kisses – loads of love.

Andy

xxxxxxxxxxxxxxxxxxxxxxxxxxxxxxxxxxxx

There was a picture in the envelope of an attractive man in his thirties with short blond hair and an earring in his right ear. It made me laugh to think he'd dyed his hair, and pierced his ear. His wistful smile looked out at me across the impassable years.

I re-read it and re-read it again. For the first time since I'd recovered, I wept. The tears came slowly at first and then they became uncontrollable. I just felt overwhelmed by sadness about the fact that I would never see Andy again. He was lost to me forever. What was also fucking awful was that on account of my illness, many of my memories of him were lost too. There was no chance to remind each other of things that we had gone through together.

I soon realised that I could make contact with him by summoning his ghost. But did I really want to do that? It was one thing summoning the ghosts of strangers, like Joe Devlin and Mrs Syme when I was trying to adjust to my return to the planet; it had been fine to catch up with Peem Duthie. But when I'd summoned the ghost of my father, it hadn't been a disaster but it hadn't solved things between us. And how could it! He was dead, after all. Dead and gone. What would happen if I summoned the ghost of Andy? It would be good to chat with him, of course, but nothing could change. I couldn't bring him back to life. I couldn't have sex with him. And I wasn't going to join him in his ghost eternity, this was not Brigadoon. My memories of him would be with me somewhere in my subconscious and sometimes some of them would come into my consciousness. That was all there could ever be.

I was crying with the pain of realising that he had gone out of reach but I really had made up my mind about this. I was not going to live in some shadowland. I'd been forced into one kind of shadowland for twenty years and I did not want to choose another one, however comforting it might seem at this moment. I'd get in touch with his sister and maybe we could talk about him. She had always been nice to me and she'd got on with him, at least as well as any teenage girl does with her older brother. Maybe, she'd even have some photos she could give me. I was a bit amazed at myself about making a decision so quickly. Andy had been an important part of my past and he would remain in my memory and my imagination but I didn't want a life with ghosts. I wanted a life now. I was sure that Andy would have understood. It all helped me to decide to put all my ghosts behind me. Thanks, Andy, for helping me to see how to get on with the business of living life now.

22

STRICTLY CONFIDENTIAL

Report for the Kerbit Trust by independent consultant, Reuben Donatello, regarding EUAN SADDLER

It is now one year since Euan Saddler regained consciousness and eight months since he went into the care of the Kerbit Trust at Wedderburn House in Broughty Ferry, Dundee.

The medical reports which have been made available to us by Professor MacIntyre of Ninewells Hospital indicate a remarkable level of recovery. The treatment regime has proved successful with no observed side-effects. The wellbeing reports made by Mr Jakupovic, working as a member of Professor MacIntyre's team, also indicate a high level of progress.

A one-to-one interview with Mr Saddler, conducted by myself, indicated a high level of social and emotional wellbeing. He was also asked to complete an internationally recognised Emotional Autonomy Scale, where he achieved a high score.

We understand that he has plans to move into a flat in Calcutta Street with a friend, a teacher by the name of Stephen Fitzpatrick. Our research into his background has indicated no criminal record on his part, nor any other factors of concern. He is involved in a number of voluntary organisations in Dundee. This move into rented accommodation may well mark an important step on his way to leading a fully autonomous life.

He has further expressed an interest in resuming his studies and taking up a place at a university. There may well be complicating factors with funding these studies in higher education. He has recently enrolled on an access course in Dundee as a first step on his return to the world of education.

Appendices on current prognosis, treatment regime history and emotional wellbeing are attached.

23

It was a big turnout for an old lady. Nan Saddler had outlived most of the people she had grown up with. She had also, sadly, outlived the interest of most of those who had once depended on her. But she came from a well-known family in a community where people still bothered to show their respects on the deaths of their elders and so her funeral service was packed to the gunnels. The gallery of the Balkerro church was seldom used in these material times but this day was an exception. It was a nineteenth-century building with the detailed carvings and crevices much favoured in that period. There were some who remarked that it could have benefited from a wipe, or even a bit of a dust, to make it a more fitting place to say goodbye to this pillar of their community; others pointed out that the difficulty in finding cheap, reliable cleaners was symptomatic of the age. One neighbour of the Saddler family counted two hundred mourners but she decided not to mention that to her husband since his mother had barely reached a hundred for her send-off.

Nan had simply passed away in her sleep. After years in a care home, she was increasingly frail and it was old age rather than any specific illness that took her in the end. The young care worker who found her had been upset but everyone else acted as though it was only to be expected. Nonetheless, there were lots of guilty feelings. Euan felt guilty that he had only visited her once after his illness; he had hoped that she had recognised him but he couldn't begin to imagine how she might have felt about his failure to make a return visit. Wilma felt guilty that she had not been able to persuade Amanda to come to the funeral but since she had turned 16 and got involved with this lad in a band, there was no way of knowing what she was doing. Irene felt guilty that she had not made more effort to drop in on her mother when she was travelling across the world; she also felt guilty about the fact that she was worried about missing the opening session of the conference in Chile where she was going to be a keynote speaker later in the week. Alistair felt irritated, more than anything else, by the slow pace of the service and he was the only one to say directly that he felt guilty about not spending more time with her after she was, as he put it, "sent awa". The others all kept their feelings to themselves and tried to concentrate on making her funeral service as meaningful as it could be.

The music was dreich in the extreme; the idea that you might celebrate the joy and wonder of someone's life after their death was a concept that had yet to reach Balkerro. Nan had been a music lover all her life but there was not a whisper of her favourite songs and melodies. Someone had mentioned Kathleen Ferrier but it wasn't clear if she was available on CD and no one made the effort to find out. As it was, the mourners all knew where they were with the 23rd Psalm.

It was easier for everyone at the hotel after the service was over. Someone had written the words **Dundee is not Rwanda** on a hoarding in the hotel car park but it had generated no comment. The hotel itself was indistinguishable from others in a national chain and had been designed to accommodate large gatherings – "Quality time for quality people" was one of its mantras – but privacy and the sharing of intimacy were not part of the package. The men clustered in groups near the bar and the women hovered near the buffet; but the whisky and the sherry soon took effect and before long there was a buzz, the groups mingled and decorous laughter was heard; men loosened their ties and women removed their hats. On an occasion like this when folk saw other folk that they had once known really well but later lost touch with, there was a sense of unfinished business in the air. It is hard to banish the past from a funeral. Things that had been said, or not said or maybe would never be said, hung over the crowd of mourners like a threatening cloud.

Euan realised that he was not the centre of attention at this gathering and that was both a relief and a cause for discomfort. Most people seemed to be clinging close to someone else but he had no one to cling to. The change in the pattern of his medical treatment meant that he spent less official time with Haris than he had done previously. He knew that he was missing his company but he wasn't sure if that was because of the break in his routine or because of something deeper. Haris had promised to drop in later but it wasn't clear if that was as a psychologist or in some more informal capacity. Euan realised that he wasn't quite sure about the way that friendships worked in the new world that he was living in. He wandered through the reception area and was pleased to see Gregor, who, in an unfamiliar suit, looked like a boy in search of a role for himself too.

'I thought some of the old people, I mean the really old people, would be looking scared but a lot of them look quite happy,' said Gregor. 'Mum's Auntie Bella was telling stories about things that she and Granny used to do when they were young and everyone was laughing and enjoying themselves.'

'But why did you think they would be scared?' They sat down on a sofa together.

'They might be thinking it was their turn to die next and that wouldn't be a very nice thought. I wouldn't like that at all.'

'But you're eleven, Gregor,' said Euan. 'It would be all wrong for you to be the next one to die. Maybe, these old folk have stopped worrying about dying because they've had long lives and they want to enjoy what's left to them.'

'Amanda's decided that she wants to enjoy her life a lot more and that's not because she thinks she's going to die soon. Since she had her sixteenth birthday, she spends most nights of the week with her boyfriend.' He was enjoying talking about something which he knew was supposed to be naughty.

'Is that the one who sings in that band that's called ...'

'Endriggs. Dad always said that was a silly name for a band and he says that Ludo is an even sillier name for a boy. Actually, he used a bad word about his name. Ludo likes big girls; Elaine Petrie was his last girlfriend and she's as big as an elephant...'

'Gregor! That's not a very nice thing to say. I'm surprised at you.'

'It's true and maybe that's why he likes Amanda because she's a bit fat too.' Gregor could see from Euan's face that this was not going down well and he started to back track. 'Amanda was always going on diets but since she started going out with Ludo she's stopped all that kind of thing; she says that she doesn't have to hide away when she's with him. At least, I think that's what she said but it's all very complicated knowing about boyfriends and girlfriends. Do you think you'll have a girlfriend soon, Uncle Euan?' He paused. 'Or maybe a boyfriend?'

Euan was unsure what to say about all this but Gregor continued anyway.

'You can have either a girlfriend or a boyfriend nowadays, whatever you want. It's different now from what it was in the olden days when you were young. Adam's cousin, Lorraine, has a girlfriend and because they wanted to tell everyone about themselves, they decided to come out of the wardrobe.'

All kinds of thoughts were going through Euan's head but he didn't know how to start talking about them with an eleven-year-old boy, even if that eleven year old was Gregor.

'They didn't come out of a *real* wardrobe; it's like in poetry when you have a simile. Miss Carnegie explained to us that when Robert Burns wrote that his love was like a red red rose, she didn't actually look like a rose with prickly bits, it meant that she was as beautiful as a rose. So, coming out of the wardrobe is like that. In a wardrobe, you have lots of different types of clothes, men's clothes and women's clothes, and men don't have to choose the ones that are made for men, they can choose whatever ones they want. But that's a simile too because you don't really have to wear women's clothes if you're a man with a boyfriend. If you came out of the wardrobe, you'd just be telling people that you want to have a boyfriend rather than a girlfriend. Maybe Adam's cousin could explain it better; I'm still only a little boy and I'm no' supposed to know about big people's stuff yet.'

Euan put his hand on Gregor's shoulder but before he could say anything, they were interrupted by the arrival of the minister who took the opportunity to tell them how lucky they had been to have Nan Saddler in their lives. This could have gone on for some time but when Gregor spotted his Auntie Irene, he pulled Euan away, leaving the unfortunate cleric gesticulating at a bemused waiter with a drinks tray. A man in a clown costume walked in, paused, turned round and walked out, probably realising that he had not been booked for this particular event.

Irene was talking in an animated fashion with Alistair and Wilma when they reached her; she seemed to be in United Nations mode rather than Balkerro mode. 'The reason why micro-credit is usually paid to women in Bangladesh is not because of what you call "women's lib", Alistair, but because they are the ones who have to cope most directly on a daily basis with the poverty in their lives and, therefore, they are the ones with the greatest incentive to find a way out of that poverty. It's a better system than traditional methods of aid because it enables the borrowers to set up their own enterprises which have the potential to be sustainable. Women also have a good track record in paying the loans back on time, considerably better than men.' She paused briefly when she realised Euan and Gregor had joined them. 'This might be as good a time as any to talk about finances while we're all here together.' She straightened her back.

'This is our mother's funeral, Irene,' said Alistair. 'Can it no' wait a bit?'

'I'm off to Chile tomorrow, Alistair, and I'd really like to get things sorted out before I depart. I've seen mother's will and there are issues that we need to discuss; it would make sense to discuss them while we are all here together.'

Alistair realised that this was going to be a difficult conversation and so he shouted at his son. 'You're no' needing to hear this, Gregor. Away and find somebody to play with.' Gregor, like everyone else, knew that playmates were unlikely to be plentiful at a funeral but he decided that the best thing was probably to move a few feet away; there was always less trouble, in his experience, if adults were appeased when they became angry for no obvious reason.

Euan was rather stunned by all this. He knew that his mother had left him and Irene several thousand pounds each; not exactly a fortune but it could make a big difference to his plans. He also realised that his mother had been a director of the company that ran the farm and that was where all her money had been invested. He accepted the fact that the bulk of his parents' wealth should go to Alistair because he was running the farm. The farm was where they had all grown up and Euan had no desire to see it all broken up or sold off. Nonetheless, he wanted to make sure that he got what he was entitled to and that would mean Alistair finding the money from the farm reserves.

He realised that reaching an agreement about this money might involve him being what Andy had called assertive. He had spent the last few months feeling his way around his new world and asking questions and trying to understand. Maybe, it was now time to become a participant in that new world rather more than just an observer. Maybe, it was also time to take Gregor's advice and be more open and honest about what he expected from life; coming out of the wardrobe was not just an idea that related to sexuality. No one would know what he was thinking if he didn't speak up for himself; it would have been easier if it hadn't been about a family will but you couldn't choose the crises that you found yourself embroiled in. Alistair and Irene were arguing away, regardless.

Alistair was getting very heated and his face had turned bright red. 'You can't expect me to run a business to support my family if I have to make great big handouts like this. You wouldn't want me to have to sell up just to pay you two off.'

'Of course, we don't want you to sell up,' said Irene, in a resolutely calm tone. 'Euan and I grew up on this farm and we know the land here better than anyone else, apart from you. We know the fields where the land becomes easily water-logged; the fields which are dry and stony; we know that you think about the fertilisers you use in a more intelligent way than our father's generation never did; we know that you appreciate the value of trees to the quality of the soil; you manage it really well and you should be proud of that, but we have to start finding a way to pay off these legacies. There has to be some way of reaching an agreement.'

Alistair was pleased to hear Irene's compliments but he knew when he was being soft-soaped and he was not going to be rushed into anything damaging. 'I've got children to think of – and that's something that you two don't have to contend wi...'

Euan decided that this was the moment when he had to intervene in the conversation, even though he wasn't really sure of all the details. 'I'm sorry to interrupt you but I want all the money that's owing to me as soon as possible.' It all came out very bluntly and maybe even sounded aggressive. Alistair and Irene had clearly not been expecting this from their sick young brother and both fell silent. He repeated himself.

'I want all the money that's owing to me as soon as possible. We'll maybe have to work out some kind of instalments system but it has to be done. I am, as we all know, back in the land of the living, not comatose any more, and so, we have to adjust to the different circumstances. I can see that it's going to be difficult for you, Alistair, but I can't afford to go on subsidising you any longer.' He was sweating with the effort of expressing himself.

Alistair's face turned an even brighter red, tomato red. He shouted at Gregor again. 'Did I no' tell you to go and do something useful.' Gregor knew that that was not what he had been told to do but thought better of correcting his father; he burst into tears. Alistair now turned his wrath on Wilma. 'Awa and see tae that laddie, there's nae need for a' that carry on, he needs to get toughened up a bit. I'll see tae him later.'

Euan and Irene saw a steely side in Wilma that was unfamiliar to them. 'I'll make sure that Gregor's Ok, don't you worry. It's bad enough having one child leaving home without you making the other one miserable as well. If the three of you could just behave like adults and sort out your tight-fisted father's will, that would be great. Now, just get on with it and don't bother to come and find me until you have got it all sorted out. Your father was a real bully and I'm sick to the back teeth of the way you let his bullying still hang over members of my family. Sometimes I think the old bastard's ghost is just sitting there smirking at you all falling out with each other. There's ways of finding enough money to pay off Euan and Irene three times over. There's four hundred acres on that farm of yours, so it's not beyond the realms of possibility to find some money with all that as a security. So just find it quickly. I mean it, don't come near me till you've got this sorted out.'

'And where am I gonna get money like that?' Alistair looked as though he might either explode or burst into tears or, conceivably, do both simultaneously. 'It doesn't grow on trees, you know. There's no bleeding heart credit union here for farmers like me.'

'Maybe not,' said Irene, 'but there's a thing called a bank and I can see the bank manager over there, sipping away at some beverage or other. We could go and get him over here now to start the ball rolling, if you want. I'm sure he's here because you're such a good customer rather than out of any love for our mother.' She actually looked more relaxed now that the argument was progressing.

Euan could see Alistair just oozing with anger at the very notion of being challenged, another one of his father's little legacies. But he did not feel intimidated by it. 'Maybe I should get a lawyer to represent me and draw up some kind of formal agreement; I certainly don't want some under the counter shenanigans.' He could feel himself trembling but he continued. 'I know a lawyer that I could speak to about all this.'

'What lawyer?' barked Alistair.

'Her name's Heather, she's a friend of Stephen, my flatmate.'

'That'll be Heather McKelvey, she was in my class at school,' explained Irene. 'She's a partner in a firm in Castle Street called Trollope and McKelvey. They're very successful and a bit more professional than the cowboy lawyer that drew up the wills for our mother and father.'

'Bloody lesbians!' muttered Alistair, apropos of nothing except his feelings about clever women.

After more tense exchanges, Alistair agreed to speak to his bank manager, and Euan agreed to approach Heather McKelvey to act on his behalf, while Irene congratulated herself on the successful use of her diplomatic skills. Euan had spent the last few months since he came out of his coma being encouraged to develop his independence and to adopt assertive patterns of behaviour, yet as soon as he did so, it felt like a skirmish in a civil war. They always said that civil wars were the worst because you were fighting against people you knew and thought you could trust. He was shaking almost uncontrollably, amazed at his own audacity. He went outside to try to regain some self-control. He was astounded at the capacity of some folk to medicalise any human emotion that they saw him expressing. "Are you sure you're no' taking on too much?" And he did not want to be hospitalised just for standing up for himself. He thought that a walk in the grounds of the hotel would reduce the chance of that happening, as long as he wasn't seen talking to himself, as he was wont to do.

On his return, he was pleased when he saw Haris sitting on a sofa in the reception area with a beaming Gregor, clearly recovered from the recent altercation. 'Uncle Euan, can Haris and me come back to your flat for a pizza? I could order it on the phone from Patel's Pizza and then they could deliver it to your house. I don't get many chances to order pizza on the phone because we live so far away from Dundee that they don't want to deliver to us.'

'I spoke to Wilma,' said Haris, 'and she agreed that this would be a nice thing to do. I had the impression that she and Alistair wanted to have some quality time together after the funeral. I said that I would drive Gregor out to the farm after we had had the pizzas. Funerals can often be very stressful.' Unlike everyone else, he sounded very calm.

Euan was pleased to see that Gregor could bounce back so quickly from the earlier fracas but it was more than he could manage himself; he laughed rather hysterically. 'Yes, it's been stressful, believe me.' Gregor gave him a big hug.

Later on that evening while Haris was driving Gregor back home, Euan found time to reflect on his relationship with his mother. He felt particularly bad that on the day of her funeral, he had hardly had any conversation about her at all, apart from the arguments about her money. He was afraid that his real memories of her would get lost in some bureaucratic muddle. He decided to find his notebook and jot down some thoughts about her.

I was the youngest of my mother's three children and I think she maybe spoiled me in a way that she didn't do with the others. Alistair and Irene were in secondary school when I was still in primary school; especially during the school holidays, she and I would often be together in the house when all the others were out doing their own things. Sometimes she would take out old records and we'd listen to them together. There were Gilbert and Sullivan operas that we could sing along to; even though I had no sense of tune at all, it was very enjoyable and she laughed during these sessions in a way that I never remember her doing elsewhere. She told me once how she had nearly played the role of Katisha in The Mikado. She also had records by the likes of Frank Sinatra and Doris Day; I liked to sing along with Good Night, Irene, even after it had been explained to me that it was not about our own Irene. She had a collection of the complete works of Charles Dickens and encouraged me to read some of the easier ones like David Copperfield and Oliver Twist. She once tried to teach me to bake a chocolate cake; it was great fun and I was covered in chocolate but no one else would touch the cake apart from us! She took me outside as well because she said my father would think I was becoming too much of a wee jessie if I stayed too long in the house. There weren't any other children on the farm at the time and she would take me up the old kirk hill to have a wee picnic under the beech trees; later on, my father went on to chop them down because he said that having them there was just a waste of land. I remember too that she liked to listen to the birds singing and she and her friends would ring each other up when they heard the first cuckoo in the spring. It all seems very peaceful and relaxing and a long way from the kind of life she had in her last few lonely years.

But I can remember that things were a bit more tricky when I started at the Harris. I met Andy straightaway but I also became friendly with another boy called Derek. She seemed to prefer Andy because his father was a bank manager at the British Linen Bank; Derek was brighter than the pair of us put together but she didn't really approve of him because his mum was on her own and he came from one of the schemes. I realised that she could be a bit snobbish about my friendships and so while she always made it easy for me to meet up with Andy, she was never that helpful with Derek. He and I grew apart anyway; we were in our teens and he was very, very interested in girls and I just wasn't. Later he went off to join the Army and we just lost touch. She never said anything but I knew she was pleased, or certainly relieved. But despite that, I also knew that she was proud of me, proud of me doing well at school and going to university.

I cannot imagine what she must have felt about me falling ill with sleeping sickness. I understand that she came to see me every day at first but when she had a stroke, she wasn't able to drive any more and so she was dependent on someone else taking her to see me. I know that my father blamed her, as he told me himself, for the fact that I went to Kenya where I fell ill. When she couldn't drive any longer, he didn't like taking her to visit me because he said it was a waste of time talking to someone that couldn't hear you. I'm sure that he was just scared of a difficult situation but he wasn't good at helping people out and I bet she was left to cope with all this on her own. I'm pleased that I did get around to visiting her but I really regret that I only went to see her the once. I wonder if I should summon her ghost, like I know that I could do, but I'm not sure what I would do it for. It might make me feel a bit better about things but it might also make me very tearful and upset. I don't know what it would do for her; I don't know if ghosts can have new feelings or if they're always stuck in the past with all the things that were unresolved staying unresolved.

Euan closed the notebook for the day. He wasn't finding the notebook as helpful as he used to. Maybe that was because he was trying not just to make discoveries about the past but also to make decisions about the present and the future. That seemed much harder. He was pleased when he heard Stephen coming into the flat; maybe they could watch some TV together. He heard another voice in the kitchen with Stephen and was even more pleased when he realised that it was Haris.

24

A quiet life seemed to have become within Euan's reach. There was a rhythm of home, work, leisure that gave him the space to breathe and to appreciate his new life. This life began to take the shape of something that belonged to him. At home, Stephen, proving to be more than a landlord or a flatmate, welcomed him into his world. Sometimes they just watched TV together, spent time with Stephen's friends or did stuff in the community. Euan was also studying on an access course at the university and he and Dolly both enjoyed being part of such an enthusiastic group. He saw his other friends regularly and he enjoyed going out on the scene; Gregor popped in most weekends. Euan no longer felt that he was the novelty that he had been a few months earlier; people didn't feel that they had to discuss sleeping sickness with him every time they met. Anonymity was beginning to suit him very well.

He had arranged to meet Fergus and Haris one evening just at the end of the working day. They all liked a pub that used to be a bank that now went by the name of The Shoogly Nail. It served good beer and there was plenty space for watching the TV or having a laugh or an argument; it was definitely not a place for a romantic liaison.

After just a couple of pints, Fergus got on his high horse at the very mention of Radio Dighty. 'They're just a nasty bunch of dangerous fascists. All that cuddly folksy stuff that they do is a cover for their serious political agenda.'

'But tonight,' said Euan, 'they were talking about the 1966 World Cup and the way that the English media is obsessed with that. Didn't you tell me that there's even a TV quiz programme named after 1966? They were complaining too about the lack of coverage given to the Lions of Lisbon, the Celtic team that won the European Cup in 1967. I don't see any difference, Fergus, between what they're saying and the kind of thing that you say.'

Fergus was ready with an answer. 'They want to replace an English obsession with 1966 with a Scottish obsession with Celtic's victory in 1967; they just want to replace one obsession with another. They're both unhealthy. You know those distorting mirrors that you get in fairgrounds. The image that you see in the mirror is a reflection of something but it's no' a reflection of reality. Radio Dighty thinks that the obsession that the English media have with 1966 distorts the way that all football is understood. "Is this team better than 1966?", "Is this captain better or worse than 1966?" But, instead of challenging the very idea of obsessions, they want us to have our own distorted mirror of 1967. "Is this team better or worse than the Lions of Lisbon?", "Were the Lions of Lisbon better than the 1966 England team?" So, we take our eye off the ball, so to speak, because we're too busy thinking about 1966 or 1967.' He was getting louder. 'We forget about the actual football. We don't make time to appreciate the game as it is today.'

Euan shook his head and smiled. He enjoyed arguing with Fergus now that he felt more confident about himself. The folk at the next table seemed to be enjoying it as well.

'You're taking it too seriously, Fergus. It's only a phone-in programme and it seems to be popular, just a bit of light entertainment on a Friday evening. And they have some Scottish music as well, I quite enjoy that.' He knew that this could wind Fergus up.

'But the music is poison, it's pure nostalgic crap.' Fergus almost spilled his pint.

'Nothing wrong with a bit of nostalgia,' said Euan.

'They only play certain kinds of Scots music, music that has nothing to do with life today. I don't know if you've heard of a band called Endriggs.'

'Yes, they were playing at the festival in the City Square.'

'Aye, of course,' said Fergus. 'Their music is Scottish but it also draws on music from other places too. One of the band is a guy from Arbroath called Naresh and their music is a fusion of traditional Scots and Indian. Now your Radio Dighty…'

'Steady on, Fergus,' Euan protested, 'it's no' my Radio Dighty, if you don't mind.'

'OK, OK, sorry. But my point was that Radio Dighty will no' play any music by Endriggs because they say they are no' properly Scottish and they say that foreign musicians, by which they mean Naresh, are taking work away from proper Scots musicians. He was born in Arbroath, for God's sake. Endriggs are one of the most popular bands in Dundee at the moment but they get no airtime on Radio Dighty.' He was really on a roll.

'So, you're saying it's a racist radio station? I didn't know about that.'

'And it's more than that,' Fergus asserted, 'although that's bad enough; they want all Scottish life to be "pure" or untainted by foreign influences. They want all the music to be ethnically "pure"; they want all the football memories to be of a "pure" Scots team; they want everything to revert to the way they say it used to be. They don't like Margaret Thatcher, like most folk in Scotland, but they claim that it's no' just her that's the problem. Women, they say, have no place in politics because they should be in the kitchen, just like Maw Broon, and everybody loves Maw Broon. It's a very selective memory that they have and they want everything frozen in a particular way that suits their agenda.' He had seemed unstoppable but he paused for a moment to give his audience time to reflect. He drew up his shoulders and then relaxed them again.

'Well,' said Euan, 'they didn't say anything about the freezing of time tonight. It was just about football.'

'Which is why they are so clever and so successful; they can lull folk into believing that they're talking about one thing when they're actually talking about much more than that. They feed on people's discontent with life today by romanticising a segment of time gone by. You're very quiet, Haris. What do you think?'

'I am from Sarajevo, as you know, Fergus, and I do not have arguments about any forms of nationalism – ever!' Haris pursed his lips, as if it was almost too obvious to have to explain this.

'That's me telt,' said Fergus with a laugh. But he had enjoyed this discussion and he wandered off in good humour in pursuit of his many friends, acquaintances and drinking buddies all over the pub. Euan was pleased to be on his own with Haris for a change but, given the din all around them, meaningful conversation was difficult. Shouting away at each other was tiring and they were feeling hungry; Euan had a pizza in mind and Haris was up for that too. They decided to wait till Fergus came back from his foray but they didn't see him for about half an hour. When he did reappear, his good humour had gone; he seemed distracted and he seized on a half empty crisp packet on the table.

He began to stuff some crisps into his mouth. And spitting half of them into the air, he proclaimed: 'Poor fucking crisps! Just waiting there to be assaulted by some greedy pissheid like myself, and the fucking terrible thing is that if you're no' assaulted like this, then what's the fuckin point in being a crisp? You spend a' that time in the ground as a fucking tattie and then you're picked and cleaned and sliced and doused wi' some shite chemicals to make some daft bugger think that maybe you had once been in contact with some cheese and some fucking onions and then you're sealed away in some impermeable bag and then it's ripped open by some cunt like me and what can you do about it? You're a crisp, you can only wait for your destiny, wait for your fate and if your fate escapes you then you're chucked in some bin and forgotten forever. Naebody would choose tae be a fucking crisp wi' a fucking life trajectory like that, would they? Would they?'

He looked as though he was waiting for someone to challenge his analysis of the life history of the crisp. People had stopped their conversations and were looking round to see what was going to happen next. It was impossible to tell from his face whether he was going to pick a fight or burst into tears. He very definitely looked like a man who felt unloved.

Euan's response was to turn into Gregor, a polite wee boy who was puzzled and sometimes distressed by the behaviour of adults but had long realised that it was best to sit quietly until whatever had caused a particular storm had blown over. Haris took on the role of the sensible adult in charge of the situation.

'We were just talking about getting a taxi home, Fergus. Do you want to join us?'

'Hmm,' grunted Fergus. 'I know what you're bloody doin', Haris Jakupovic. But maybe you're right, maybe I should get home and see if there's anything in the fucking freezer.' He growled at anyone who was within hearing distance. 'Fucking cunts.' Haris began to talk very loudly to reduce the chance of anyone taking Fergus's remarks personally. He went on to Fergus's left side and indicated that Euan should go to the right. Euan knew that this was not the moment to mention the pizza that he had just begun to look forward to; they succeeded in escorting Fergus out of the pub without any further stramash.

As soon as they got Fergus into a taxi, he fell asleep and quickly began to snore loudly. While the taxi made its way towards Lochee, Euan and Haris discussed their next moves. 'We cannot just leave him in bed,' said Haris, 'in case he becomes sick while he is asleep and chokes on his vomit. We will have to induce him to vomit and give him a lot of water; we will have to stay with him for about an hour and only then will it be safe to leave him.'

'How do you mean, induce him to vomit?' Euan asked. Life was getting more complicated by the day.

'First of all, we give him a glass of salted warm water and then, if that does not work, I will put two fingers down his throat until he vomits a satisfactory amount for him to be safe.'

'You're joking,' said Euan. 'Two fingers down his throat!'

'I am not joking. I have had to do it before. It is not pleasant but it is necessary.'

Euan was round eyed with amazement but also relieved that he wasn't being asked to give him the two-finger treatment. 'But I don't actually understand how he became so drunk. We all drank the same amount, we all had the same number of rounds. You and I are no' drunk like that. How did it happen?'

'While he was wandering around the bar, chatting to his friends, he was also buying double whiskies and drinking them alone before he came back to us. I have seen him behave like this several times before. I do not like it but I do not know how to stop him from doing it. He will be very embarrassed tomorrow and he might even send you some flowers because you are his new friend and he will not want to upset you. I will not get any flowers but he will be very apologetic the next time we meet.'

It was only when the taxi reached its destination that Euan remembered that Fergus's flat was on the third floor. But he was somehow propelled up the stairs, the vomit was induced and the water was administered. After he had been safely asleep for an hour, Euan and Haris began to make their way home. They were well wrapped up for the cold and, though they were both quiet after their stressful experience, their silence was a companionable one. It was a fairly long walk across town but neither of them was in a hurry and neither of them felt the need to break into conversation. 'Look,' said Euan, gently touching Haris's elbow; they paused while a barking fox ran across their path into the depths of Dudhope Park. It was nine o'clock, there wasn't much traffic around and it felt still and almost peaceful, until they passed a church wall where some reclining teenagers were drinking cheap cider and interrogating passers-by about their opinions on the merits of outdoor sex.

'People get drunk so early in the evening in Dundee,' said Haris. 'It was never like that in Sarajevo.' There was just a hint of judgement in his voice.

Euan decided to forego this chance of a conversation about the comparative drinking habits of the Scots and the Bosnians. He cleared his throat. 'It's nice getting the chance to spend some time with you on our own. Now that you're no' my official psychologist anymore, we don't seem to see so much of each other. It would be good to meet up sometime, without having to go to a pub.'

Haris hesitated and seemed to be unsure whether to respond as a friend or as a healthcare professional. 'I am quite busy at work and I go to Edinburgh most weekends but I agree that it would be nice to meet up sometime.' His words came over quite nervously.

'I don't know if you fancy meeting up to go to a gym together. You know Fergus's old school friend, Murray?'

'The man who owns the Ashet restaurant? Yes, I know him.' Still uncertain where this was going.

'Well, Murray's opened up a gym just next to the Ashet.

They've got special reduced rates for anyone who joins in the first three months. I thought that maybe we could go there together sometime.' Euan was trying to be patient while waiting for Haris to make up his mind; although his health was currently good it was uncertain how long that would last or how long his medication would continue to be effective. He saw indecisiveness as a luxury that he could not afford and although he tried to look tolerant of people who took a long time to reach decisions about their everyday lives, it was a role that he found difficult. He breathed deeply.

'OK,' said Haris. 'I used to go to a gym but my membership lapsed – so that would be a good idea – to keep fit.'

'And they have a special joint membership offer...'

'Joint membership?' Haris's voice went up an octave.

'It's no' just for couples or members of the same family, it's for pals too. Murray reckons that more people will use the gym if they go there with someone they know rather than have to go on their own. So, there's a financial incentive to go with your pals.'

Haris looked very thoughtful, almost defensive.

Euan was becoming exasperated. 'Haris, stop looking so bloody worried. If I wanted to shag you, I would use a more direct method than tricking you into joint membership of a gym. I may have been asleep for twenty years, but I'm no' completely stupid.'

'So, what method would you use if you did want to shag me, Euan?'

Euan was taken aback by the question and was just about to answer it, when he caught the glimmer of a smile on Haris's face. 'You bastard!' he said, as he punched him in the gut. Haris responded with an oath in Serbo-Croat, very rarely heard on the streets of Dundee.

'Ok, Euan, ok. Let us get a pals' membership and go along to the gym, but no more violence, please!'

'I've got an application form in my bag, Haris. So, you just have to sign here; there's no time like the present,' he giggled. Haris signed the form, without even checking the membership fee. 'That's great,' said Euan. 'We're now pals, officially. Let's shake on that.'

'In Sarajevo, we normally hug our friends at times like this.'

They were warmly embracing each other, albeit in a non-erotic way, when a chorus of cider drinkers ambled along the other side of the street on their way to the chippie. 'Poof! Poof! Poof!' went the chant. 'Poof! Poof! Poof!'

25

The phone kept on ringing. Euan was cooking, rather laboriously, and distractions were not welcome but it proved to be Haris, on a bad line, explaining that his car had broken down somewhere in deepest Fife at a place with a name that he couldn't pronounce.

'Don't worry,' said Euan, 'we'll keep some food for you. There's enough food here for a biblical miracle.' Euan had decided that it was time to cook a meal for his closest friends rather than celebrate his 40th birthday; was he 20 or was he 40? It all seemed rather arbitrary and celebrating his friendships seemed more worthwhile. At least, that was the theory but when it came to cooking, he was something of a stranger to ingredient quantities and portion sizes and the task was proving more complicated than he had anticipated. The leg of lamb itself was not a problem but the herbs and the garlic rather overwhelmed him; the accompanying vegetables required more co-ordination than he was able to muster. And the phone kept ringing.

Gregor rang next to ask if he and Adam could stay over the following Friday before their screen printing course. Then he wanted to tell Euan a joke as well.

'Why did the man have to stop making yachts in his attic?'

'I don't know why the man had to stop making yachts in his attic.'

'Because the sales were going through the roof!!'

Euan grinned but, of course, you can't see a grin on a phone and he sensed that he would need to find a way of convincing Gregor, who clearly thought that this was the funniest thing he had ever heard, that he found it funny too. So he promised to tell the joke to his guests once they arrived for their dinner and that seemed to satisfy his nephew.

He wasn't now sure if Yorkshire puddings were such a good idea, even although they came from an easycook packet. They weren't really traditional with lamb but then Lakshmi, Fergus, Stephen, Dolly and Haris were hardly stolid defenders of tradition.

The phone rang again. This time it was Dolly. She wasn't feeling that well and wouldn't be able to come for the meal. Euan felt, however, that there was something on her mind and eventually she admitted that she was pregnant and pleased about it. She saw him every day on their course but decided to tell him more privately than would have been possible there.

'Craig must be pleased,' said Euan. More of a statement than a question but it turned out that a question might have been more appropriate.

'Eh'm no' sure, tae be truthful. It wiz never planned, ye ken, and he's got this bloody election on the brain, so he's no' celebrating aboot the pregnancy. He has another bairn frae his time in Spain though he never sees him. Maybe, eh'll need to start showing afore he taks it seriously. But you ken me, Euan. Eh'm no' gonna be dependent on any guy, even if there's a bairn concerned. Meh mither wiz one o' a lang line o' single mothers and it might be the case that eh'm jist carrying on whaur she left off. We'll see.'

Euan muttered some platitudes about Craig's suitability as a father but, changing the topic, he asked, 'Have you thought about a name yet?'

'If it's a lassie, it's tae be Wynette; eh dinnae think it wid be a great idea to ca' a lassie in Dundee Tammy, so we'll go for Wynette. And if it's a laddie, it'll be Pablo, like Picasso, ye ken.'

Euan was still worrying about the Yorkshire puddings but he offered himself as a babysitter, when the time came. Back in the kitchen, he realised that he should have boiled the potatoes for a while before putting them in the roasting tray; so that was going to slow him down and he became even more worried about the Yorkshire puddings.

Haris called to let him know that there had been some Bosnian-Scots linguistic misunderstanding which had resulted in the repair van going to the wrong village; twenty-five minutes had been lost in the confusion. 'Do you know how to make gravy?' Euan asked and was then relieved when the line was so bad that Haris couldn't hear the question. Apparently, there was a lot of rain in West Fife.

Stephen came in at this point and, of course, he did know how to make gravy. He promised to make it as soon as he had come out of the shower. In the meantime, his boyfriend, Jose Mateo, phoned from Madrid. He and Euan chatted for a few minutes until Stephen appeared in his towel. This delay wasn't helping the Yorkshire puddings and he wondered if he should just throw them in the bin while no one was looking.

'Jose Mateo says that you should go to visit him in Madrid,' said a refreshed Stephen.

'That's nice of him,' said Euan. 'Do you think I could go tonight?'

'Ah, trouble in the kitchen, I see,' said Stephen. 'You go and get the table ready and I'll see to things in here for a while. Did you know that Yorkshire puddings are no' traditionally served with lamb?' But there was no reply from the other room.

Lakshmi and Fergus arrived together; he was wearing a deep purple shirt and she had abandoned her customary denim for a cream linen top with green velvet trousers. Euan felt a bit of a scruff in his well-worn jeans and a t-shirt that looked as though it had been retrieved from a time capsule. They were all in a good humour and the wine was soon flowing copiously; he told them Gregor's joke and they all groaned. The meal was judged a great success and Lakshmi remarked that this was the first time she had ever eaten Yorkshire puddings with lamb. The parsnips were praised for their crispness but Euan sensed that meant that they were undercooked.

Once they were tucking into their dessert, a classic Carse of Gowrie strawberry cheesecake, the conversation turned to politics and very quickly focused on the coming election for Lord Provost. There was a distinct lack of enthusiasm for this new post but everyone was a committed voter and there was no doubt that they would all turn out on the day.

'This'll be my first vote since the referendum in 1979,' said Euan, 'but I'm hoping I'll be a bit luckier this time around.'

'I'll be your voting escort, if you like,' said Stephen.

'I'll come along too,' said Fergus. 'A critical mass of support and anyway, lightning never strikes twice in the same place.'

'Have you all decided who to vote for?' asked Lakshmi.

'I'm looking for a bit of vision,' said Stephen. 'I'd never vote Tory but I'm no' impressed with the suits from the three other main parties; so, I'll be looking at the minority candidates. I'll probably go for Craig Baxter, I got to know him a bit through the Planet Scotland Festival and he seems a good guy.'

'He definitely likes to see himself as a man o' the people,' said Fergus, 'but it's strange that he's no' associated with a political party. It's all very well being independent but it could mean that he lacks discipline and, of course, it's easier for outside interests to buy over an independent.'

'What kind of outside interests?' asked Euan.

'There's always property speculators on the go in Dundee, somebody wanting to knock something down and put up something cheap in its place; cheap but also profitable for them. The municipal history of Dundee sometimes feels like the history of a building site.'

'The other independent candidate is a woman,' said Lakshmi, 'and that's a good thing but I haven't been able to find out very much about her. All I know is that she's called Daphne Pattullo and, although she was born in Dundee, she didn't go to school here. She's the manager of some football club down South, so she must be fairly tough to cope with that.'

'A ballsey woman, you could say,' said Fergus.

'Aye, you could, if you were lacking in imagination and wit,' Lakshmi sighed.

'I wonder what Radio Dighty will think about that,' said Euan. 'They won't feel happy about a woman stepping out of her traditional role but they may well think that a candidate with a real interest in fitba is worth supporting.'

'Apparently, they are going to research all the candidates and make an announcement near the time of the election about which one is the most Scottish,' said Lakshmi. 'I thought that Scotland First might put up a candidate but it seems they were caught on the hop by this election.'

'Maybe, they don't have any real supporters,' suggested Stephen optimistically, 'apart from the handful of bampots that you get sounding off on Radio Dighty.' He hiccupped a couple of times.

The very mention of the name, Radio Dighty, was making Fergus bristle. Stephen decided to swerve the topic of the radio station that they all loved to hate and began to talk about something he remembered from his school days. 'I don't know if any of you have heard a limerick about the Dighty Burn?' Everyone shook their heads. 'Ok, here goes, bringing a bit of culture into the evening.

'A bleacher at Mid-Mill cried Mighty
A full rigged ship on the Dighty
A voice cried oot Havers
Eh fell in at Clavers
It's just me masel' in ma nighty.'

'Like you say,' said Lakshmi, 'we really needed a bit of high culture! I suppose young folk nowadays would think that a bleacher was somebody goin out to impress on a Saturday night.'

'Wait,' said Stephen, 'I'm no' finished yet. That's the pure Dundee version that you heard with all the gh-sounds pronounced in a hard Scots way that makes you think the speaker is clearing his throat. There is another upmarket version, a low fibre version, you know, where you pronounce the sounds very differently.

'A bleacher at Mid-Mill cried Mai-ty
A full rigged ship on the Dai-ty
A voice cried out Hav-ahs
I fell in at Clav-ahs
It's just me myself in my nai-ty.'

'That's no' even pan loafie,' cried Fergus. 'The Queen, mair like!'

'Were you taught that at school?' asked Euan.

'No, no. It was just the sort of stuff that we said round the back o' the proverbial bike sheds, when we were trying to prove that we were real tough Scotsmen, as opposed to wee English fairies.'

'No' very successful then,' said Euan, preparing himself in case an object was thrown at him. But he was saved from any such missile by the phone. Haris was on the move again and was driving back to Dundee.

'He seems to be spending a lot of time in Edinburgh these days,' said Fergus. 'I wonder if he's seeing anyone there.'

'No,' said Lakshmi. 'I'd know if he was up to anything like

that. I wondered if he might be interested in someone nearer home?'

'There's no point in looking at me,' protested Euan. 'Just because we go to the gym together doesn't mean anything more than, well, the fact that we go to the gym together. Lots of guys do that.'

'But they don't all go beetroot red when they're explaining their training schedule!' said a delighted Fergus.

'Everybody blushes in my family,' said Euan. The colour of a traffic light by now.

'Gregor blushes all the time. They think it's genetic, but, of course, it could be exacerbated by my medication.'

Lakshmi took pity on him and began to talk about Amanda. 'I saw your niece the other day in The Whalebone. Endriggs had a gig there and she was playing the accordion; she's very good. It must be difficult not to be overshadowed by someone as charismatic as Ludo but she did get one or two solo slots.'

'Aye, and she had an incredible post-punk sort of hairstyle,' said Fergus. 'It would be my guess that she probably didn't get it cut in Broughty Ferry.' He could see that Euan was looking perplexed. 'The left side of her head was shaved really close but she had a left parting and all her hair of normal length was brushed over to the right. And, I might as well go on now that I've started, she had three piercings in her ear.'

'Oh, god,' said Euan. 'I wonder if Alistair and Wilma know about all that. To think she was once gonna be a vet!'

'There's no barrier to women with piercings becoming vets,' said Fergus, although part of him wondered why he was saying this so authoritatively.

'Gregor has never mentioned it, has he?' asked Stephen. 'I'm sure he would have told you if he'd known.'

Euan was, as they used to say in the farmlands of Angus, dumbfounded. So much so that he didn't really register that the phone was ringing. Stephen went to answer it and came back to tell him that it was Dolly. 'She seems upset about something.'

He was gone for an age, certainly long enough for the bottle which he had just opened to be empty by the time he came back. The other three stopped laughing when they registered Euan's face.

'She's been dumped, Dolly's been dumped. She told Craig about her pregnancy and he dumped her, just like that...'

'Hey, hey' said Lakshmi. 'Why don't you start at the beginning? I never even knew she was pregnant.'

Euan explained what he knew about the pregnancy. After the previous conversation, Craig had turned up unexpectedly at Dolly's flat; when she tried to discuss the pregnancy with him, it soon became clear that he wanted nothing to do with bringing up a child. To make matters worse, it also became clear that he had specifically come round to dump her or, as he put it, to discuss making the relationship less intense and less exclusive. That was when she had told him to go and fuck himself. He protested that he would support the child financially, presuming that it really was his. Euan wasn't entirely clear about what had been said at that point but he knew that she was on her own in the flat. He had offered to go round but she preferred to be on her own while she tried to calm down.

There was a moment's astonished silence.

'There's more,' said Euan. 'Apparently, he wanted to discuss making the relationship less intense, blah, blah, blah, because he's getting engaged to someone else. A chiropodist from Blairgowrie.'

'Blairgowrie!' said Fergus, almost as if it would have been acceptable had she come from Aberfeldy.

'Here was me thinking that he's a man of principle,' said Stephen. 'And he's obviously just looking for someone who'd make a more conventional Lady Provost.'

'Men!' was all that Lakshmi could say.

'That man!' said Fergus.

They only said these three words but as they glanced at each other, a whole undercurrent of pain, argument and negotiation could be heard stirring. But it was clearly something that neither of them wanted to touch upon there and then.

'I need a drink,' said Euan.

They were drinking and talking across each other about the implications of the end of Craig and Dolly's relationship when the phone rang again but no one really wanted to answer it in case it was more difficult news. Lakshmi went to take the call and came back to tell them that it was Haris; all the off licences in Fife were closed and he just wanted to check that they still had some wine for him to drink. He was really looking forward to relaxing with them all after his car problems.

'I think that was the last bottle we just finished,' said Stephen with a hiccup. 'And all the off licences will be closed here too.'

'There must be one of those late night convenience stores that sells booze at this hour,' said Lakshmi.

'Don't look at me for advice about this,' said Fergus peevishly. 'This is no' a part o Dundee where I've ever had to go and buy booze late at night.'

Euan tried, unsuccessfully, to smother a laugh at this unexpected self-righteousness. Soon they were all laughing and they agreed that they'd just have to go out looking for one of these stores. It was while they were getting their coats on that Fergus began to talk about Neddy Scrymgeour.

'Does he have a late night offie?' asked Euan.

'No, no, he was the Prohibitionist MP for Dundee between 1922 and 1931. The only Prohibitionist MP in the country and he came from Dundee. I mean, who would have guessed it? I wonder what he would have thought about us heading out into the dark in search of the working man's ruin. Marx said that religion was the opium of the masses but it was obvious that he never visited the Dundee Seagate when the pubs are throwing out. Neddy had his problems with the Communist Party but he would probably have been MP for much longer if it hadn't been for that scab, Ramsay MacDonald.'

Euan was struggling to keep up with all these ideas, when Lakshmi took charge.

'Right, two of us should go in one direction and two in the other and come back here as soon as we find a bottle for Haris. Stephen, you and me could head east and we'll leave the two prohibitionists to go west.'

'*Go West, young man, go west*,' warbled Fergus as he and Euan staggered together down the tenement stair.

Back in the flat, the phone rang but there was no one there to answer it. It rang and rang and rang.

26

There are those who surmise that democracy is something more cherished in its absence than by its presence. This is not to say that folk were not interested in the election for the new post of Lord Provost but they could not be said to be excited about it; it was definitely no' the speak o' the town. But politicians were very interested in it; you never hear of a place that has run out of politicians and Dundee was no exception to this rule; there promised to be an enormous line up for the populace to choose from. Euan did not see himself as a political activist but he had always been a thoughtful observer; when it came to politics, you could say that he was a bit of an optimist. He was sure, if he had indeed voted in the 1979 referendum, that he had voted Yes; it wasn't because he hated the English or even the Westminster government. All he wanted was a chance for Scots people to decide things for themselves; now the good folk of Dundee were getting such a chance.

The organisers were concerned to maximise the involvement of the citizenry because of its importance, not just for Dundee but also as a precedent for the rest of the country. One of their big ideas was to organise the hustings around themes rather than localities; the meetings on health, education, young people and traffic had all been well attended and useful discussions had ensued. But the level of interest expressed about the hustings on football was so enormous that the Caird Hall in the City Square had been booked. Truth be told, there was no other city in the country, let alone the world, that would organise election hustings to focus solely on football. Some Dundonians lamented the backwardness of democracy in other places that would ignore something so central to the everyday lives of men, and, of course, women as well, always assuming that they could organise childcare.

Fergus, with all his political antennae, was in his element. He devoted considerable time and energy to researching the backgrounds and the wider interests of all the candidates. There were no surprises with the more deeply embedded local candidates but he uncovered lots of interesting data about the little known Daphne Pattullo; it turned out that she had connections with property development that he believed would, and should, be of interest to the footballing democrats of Dundee. Her most ambitious proposal was to draw private capital into the city to assist in the building of a Football Village, which could replace the rather elderly stadia of the two local teams as well as provide employment for significant numbers of Dundonians. Fergus was researching her financial connections right up until the time of the meeting.

Euan had attended the hustings on health and education, both issues close to his heart, and, while he was interested in football, he went along because he suspected these hustings would have much more drama and conflict than any of the others. He set off there with Fergus and Stephen; Fergus was rather agitated and had spent what seemed like hours choosing the right colour of shirt before settling on a brilliant yellow one with black polka dots. Where they got off the bus, there was a large graffito proclaiming **Dundee is not Amritsar** but they were all so focused on the hustings that it was never mentioned.

There were scores of leafleters dodging around the pillars at the front of the Caird Hall; they were taking the opportunity to warn the audience about all conceivable social and political dangers; one guy was advocating veganism as an alternative to the perils of chemically enhanced meat; more typical were those who identified the imminence of betrayal by political leaders; Scotland First supporters were urging voters to remember family values. Kyle Fullerton was standing near the entrance but didn't appear to be part of any group of leafleters.

As they walked up the steps and into the entrance hall, Fergus remarked that Paul Robeson had performed here once.

'And David Bowie,' said Stephen, ever the teacher setting the context.

'But no' at the same time, I take it?' asked Euan.

There was a bit of a stushie at the door when stewards tried to stop some fans walking in with large carrier bags full of cans of Export. They claimed that access to Export was their human right in view of the absence of a licensed bar in the hall. But while the stewards may have been less than familiar with the intricacies of international law, they were up to speed when it came to seeing through excuses and evicting anyone who argued with them. 'Bloody teuchters,' complained one overweight man as he was thrown unceremoniously on to the pavement by a wee Aberdonian steward several times fitter than him.

Euan and Stephen were feeling quite relaxed as they made their way in, when they saw a man in army casuals going over to Fergus. 'Well, well, Mr Nicol,' he said, sneeringly. 'I see you've come along with your latest good cause. The poor man's asleep for twenty years and what happens when he wakes up? He's befriended by Fergus Nicol, the underdog's mascot.' Fergus proceeded to lock horns with him.

'Is he talking about me?' said Euan to Stephen.

'I think so. Do you recognise his voice?' Euan shook his head. 'That,' said Stephen, 'is Millar Gibb, the great star of Radio Dighty. He was at school with Fergus and likes to goad him every now and again. Makes a really big deal of the fact that Fergus has an Asian girlfriend, or, as he calls her, an oriental sweetmeat.'

'He doesn't say that to Lakshmi's face, does he?'

Stephen laughed. 'You bet he doesn't.'

Voices were raised and when Euan and Stephen heard this, they moved over towards Fergus.

'Oh, fuckawaywiye,' said Fergus as he turned his back on his old schoolmate. 'Once a bully, always a fucking bully.' Millar seemed not to have heard this and was smiling smugly at his ability to rattle his former schoolmate and political opponent. Euan had expected drama and it had begun before he'd even taken his seat.

Lakshmi emerged speeding from a rather grand mahogany panelled press office to say hello. 'It's amazing how much international interest there is in these hustings. I suppose no one's ever done hustings like this before and there's folk all over the world that like football. I've just been explaining to them that the Arabs and the Dees are football teams and no' ethnic groups. I thought I was making some headway until the man from *El Pais* asked if they were like the Moors and the Christians that they have in Spain. Still, it's a great turnout. Hope they all mind to vote on the day.'

'Did you ever find out whose idea it was to have the election on a Tuesday instead of the traditional Thursday?' asked Stephen.

'I just know that they chose that day because it was St Andrew's Day. I suspect that if they get a good turnout, everyone will be claiming it was their idea. If it's a poor turnout, it'll have been someone else's idea!' she remarked with a cynical smile.

'Anyway, my dear,' said Fergus. 'We'd better love you and leave you, while there's still good seats.'

'With a shirt like that, there's no chance of you being missed when it comes to the questions,' she said as she headed past an Argentinian band singing some old Latin American song. Each verse of what seemed like a complicated narrative about the beauty of football was concluded with a chant of *Rio Plata, Rio Tay*!

Euan fancied walking up the marble staircase to a balcony seat but Fergus said that would make life difficult when it came to asking questions. They headed off into the main body of the hall to find the organisers had placed a troop of stewards around the organ loft to protect it from any excitable voters. They were just taking their seats when Stephen nudged Euan. 'Do you see who that is in the middle of the front row?' he asked.

'My god, it's Dolly! She's never willingly turned up at anything to do with football before.' He, in turn, nudged Fergus. 'Do you see Dolly there in the front row?'

'Aye, you're right,' said Fergus. 'Could her heels be higher or her skirt tighter?'

Euan craned his neck round to see a bit better. 'She said she'd let Craig know what she thought of him. I wonder if this is her chance.'

Just at that moment, all eight candidates trooped on to the stage to explosions of noise and waving of banners from all over the hall. There were over two thousand football fans in the hall and the noise was little short of deafening. Perhaps Craig was taken aback when he spotted his former girlfriend and, given the seat she was in and the outfit she was wearing, there was no missing her, but he did not appear to even blink. Mister Professional Politician to a tee. They all took their seats and the oldest man on the stage got up to open the event.

'My name is Willie MacToran and I am to be the chairman for tonight. The format is this: each of the candidates will have three minutes to declare their position on football in this election and then we'll throw open the meeting to questions and discussions. The order in which the candidates speak has been determined by taking the names out of a bonnet.' He read the names out and Craig was to be last and Daphne Pattullo second last. Fergus had his notebook out, ready to record anything of interest. At last, he looked as though he was beginning to enjoy himself. The first six candidates trotted out their party lines on football and it has to be said that there was no danger of the heather going on fire.

When Daphne Pattullo got up to speak the fans were not sure what to expect from this independent candidate. She was the only woman on the platform and she also spoke with a privately educated accent; she was completely unapologetic about the two factors which might well prove to be disadvantageous to her campaign and even seemed oblivious to their possible impact. The fact that she wore pearls, a twin set and a tweed skirt told everyone a lot about her high level of self-belief; there was no air of pretence about her at all. Her speech reached its culmination when she spoke of her vision of a Football Village.

'My vision is to put Dundee on the world map of football. For too long, we have settled on second-best role, almost as though we've been afraid to come out of the shadows of mediocrity. My dream of a Football Village will bring a new sense of excellence to Dundee and make us all proud of what we can offer to the world of football. Working in partnership with the existing football teams in the city – and I am one of those people who supports both teams – I will be able to introduce them to new funders from the private sector who will give us a site that will soon be the envy of football teams the length and breadth of the country. My experience as a football manager down South has brought me in contact with stakeholders who have an interest in contributing to the revival of football in Dundee. With their support, the Football Village will be a site that will provide employment and draw tourists to our great city...'

She continued in this vein for some time and while she skated over potentially tricky issues like the fate of the two existing stadia and the identity of the new funders, she did succeed in inspiring some sections of the audience. There was no question but that she came over as refreshing and those who were minded to let some fresh air into what could have been an inward looking, stale debate were stimulated by what she had to say.

Craig Baxter was certainly stimulated by what she had to say and was very pleased that he was speaking after her rather than in the midst of the indistinguishable apparatchiks. He was, of all the male candidates, the only one not wearing a tie; he was turned out like a family man on his way to a football match, a smart bomber jacket with matching shirt and chinos. Fergus noticed that he was wearing a ring on his wedding finger, presumably in anticipation of his nuptials to the chiropodist or perhaps he had already celebrated them unbeknown to his potential voters. Either way, it added to the image of the football-friendly family man.

He spoke as a former teenage footballer; he made connection with all those in the audience who had had a similar youthful dream about their own individual potential; he made a link with the potential of football to rebuild a sense of community throughout Dundee; he saw the people of Dundee as its greatest asset and that was what he would build upon. He was aware of the networks of amateur football clubs as well as supporters' clubs throughout the city and he vowed that one of his aims as Lord Provost would be to strengthen them and make them a force for community cohesion. Unlike any of the other speakers, he recognised the danger of racism and sectarianism not only to football but to the city as a whole; he was the only one to welcome the growing force of women's and girls' football and to incorporate them into his plan to revive the city's football. He also addressed the financial question but for him, the answer was not to be found in the private sector but in the redistributive funds of the European Union.

'Everyone in this city loves football, some to play and some to watch, and what I want to do is make it a force for change and to place it at the heart of my project for renewal. The football networks which already exist are our building bricks and it will be my job as Lord Provost to construct something innovative and sustainable from those bricks; it will be my job to help make Dundee not just the football capital of Scotland but also a source of inspiration to other communities throughout Scotland.'

The last two speeches had provided contrasting visions of the future of football in Dundee and there was a murmur of discussion throughout the hall. But the first questioner, sitting next to Millar Gibb, appeared not to have listened to any of the speeches; his pre-prepared question focused on what he called 'the flow of aliens on to our Scottish football pitches'.

Fergus was next to access the travelling microphone and he sought clarification about the funding implications of Daphne's Football Village. He was so nervous that his sweat-soaked shirt was sticking to his back. 'I am seeking assurances that the two current stadia in Dundee will not be sold off to property developers. Dundee has a long history of property disasters and I would not want to think that any such plan would result in the footballing fans in this city being ripped off by any such initiative.' He had planned to stop there but his nervousness led him to continue. 'I ask this question particularly of Daphne Pattullo because I understand that your husband is Daniel Harrington-Brown, the property developer who has a long history of mysterious involvement in brownfield sites in struggling cities down South.'

'Perhaps I can remind the questioner,' Daphne came back with lightning speed, 'that I am the candidate here, and not my husband. I have considerable experience of football management down South and that is one of the qualities that I bring to this election. Can I also remind him that Dundee has a long history of independent working women, I am sure that the ladies in the audience know what I am talking about. I am part of that tradition. I hope that I will be judged on what I have to offer and not on anything else.'

There were cheers from most of the women in the hall. She looked pleased with the way that she had tackled this question about her marriage and thus side-stepped the issue of property development.

Fergus knew that he had got this wrong but he was not one to give up easily. A woman in front of him shook her head in dismay.

'It's quite a simple question. Are you or are you not married to the property developer, Daniel Harrington-Brown?'

'Sit doon, ye bloody male chauvinist,' a woman at the back called out to widespread applause.

But there were other ripples of noise, as people began to engage with the implications of her married name, whether she chose to use it or not.

'Daphne Broon! Daphne Broon !' cried a lone voice. But soon it was echoing throughout the hall. 'Daphne Broon! Daphne Broon!'

'Whaur's the bairn?' shouted someone at the front.

Daphne, smiling with satisfaction at the way she seemed to have got the audience on side, responded, 'My child is at home with his grandmother ; I expect she's asleep by now.'

'Is that yir ain mither or is it Maw Broon?' another voice cried out from the back.

The chairman had begun to realise, even if Daphne had not, that the debate was going awry but as he stood up to call the meeting to order, he was interrupted by shouts of 'Oor Wullie! Oor Wullie!'

Lakshmi was busy in the press box trying to explain that these were all well known and much loved cartoon characters. 'Like Tintin?' said the man from *El Pais*, struggling to grapple with the strange cultural configurations of this city. Nor had he, even as a Spaniard, been prepared for Dundee to be such a noisy city, as two thousand fans shouted their views on the probity, or otherwise, of Daphne Broon.

The remainder of the meeting was nothing short of chaotic. Every time a question was asked, some wag in the audience would generate a reference to the large Broon family.

Daphne Pattullo found it impossible to make herself heard. It seemed that, while the stewards had managed to prevent the smuggling of beer and cider into the hall, their success rate with smaller, less visible bottles of spirits was rather more patchy. Singing broke out in various parts of the hall and brought Craig Baxter to his feet in an attempt to bring some order to the event. There was a bit of a lull for about ten minutes but the damage had been done. The chairman brought the hustings to an end and the fans made their way out. The Argentinian musicians, responding to the flow of the meeting, had a handle on the situation and improvised a chant of 'Dulce Bruno, Dulce Bruno!' to an interminably long song about the travails of a lonely lovelorn footballer.

'Aye, lad,' said a passer-by to Fergus. 'You fairly kicked her ba' up on the slates there. I wiznae sure how to vote but, after your question tae Daphne Broon, Craig Baxter's got my vote.'

Fergus was opening his mouth to reply but the man had moved on.

'Well,' said Stephen. 'That's some kind of result for you. You've brought the whole question of corruption and dodgy dealings into the election.'

'And misogyny as well,' replied Fergus, flustered and angry.
'There was no discussion worthy of the name but plenty of sexist
name-calling. That was never my plan. I'm off to the Shoogly
Nail.' Stephen joined him, looking forward to a relaxed couple
of pints but also well aware of the probable need for the finger
down the throat treatment within the next few hours.

Euan decided to stick around to find Dolly. He wasn't quite
sure what to do when he noticed her having a tense-looking
conversation with her ex but the decision was taken out of his
hands when Craig spotted him and, like the successful politician
he was, greeted him with an outstretched hand. 'Good to see
you, Euan. A bit of a rammy but a lot of good issues were raised
tonight. I hope that I can count on your vote on the thirtieth.'

Voting intentions had not been foremost in Euan's mind when
he came over to find Dolly but he agreed that he probably would
vote for Craig. He would definitely vote for him, in fact, but he
was reluctant to show his support too openly because of Dolly.
She said nothing but was clearly raging and, Euan surmised,
Craig used the opportunity offered by his arrival to head off to
engage with potential voters rather than stay and engage with
his erstwhile girlfriend.

'Fuckin low life,' Dolly muttered at the sight of Craig's back.
'He said, the bastard, that he hoped eh wiz taking good care o'
masel, in meh condition. He seemed to be sayin there wiz nae
place for me at election meetings when eh should be at hame,
knittin or whitever it is pregnant wifies are supposed tae dae. He
never even let on that eh wiz there. It wiz meh plan, tae be
truthful, tae get up and mak a bit o' a scene at the meetin but
when it cam tae it, eh jist decided eh would be makin a fool o'
masel. There was enough shite bein thrown aboot at Daphne
withoot some ither daft wummin jumpin up and doon. Eh ken
the media would love it if there wiz some story aboot Craig

Baxter dumpin his pregnant mistress, but, for the bairn's sake, eh'm no' gonna dae that.'

'Oh,' said Euan, 'there could be some great pictures of you looking glamorous but defiant, gazing out of an....'

'Jist watch it, pal. Ye're skatin on thin ice.' Her words were assertive but the way that she hit him with her bag helped him feel that her sense of humour was returning. They talked away for a bit and Dolly did begin to calm down but rather than go to the pub, she made moves to set off home to Bannockbrae for a cup of tea.

'Eh jist hope the bastard disnae realise eh'm gonna vote for him.' Dolly pulled her face in distaste at the very thought.

'Same here,' said Euan. They both laughed, slightly hysterically, about the condition of democracy in Dundee.

27

'Good evening, Scotland, you are listening to Radio Dighty – the radio station where you can always be sure of hearing Scots voices. This is Millar Gibb and tonight, before we hear some grand Scots music, we will be focusing on the election for Lord Provost that's to be taking place on the 30th of November. That is, of course, St Andrew's Day and many of us here think that should be a public holiday rather than a day for something like an election. But we have argued that, if there is to be an election on that day, then we should make sure the result is as Scottish as possible. Let's send out a message from Dundee that Scots will not tolerate any meddling in their affairs by alien forces.

'When we look at the candidates who are putting themselves forward for election, we see a sorry bunch. There are the unionist parties, and I won't bother to mention their names because we all know who they are and we have heard their names more than often enough. I'm no' being rude when I say they could make a lassie puke. Whether they are of the right or the left or whether they've fallen through a hole in the middle, their first loyalty is to preserve the Westminster system. They are a parcel o' rogues, nothing more, nothing less. Even those parties that call themselves nationalist but still send MPs to London are in thrall to a rotten system; they may think they are confusing folk about their real agenda but they do not confuse Radio Dighty. We know that they just stand for another brand of unionism.

'I can explain what I think o' the whole spectrum of unionists when I say that they remind me of Patrick Sellar, who was the driving force behind the Highland Clearances in the nineteenth century. The Duke of Sutherland was the main beneficiary of these genocidal campaigns but he would have been powerless without the support of Scotsmen like Sellar who used their local knowledge to drive their fellow Scots from their traditional homes. Some say Sellar was motivated by personal greed; some say he suffered from over-deference to landowners like the Sutherland family. All I know is that he was prepared to betray his fellow Scots and we here on Radio Dighty do not thole traitors. At least, we can encourage the English exploiters in our midst to go back home to their own country and to leave Scots in peace. Traitors like Sellar are far, far worse because they are like a cancer threatening the wellbeing of our body politic and sometimes radical surgery is the only option for cancerous tumours. But Scotland has a proud tradition of education and we should be ready to make resources available to re-educate these unionist traitors. We will know that the process of re-education has been successful once they've thrown off their tartan-lackey mentality and begun to focus themselves on the reconstruction of Scotland on Scottish terms.

'There are some other smaller groups whose primary loyalty is not to Scotland or to Westminster but to internationalist ideology; they call themselves parties but they are more like sects. Many of us imagined that Communism had died with the collapse of the Soviet Union but we may have been optimistic. There are still small elements that are devoted to the teachings of Leon Trotsky or Che Guevara. Neither of these men was proud enough of the land where they were born to stay there. In fact, both these men can best be described as rootless cosmopolitans; they, and their like, had no regard for national traditions that are so necessary to any reconstruction process. The internationalist politicians in our midst may speak with local accents and may live in the more deprived areas of our country but their hearts are elsewhere. One of the strange things about them is that they are both over-educated and under-educated. They are over-educated insofar as many of them have studied historical and economical developments across the world in great depth; if you're daft enough to want to know about the Bulgarian Peasants Party in 1947, these are your men. They are under-educated in that they know next to nothing about the everyday lives and dreams of their fellow Scots; to use a footballing metaphor, they follow the teams but they don't understand the offside rule. They are not grounded in modern Scottish life. These rootless cosmopolitans spend all their lives in meetings, grouping and regrouping, plotting and counter-plotting. It's hard to believe but they can spend hours, or even weeks, arguing over the minutes of the last meeting they attended. They are few but they are obsessive and they can distract young Scots searching for meaning in their lives. They distract their fellow Scots from making the necessary changes to their lives. I urge all true Scots to beware of them.

'The two candidates in Dundee who are commanding the greatest interest in the opinion polls are the independents. While opinion polls are not to be trusted, it says a lot about the common sense of Dundonians that they have not been taken in by the baseless rhetoric of the unionist parties or the internationalist sects. And we here on Radio Dighty congratulate you for that. Craig Baxter and Daphne Pattullo are to be credited for standing as independents because they have clearly seen through the havering of the unionist parties and the internationalist sects. As those of you who attended the hustings over the last few weeks will know, they have both given serious thought to what is needed for Dundee and that's no' to be sniffed at.

'Let's start with Daphne Pattullo. I'm an old-fashioned sort o' guy and I still believe in Ladies First. Daphne says she grew up in Dundee but you just have to listen to her speaking for about thirty seconds to know that it must be a long time since she did that growing up. She's no' an incomer but she's been away such a long time that she might as well be. She also tells us that she's married and she has a couple o' bairns; in these unstable times, there's something to be said for a woman that's stayed married to the same man. But I'll warrant that many of our listeners will want to know how a proper wife and mother can think o' taking on a demanding job like Lord Provost of Dundee. If one of her bairns was ill and taken to hospital, you'd expect the mother to be at the bedside; but, in that case, who would be taking care o' Dundee? Some kind o' civil servant, no doubt, but we're no voting for civil servants; we're voting for a Lord Provost. The enemies of Radio Dighty and Scotland First will say that I'm being sexist here but I'm thinking about Dundee and Dundee needs more than a part-time Lord Provost. Radio Dighty believes in traditional family values and we cannot support a woman whose man also has a full-time job for election to this position.

'So, that leaves us with Craig Baxter. A man o' the people with a good Scots tongue in his head, or that's what he'd like us to believe. There's no' many ordinary Dundee men that could afford the kind o' suits that he wears and you wonder how he can afford them. You might also wonder who it is that's backing Mr Baxter. His campaign manager is the owner of a Chinese restaurant that goes under the name of Ashet and I'm no being funny but what kind o' Chinese restaurant hides behind a Scottish name like that? There's something that's being hidden there and there may well be some financial shenanigans that are being hidden as well. On top o' that, we all know that Craig Baxter is a trade union official and those of us with long memories can remember how it was that trade union squabbling prevented the opening of an electronics plant by Ford less than twenty years ago. We wonder if, when push came to shove, Craig Baxter's major loyalty would be to his trade union pals or to Dundee.

'And another thing, some of you will remember how he talked about European funding at the hustings. How can he be so sure that he'll be able to bring that here to Dundee? One of the reasons might be because he spent years working in Europe and he's supposed to be fluent in both French and Spanish. That's the kind o' thing that makes you question his priorities. When he's swanning off to Europe to win funds for Dundee, will he be thinking about this city of ours or will all his attention be on the European gravy train? Mark my words, if he's elected, Dundee will only be a springboard for his greater ambitions. He'll be after a job in Brussels that will enable him to buy even more expensive suits than the ones he already has. Craig Baxter's no' a man to be trusted; there's far too many loose ends and unanswered questions about him. He's no' a man that deserves your vote.

'Some of you will maybe be getting a bit depressed at all this doom and gloom about the election but you know that you get the unvarnished truth on Radio Dighty. I would be insulting your intelligence if I told you everything was ticketyboo when that's far from the case. Some of you will be wondering how there's no' a candidate from Scotland First to put forward the kind of ideas that we support here on Radio Dighty. And I can answer that question very easily. Scotland First is a new organisation and these elections were called so quickly that there was no time for them to get their nomination papers and their manifesto sorted out. The eight candidates that are standing have got some kind of bureaucratic backing behind them. Given some more time, then Scotland First could have got its organisation in place but they've been concentrating on grassroots issues rather than bureaucracy building. Some folk are asking if the election was rigged in such a way as to prevent organisations like Scotland First from taking part.

'At Radio Dighty, we know that our listeners will be looking to us for some kind of steer about how to use your vote. A lot of folk will be feeling really scunnered about this election and will maybe no' even bother to turn out and vote. We would encourage you all to make sure you *do* vote but leave your ballot papers blank. If there are a large number of blank voting papers that will be a major statement about what you think about this rigged election. The electoral process is certainly letting the people of Dundee down. When that happens, folk may well turn their backs on the democratic processes. We should not be surprised if younger Scots decide to take the law into their own hands. Sometimes folk feel that when the law lets them down, it's no' worth supporting that law any longer. We just have to hope that things do not get out of hand in the event of any such extra-legal activity. But if you are going to vote on St Andrew's Day, the most Scottish way to vote is by leaving your voting paper blank.

'But now we can all stop worrying about that and sit back and listen to some grand Scottish fiddle music with a Radio Dighty favourite – *Bunty Dargie*!'

28

Hogmanay has always been the big one. Times change and ways of celebrating events change too but wherever you go in Scotland, you will find folk of all ages and classes saying farewell to one year and beckoning in the next. Not many people talk of Jock Tamson's Bairns these days but the atmosphere at Hogmanay brings to mind the notion that Scotland is a land that welcomes everyone, whatever their age or background. It's a time when folk will offer a dram to strangers and men will hug other men in public places. Hogmanay is a time like no other in the Scots calendar.

Euan had been back in waking life for a year now but this was to be his first New Year since he was a boy back in the Seventies. It was an extra special New Year because it would (whatever the purists and the pedants might say) mark the end of one millennium and the beginning of another. It was a cold dry day, with no threat of rain or snow, and it would be ideal weather for being out and about; whether there would be any chance of first-footing was unclear but he liked the idea of crossing the threshold of someone's house and sharing a sense of hope together. He knew about new beginnings and he liked the idea of a festival that was there to celebrate the possibility of new beginnings for everyone.

He was sitting impatiently in Fergus's flat, watching the clock until such time as they could go out and start celebrating. The plan was that he, Fergus, Lakshmi and Haris would have a meal in Ashet; after that, they would head down to Victoria Dock to hear the foghorns usher in the New Year; then the first footing could begin.

'Have you ever done the New Year's Day swim at Broughty Ferry?' Euan asked Fergus.

'The dook? Well, I've thought about it several times but, well, let's just say that circumstances have never permitted me to do it!' He laughed, in memory of all his New Year's Day hangovers. 'I watched it last year. It was a good laugh; folk go into the water in fancy dress and some of them actually swim!' But Fergus's mind was really focused on choosing a shirt that would be suitable for a meal at Ashet, for going first footing and, quite probably, for the over-consumption of alcohol.

'Well, I'd at least like to go and watch it,' said Euan. 'I'd like a memorable start to the year 2000.'

'Apparently, Craig Baxter is going to open it, or ring a bell or fire a starting gun or something. It'll be his first official appearance as Lord Provost,' said Fergus, now attired in a deep green shirt fresh from the Breeks and Semmits New Year Sale. 'That'll be the easy part. It's a job and a half he's got for himself.'

'I am glad that he won, but I don't envy him,' replied Euan, who had given no such thought to changing his attire to mark the change of year. 'There's so much that needs doing in Dundee and everybody expects him to be a miracle worker. I hope he realises he owes you something for getting him elected. Your question about property development at the hustings finished off any chance that Daphne Pattullo might have had of winning the election.'

Fergus wasn't convinced. 'Aye, maybe, but it unleashed a whole load of sexist crap about her too. I know that I got the point over but it's never the way I would have wanted to do it. Still, I'm no' unhappy that Craig's been elected and at least I think he knows what a hard time he'll have. He'll be strapped for resources, no' to mention all that negativity coming from the likes of Scotland First and Radio Dighty.'

'I know that they're horrible but maybe they're just all hot air. I mean to say, Scotland First didn't even put up a candidate in the elections.'

'Aye, there's that,' replied Fergus. He was concentrating on using a gadget to remove hairs from his nose. 'But he emphasised the role of community development and so he'll have to make sure that he gets the community on his side; Radio Dighty will do all they can to make that as difficult as possible. They're bound to accuse him of being untrue to Scottish values, whatever he does.'

'I wonder how he'll feel about showing his face in Bannockbrae. All Dolly's pals will know about how he's dumped her; they'll maybe be less than friendly to him. Mind you, I'm more concerned about her than about his political plans. It's just as well she's as tough as she is; bringing up a child on her own will not be a barrel of laughs. I'm trying to persuade her to stick with her course but it's easy for me to say that, when all I've got to worry about is getting my essays in on time. Maybe we could go and first foot her.'

Fergus was popping back and forward to the window, as if his presence there would magically make Lakshmi and Haris appear on his doorstep. The intercom rang and he let Lakshmi in. She bounded in as if she was in a race.

'You'll never guess what's happened?' she said, as Fergus attempted to give her a kiss. 'A bus has been hijacked on the Nethergate!'

'Somebody's idea of a Hogmanay joke,' said an unthwarted Fergus.

'No, no, it's serious. It's something to do with Scotland First, They want this to be the start of a truly Scottish millennium and they've made some kind of declaration of Scottish values.' She answered her mobile and kept on saying OK to whoever was on the other end of the line.

'They're broadcasting their declaration on Radio Dighty at eight o'clock,' she said.

'That's now,' said Fergus, as he fiddled with the frequency on his radio. 'Fuck me, it sounds like Millar Gibb.'

'Some of you will be aware of the news that a bus has been halted in the centre of Dundee. At this point in time, there appears to be a news blackout and our listeners may well be confused as to why this has happened. Radio Dighty, of course, condemns any action which disrupts the everyday lives of Scottish citizens but this particular action is in defence of Scottish values and we see it as our public duty to transmit their message to our listeners so that you can at least understand what has driven these young men to take such action. We understand their frustration at the way in which the institutions in this great land of ours are being taken over by un-Scottish forces. Like many others, Radio Dighty was fair scunnered by the mockery of democracy that took place in the recent elections for the Lord Provostship of Dundee. Although we do not support those who take the law into their own hands, we can sympathise with their sense of despair. We have obtained a copy of a message which these young heroes made before they seized control of the bus.'

'You notice that he doesn't use the word hijack,' said Lakshmi.

'Slimey cunt!' said Fergus.

'Sshh,' said Euan.

'This is an important turning point in Scottish history and, remember, that you heard about it first on Radio Dighty. I will now play you the tape that was sent to us.'

"We declare that the Scots are a proud and ancient nation. From the time of the Battle of Bannockburn (1314) and the Declaration of Arbroath (1320) we have led the world in terms of both nationalism and democracy. The Presbyterian Reformation

of John Knox (1560), the Solemn League and Covenant (1643) and the Sanquhar Declaration (1680) also showed the world the path to true religion and proper values. We are proud to make this declaration only a few miles away from Forfar, the historic town where Malcolm Canmore, King of Scots, held the first parliament in 1057; his wife, St Margaret, also did lots of good works in Forfar and she has been a great role model for Scottish women over the centuries, even if she was born in Hungary.

We believe that current events are threatening nationalism, democracy and religion in our great land.

We call for all true Scots to rally to our cause and to support our Declaration of Scottish Values. This Declaration states that:

- Scotland is a proud nation that bends its knee to no one;
- The Scottish people will refuse to submit to the yoke of England or any other foreign body;
- Scottish education should be based around the values and beliefs of Bannockburn (1314), the Declaration of Arbroath (1320), the Presbyterian Reformation of John Knox (1560), the Solemn League and Covenant (1643) and the Sanquhar Declaration (1680);
- Scottish jobs should be given to Scottish people;
- Scotland should negotiate trade treaties with other countries where there are large Scottish communities like Canada or New Zealand or South Africa;
- Scottish hospitals should give priority to Scottish patients;
- Scottish land which is owned by non-Scots should be nationalised and handed over to true Scots;
- A strict licensing system should be introduced for

meeting places for any of the groups that are disruptive to the purity of Scotland, whether that is a mosque for the Pakistanis or a nightclub for the gays;

- *Scottish married couples should commit themselves to staying together according to the principles of Scottish love;*

- *Anyone who is not obviously a true Scot, because they are a Catholic or a Pakistani or a gay or because they have some other handicap, should sign the Declaration and commit themselves to attending re-education classes in Scottish values;*

- *Anyone who does not sign this Declaration should leave Scotland.*

As long as there are a hundred of us willing to fight for Scotland, that fight shall continue.

Long live Scotland!"

'This is a truly historic document, listeners, and you will be able to tell your grandchildren that, thanks to Radio Dighty, you heard the first broadcast of this Declaration of Scots Values. It is my understanding that the bus which has been the subject of news stories has now been redirected to Carrot Hill. I would submit to you that there is no finer name to give to the declaration than the Declaration of Carrot Hill. Many of our listeners will be shocked by this kind of behaviour but, while we have no connection with the planning of this activity, we feel sure that it will be conducted with all the grace and generosity that you would expect from folk who adhere to Scots values. We will be proud to keep you informed of any developments in this exciting episode in Scotland's history.'

There was a moment's stunned silence as they tried to absorb the information.

'I wonder who the actual hijackers are?' asked Fergus.

'Probably some of the Wullie Wallies,' said Lakshmi. 'Or they could be just some bampots that took seriously all that stuff that Radio Dighty broadcasts. I wonder if they're armed.'

They were speculating on various theories about the identities of the hijackers, and their aims, when they were interrupted by Euan.

'Where's Haris?' said Euan. 'He was coming here from his flat in Baltic Street and the bus goes through the Nethergate. And, he's late! He always calls if he's going to be late.' He was distraught and pacing around as if the room had been placed under siege.

'He's not answering,' said Lakshmi, with her mobile to her ear.

'We have to do something,' said Euan.

'Let's go to Carrot Hill, then. Fergus, have you had a drink?'

'No, I was trying to be sensible and wait till we got to Ashet before I started.'

'OK,' she said. 'You can drive then. Have you got a torch? I've got a wee tape recorder here and a notebook. Have you got a map?' She was taking charge.

'We don't need a map,' said Euan. 'I can remember the way. We go out past Claypotts, on to Baldovie Toll, up to Luckyslap and then take a left turn; I'm no' sure what the name o' the farm is but there's no' a lot of left turns; and if we get lost, we can just walk the last part. Are you ready yet, Fergus?'

'That sounds like a good route,' said Lakshmi. 'I don't know if the police will try and block off the roads but that sounds sufficiently obscure for them no' to bother about.'

Euan was twitching anxiously. Fergus was going through

another shirt change and opted, in the end, to wear the same one as he had decided to wear anyway.

'Come on,' said Fergus, touching Euan's arm. 'I've found my keys and I filled up the tank earlier. You did say you wanted a memorable start to 2000. Carrot Hill, here we come.'

29

'You are listening to Radio Dighty on New Year's Day in the year 2000. A Happy New Year to all our listeners. Radio Dighty is the one station where you can always be sure of hearing a Scots voice whenever you turn on. This is Millar Gibb and before we do anything else today, I want to update you on the unfolding of events at Carrot Hill. Due to a media blackout, Scots have had little chance to learn about what is happening there.

'The first thing we can report is that the young freedom lovers who redirected the bus acted in a spirit of Scottish generosity when they released most of their fellow Scots in time for the bells at midnight. We would have expected nothing less of them. True Scots do not punish other true Scots. Oh, no. Eleven true Scots were accordingly released in time to celebrate the beginning of this new millennium in the fresh air of Carrot Hill. In exchange for this release, items of food and drink were accepted on to the bus in consideration for the wellbeing of all remaining passengers. Those who remain on the bus with the young freedom lovers are all either foreigners or Scots with problems that will require them to be subject to re-education processes. The driver has not been released but we are informed that she is remaining on the bus for reasons of safety and security rather than on account of any ideological weaknesses.

'I am informed that the William Wallace Youth League is setting up booths on the High Streets of Scotland asking people to sign the petition in support of the Declaration of Carrot Hill. You can read the declaration on the Radio Dighty website. They are in no way asking Scots to support the redirection of the bus but they are asking for support for the principles behind the Declaration. In my view, massive support for the Declaration could lead to the young freedom lovers enabling the passengers to resume their interrupted journey. This is a time of great flux and uncertainty and, when these booths are set up, I would ask all listeners to Radio Dighty to sign this petition.

'The police have leaked the names of the two freedom lovers and because of that, I feel able to refer to them. They have not sought to glorify themselves or to seek fame in any way but because their confidentiality has not been respected, I feel able to say some words about them, words to set their behaviour in some kind of context. Their names are Kenny Horsburgh and Kyle Fullerton. These are not hooligans; I know them both through their work for the William Wallace Youth League; you may have heard Kenny here several times on this programme on Radio Dighty. Some very negative stories have been doing the rounds about these two fine young Dundonians, the most dangerous of which is that they are drug users or drug addicts. I can assure you that is one downright lie. We all know that drugs are a major problem among young people in Scotland but that is one of the things the William Wallace Youth League has set its face against. Such slanders against these two fine, clean living young patriots will not be tolerated on this programme. As the Carrot Hill Declaration shows us, they are both keen students of Scottish history. The research for the Declaration was something that they did in their own time under their own steam. Such self-motivation is something to be commended.

'I know there is an enormous amount of interest in the Declaration of Carrot Hill because of the calls, emails and other messages I have received from you. The inbox is fu' to bursting. Some of you have expressed the same sense of frustration which these young men feel about the recent rigged election in Dundee.

The election has felt to you like an alien imposition on Scotland, yet another attempt to prevent Scots from feeling at home in their own homeland. Another quisling elected as Lord Provost and that's Craig Baxter I'm talking about.

'Time prevents me from reading out more than a tiny percentage of these messages but here are some now that particularly caught my attention. To protect listeners' confidentiality in these difficult days, I will not read out the names of the folk that sent me these messages but I will mention the names of the places where they come from. A listener from Aberlemno said: "At last, someone has spoken up for real Scots. We should all be grateful to these two laddies for saying in public what so many of us have been saying in private." Somebody from Wormit said: "It's high time that we stood up for this grand land of ours. We've put up with outside meddling for too long and the Carrot Hill Declaration makes it clear who should be the boss here." An elderly lady – I hope she won't mind me telling you that she is 85 years old – phoned in to speak to me personally; she explained that she was too old for email but she just wanted to remind us about the sacrifices that had been made by Scotsmen in the past. She had lost three of her older brothers in the First World War and when the fourth one looked old enough to fight, her mother sent him off with pride in her heart. He never returned but his mother went to her grave knowing that she had made the greatest sacrifice any mother could make, to send her sons off to war to fight for their homeland. She feels sure that the mothers of the two young freedom lovers on the bus will understand what she's talking about. I appreciate her call and, of course, it helps to show that the Declaration and the rerouting of the bus have struck a chord with folks of all ages; this is no' just something of interest to young hotheads. Oh, no, it cuts across all ages.

'My last message is from a listener in Perth, who describes

himself as a fan of St Johnstone. "I am glad to hear that two real Scotsmen have said what needs to be said. There's far ower much nonsense these days about un-Scottish stuff like poofs and women's lib. I checked out the St Johnstone website only the other day and there are two poofters trying to set up a gay supporters' group. Apparently, they liked the goalie's legs. Have you ever heard the like? We need to get back to Scottish basics and these boys on the bus are helping us to do that. It's a great start for the year 2000." As I say, that's only a handful of the messages that we have received but I can tell you that there is a great body of support out there for Kenny and Kyle. What folk seem to be saying is that things in Scotland have just gone too far and the rerouting of the bus is acting as a wake-up call. Folk have had enough! Folk are fair scunnered!

'Before I go today, I should warn listeners that Radio Dighty may well be prevented from broadcasting while the stand-off at Carrot Hill continues. You might have thought that in a free society an independent radio station like ours would have been welcomed; who else speaks up for the ordinary man in Dundee if Radio Dighty is taken off the air? We have, however, received threats from folk who themselves feel threatened by what we have to say. It's strange how these human-rights boys only seem to be interested in human rights for folk like themselves and the cultural misfits in our country. Human rights seem no' to be necessary for ordinary hard-working Scots folk like ourselves. So, I just say this as a warning to you. If you can't find Radio Dighty next time you turn on, that's probably no' because o' some problem with your radio. It's probably because we've been suppressed. But, have no fear, we will find other ways of spreading the word. As the Carrot Hill Declaration said, echoing the Arbroath Declaration of many centuries ago: "As long as there are a hundred of us willing to fight for Scotland, that fight shall continue."'

30

It was over sixty hours since the bus had been driven to Carrot Hill but it felt like a lifetime to everyone involved. Folk had been gearing themselves up for the coming of the new millennium but the bus hijack had thrown them off that course completely. No one could stop talking about the bus and everyone had at least five different interpretations of its significance.

Several things had become clear after eleven 'true Scots' had been released in time for the bells. Apart from the hijackers and the driver, Haris was one of a group of seven or eight 'social misfits' still on the bus. The released hostages had been able to tell the police that the hijackers had weapons; the details were not clear but they had at least a rifle and a handgun. It was reported too that Kenny had a bag containing something he was very nervous about; the speculation was that it might be some explosives. No one really knew what to expect. Anyone wishing a toilet break was only allowed to do so under armed guard; the smell was unspeakable. Kyle was responsible for managing the hostages and everyone remarked on how calm and thoughtful he appeared to be; he didn't say anything but he made sure the hostages were as comfortable as possible. He was taking his responsibilities very seriously and though the hostages were tied to each other like a chain gang, there was no bullying.

Kenny was something else. He was the one who had interviewed the hostages to decide who was to be released. He seemed completely driven by ideology and, as a result of exhaustion, he was becoming increasingly agitated, both in his behaviour on the bus and in his announcements to the wider world. He used a megaphone to make demands for food and drink, as well as occasional statements about why they had kidnapped the bus. At first, he only made announcements every three or four hours but as time passed, he resorted to making himself heard more and more often. About three o'clock on the third of January, he leaned out of the window and shouted through the megaphone; 'We are now into the third day of this event and we're no' nearer a resolution. We call on all true Scots to make their feelings known about the dangers facing our country today. We call on all our supporters to make their voices heard about the menace of un-Scottish values being imposed upon the land of John Knox. This great man gave Presbyterian values to the world and now the traitors and cheats that run this land are willing to sell out these values at a time when Scotland needs them more than ever. Increasingly, Scots feel like strangers in their own country, swamped as they are by aliens and alien ideas. Time is running out and our patience is wearing thin with the lies and hypocrisies that are being spoken about us.

'For many of us, the election of Craig Baxter as Lord Provost was the last straw. A clever, clever guy that speaks more foreign languages than is good for him. A guy who trusts his fellow Scots so little that he makes his Chinky pal his campaign manager. A guy who has a lot of money to spend on suits and we wonder where that money comes from. A so-called football fan who welcomes all and sundry into the two great Dundee teams without any thought of what that might do to the city's sense of Scottish purity. But we know that the problem is much bigger than Craig Baxter. There is a widespread lack of respect for everything Scottish and that is what makes many of us angry.

'We have tried to be positive and we produced a declaration of the cultural values that could transform Scots life. None of our so-called political leaders have bothered to respond to the

Declaration of Carrot Hill. We know that their priorities are elsewhere and we should not be surprised but we are disturbed at their lack of interest in the ideas contained therein. All true Scots know that these ideas are the one true agenda for the reconstruction of this great land of ours. So, why are our elected leaders and unelected masters so un-interested in our proposals? Why is there a media blackout on our action here? We're scunnered by the lack of interest of these self-hating Scots and that is what has caused us to take this extreme action here.

'We have based many of the ideas in the declaration on the teachings of John Knox. We understand that these are difficult ideas but these are difficult times. We believe that if Scotland returned to a kirk session regime of the kind that used to exist throughout most of Scotland, we would be a healthier and more moral nation. The kirk session could, among other things, lay down rules and regulations for the non-Presbyterians to live by. Scotland would once again become a nation governed by values.

'What I ask for now is some kind of negotiation with the police here on Carrot Hill. We are willing to make some concessions in return for some concessions being made to us. There are some folk here on the bus who are visitors to this great country of ours; they are keen to return to their own homes and they have promised us that they will spread the word about the Carrot Hill Declaration there.'

He pulled a young Frenchwoman to the window; she was dishevelled and tired and her make-up was reduced to untidy blotches; she only spoke a few words but she promised to support the Declaration of Carrot Hill in any way she could.

'I think these remarks show that people will support us if only they are given an opportunity to learn what our mission is. We appreciate their generous offers of support and we are willing to release our foreign friends but, in return for their release, we need some concessions. For starters, we need some hot food to be delivered; we've had our fill o' cheese rolls and Tunnock's Teacakes; in addition, we need a guarantee of safe passage to take the other remaining passengers to a secure place where we can begin work on an education programme with them. If these demands are not met, we cannot guarantee anything but rest assured, whatever happens, we will not go down like cowards. We want the world to know that cowardice is not, and will not be, part of Scotland's future. We look back to the heroism of the Covenanters who were true to the values of John Knox and strove to defend Scotland against alien forces. As they said at the time: "The work goes bonnily on." The police have ten minutes to get back to us.'

There was some anxiety among the police about how best to respond to this, made worse because the team of negotiators from Glasgow were all hospitalised after a car accident on the black ice at Powrie Brae. Other negotiators were reported to be on their way but there was no chance they would reach Carrot Hill in anything like the time demanded by Kenny.

Euan, Lakshmi and Fergus were just behind the police lines, but well within hearing distance of Kenny's tirades.

'He's getting tired,' remarked Fergus, shivering in a coat that had not been designed for spending a night out in the winter.

'And unpredictable. Even he doesn't know what he's going to do next,' said Lakshmi. 'I knew that they were big fans of a Presbyterian Scotland but all this stuff about government by kirk sessions is news to me.'

'And maybe to him as well,' said Euan.

'The stuff about the Covenanters is worse,' explained Fergus. 'Back in the 1640s, they took several hundred Irish people prisoner and massacred them. One of their ministers is supposed to have used that same phrase that Kenny used about the work going bonnily on. It's all a bit of a guddle and I'd be surprised if they really saw themselves as latter-day Covenanters.'

'But they like to see themselves as extreme as the Covenanters were,' said Lakshmi, shaking her head. 'Great! A couple of exhausted bampots with delusions of historical grandeur. That's all we need.'

Euan was quiet but he was having a brainwave. Kenny had asked him several times to speak on Radio Dighty as part of their Scottish Heroes series; he had always made some excuse but he was sure that Kenny and Kyle would remember his name. He thought it might be useful if he were to offer to speak to them; if nothing else, it might delay things until the negotiators arrived. He wanted to see an end to the stand-off, but more than anything else, he was driven by a desperate fear that something might happen to Haris. A gay Bosnian was not going to be top of the list of the hijackers' favourite people. He went over to speak to some senior police officers with his suggestion. They were not keen to involve him because of the risks to his own safety but they did acknowledge that everyone knew the name of Euan Saddler. Eventually, they agreed that some kind of conversation at a distance through a megaphone might act as a stalling device.

'Kenny, Kenny, can you hear me?' called out Euan, struggling to make himself heard through the howling wind. 'This is Euan Saddler here. You'll maybe remember that you asked me to speak on the Scottish Heroes programme. Anyway, I'm here now and I want to speak. I want us to see if we can find a way to reach some kind of agreement.' Euan was using the kind of words that had been suggested by the police but what was dominating his thoughts was the prospect of something happening to Haris. He had once decided, very rationally, that he did not want to rush things between them but now he felt as if he'd just been pussy-footing around. He wasn't sure whether he felt angry at himself or just pathetic. He didn't really know the words to describe his feelings for Haris but they were strong feelings and he wished that he'd found a more intimate way of expressing them rather than through a police megaphone.

Kenny wasted no time in returning to the bus window. 'We appreciate your offer, Euan. The way you returned from the dead and took control of your own destiny makes you one of the great Scottish heroes of the day but we want something more substantial than an offer to talk. Where are our so-called leaders at a time of emergency like this? It's them that we need to hear from. I'm telling you, Euan, you're just being used as fodder by a clique of self-hating Scots. Folk that have lost their way from the ideals laid for us so many years ago by the greatest Scottish hero of all, the Reverend John Knox. We are coming near to the time when sacrifices will have to be made.' He slammed the window shut.

Euan was distraught. All that was really on his mind was Haris; everything else was secondary to saving him. But when he heard Kenny's growing obsession with John Knox, his desperate imagination led him to devise a plan that might just bring Haris back into his life. He had summoned all kinds of ghosts from the past, some strangers as well as people he had known. Why not summon the ghost of John Knox? This was definitely not something for discussion with the police or even with his friends. He would be led away by men in white coats and would never have a chance to see Haris again, let alone hold him.

There were practical difficulties too; he had only ever summoned people from the twentieth century; perhaps summoning someone from four hundred years ago would be beyond his powers. But when it came down to it, all that really mattered was getting Haris off that bus; all that really mattered was being together with him. A life with Haris was the only thing he knew he wanted; a life without Haris was unimaginable. There was nothing he would not consider doing to save Haris's life. They weren't even lovers but he knew that they should be. He surprised himself by the sense of ruthlessness he felt about saving Haris. He knew now, more clearly than ever, that he loved Haris but any feelings of tenderness he had for him were overwhelmed by this unstoppable ruthlessness. Only a man possessed would decide that the summoning of John Knox was a feasible notion.

The summoning of the founding father of Presbyterianism sounded crazy, even to him, but he could think of nothing else. He wasn't sure about how you would talk to someone from the sixteenth century; it was possible that they might not understand each other at all. But when he reflected on it, dialogue was not what this was about. He really wanted to overawe Kenny and Kyle and use that as an opportunity to get the hostages off the bus. He realised that he still had a flask of whisky in his pocket for first footing purposes. Could Mr Knox be lured by a smell of the stuff? He convinced himself that the smell of whisky would probably be more powerful than words could ever be.

So, this was it. He decided to move behind some shrubbery so no one could see him or become suspicious about his strange behaviour. He needed to be in a private place to summon ghosts and while this wasn't perfect, everyone else was focusing their attention on the bus. He pulled his scarf up over his head. Usually, it was enough to breathe deeply and concentrate for a ghost to be summoned but this required more effort. He closed his eyes, held the flask in his hand, breathed really deeply and intoned the name of John Knox. Nothing happened at first and so he repeated the exercise. He decided to open the flask and deliberately spilt some whisky on one of his gloves. He repeated the name of John Knox, again and again. It was dark where he was standing and he became fearful that he might not spot the arrival of the old man. Suddenly, there was an incredibly loud bang, smoke everywhere; Euan lost his balance and collapsed on to the ground, completely overwhelmed. He passed out.

31

Dolly was waiting for the midwife when Lakshmi arrived. Neither of them had been in any direct danger during the hijacking of the bus but they both felt exhausted. Dolly was wearing an old red tracksuit, normally kept for private occasions when there was no chance of anyone else seeing her. Lakshmi was well wrapped up in an Arran sweater that she would have taken with her to Carrot Hill, if she had realised that she was going to be there for nearly three days. Some of the Bannockbrae flats were notoriously damp but Dolly had been lucky and hers was dry and warm. God shining on the righteous was one of her explanations for her good fortune.

'Ye dinnae hae a fag on you, Lakshmi?' asked Dolly.

Lakshmi looked surprised and shook her head; she thought that Dolly would have known she didn't smoke.

'Thank god fir that. Eh'm that stressed. Eh need a fag, if ye ken whit eh mean, but eh should not be smoking or even thinking about smoking for wee Pablo's sake.' She patted her belly.

'Do you know it's gonna be a boy, or is that just the way you're feeling today?'

Dolly laughed. 'Ye mean the kind o' feeling when ye think that men get aw the fun? No, it's no' that. Eh went doon the toon this morning and got a gender testing kit, it was a kind o' New Year's resolution. It's jist like a pregnancy test; if it goes orange, it's a lassie and if it's green, it's a laddie. See here, it's green, so it's a boy.'

'Pablo Fullerton! Congratulations!' They gave each other a long hug, the warmth of which might have been as much about the end of the hijacking as it was about the gender of Dolly's baby. Someone next door started to use an electric drill on the adjoining wall.

'The wee bugger just kicked me!' groaned Dolly, bending over with the after effect of her boisterous son's movements.

'He's maybe gonna be a footballer. A few years from now and we'll be listening to a cry going up at Tannadice: "There's only one Pablo Fullerton!"'

'Ken, Lakshmi, eh feel mair relaxed already, jist a bit o' company maks a' the difference. Eh've no' telt anybody yet about the bairn being a laddie, no' even the faither, but that can wait till we've hid a catch up. It's such a relief that naebody was killed at Carrot Hill. A bloody miracle, if ye ask me.'

The kettle had boiled and tea was dispensed while they raced around all the topics that were on their minds. Dolly found it difficult to settle down anywhere and kept changing her seat in the quest for comfort.

'Haris says hello,' said Lakshmi. 'He's staying at my place for a few days, it's quieter there than it is in Baltic Street. I hardly see him in fact; he gets up late and has something to eat and then goes back to sleep again. I told him he's an ideal guest; no trouble at all.'

'He must be knackered after what he went through. Somebody said to me it wiz "only" sixty hours but they didna ken it wiz "only" gonna be sixty hours. It's hard tae imagine living wi' that kind o' tension and next tae nothing tae eat.'

'It seems like they were being fed nothing but cheese rolls. Haris says he'll never touch another cheese roll as long as he lives.'

'It must hae been hellish for you, Lakshmi, sittin there wi' nothing tae dae,' said Dolly. 'And nothing tae look forward to except one o' Kenny's rants.'

'It was hellish and we all got more tired as well. Kenny was exhausted too and that made him more and more scarey. He seemed to be losing the plot, with all kinds o' threats. I never did get to the bottom of what he really, really wanted. I knew what he didn't want for Scotland but I couldn't see what his long-term plan was. Maybe there was no long-term plan. But, on top of all that talk about the need to purify Scotland, it felt even worse when we heard they had some guns.' She shook her head as if she was scared to even imagine a worse outcome. 'When folk are obsessed about something, you just can't predict what they might do with weapons like that. And then suddenly, it was all over, one big bang and great clouds o' smoke. I was flabbergasted that it finished just like that. I was expecting it to go on for days. Thank god they didn't put up any resistance or start shooting. But the police are being a bit coy about the way it came to an end.'

'Kenny seemed to be mair and mair fixated aboot John Knox, from what eh heard. Whaur did aw that come frae?' asked Dolly. She moved from the table to the comfort of the sofa.

'Fergus got really worried when he started obsessing away about Knox and some other Presbyterians that sounded even more demented. I don't know if you heard that Euan was concussed and when he came round, he started asking about John Knox. I suppose it was just the impact of hearing Kenny ranting on and on.' She sounded puzzled, as though she didn't quite believe her own explanation.

'Mind you, eh've no' been tae see Kyle, he says he diznae want any visitors. But he saw his granny the once and she said he wiz going on aboot John Knox tae. Tae be truthful, he nivver says much but he wiz speaking aboot John Knox almost as though he'd seen him. Eh suppose it wiz wi' him no' getting any sleep fir three days.' The drilling from the flat next door came to a halt.

'Is he seeing a lawyer?' asked Lakshmi, going into professional mode. 'There will be a lot of serious charges like kidnap and unlawful seizure of a bus. I don't know if you've seen the press release that Kenny's family have put out; basically, they're saying that the whole hijack thing was Kyle's idea; he comes from a very disturbed background; they say that his mother died of AIDS and so on. Kenny, on the other hand, was just a decent young patriot doing community work on his gap year; he tried to take Kyle under his wing but it all went awry when Kyle talked him into hijacking the bus.'

'Jesus Christ! The lying wee rat.' Dolly was stunned by this news. 'But there'll be footage, will there no', o' Kenny shouting and screaming out o' the bus. They can hardly say that's under duress. Can they?'

'No, but his family's obviously preparing the ground for his defence; nice, well-educated lad led astray by disadvantaged wee schemie! They'll be hoping that will reduce any prison sentence. Kyle will need to get a lawyer and I can look out for one, if you like.'

Dolly sighed and moved to the other end of the sofa. 'That's real good of you, Lakshmi. You don't need to be doing that after what your pals went through…'

'No worries,' said Lakshmi. 'I don't know if you heard about the way that Kyle behaved on the bus. That's one of the things that makes me want to help him get a decent lawyer. Haris says that he was kindness itself. Sure, he tied folk together but there was no more cruelty after that. He kept an eye on folk to see that nobody was getting too distressed. When he saw how uncomfortable old Mr Choudhri was, he got him a cushion to sit on and he was trying to persuade Kenny to let him go early on account of his age.'

'Ye ken, it's the first time he's ever had responsibility for anything...'

Somebody in the flat above started playing the drums. Lakshmi pulled a face but Dolly just went on talking, as if it was something that she was used to hearing all the time. The builders had managed to make this block dry but they'd been less successful with their attempts at sound proofing.

'He wiz aye a bit o' a lost soul efter his mother died. Well, tae be truthful, he wiz a bit o' a lost soul afore that as weel. He spent years jist sitting around in her flat wi' her and her pals shooting up and then passing oot. She wiz never deliberately cruel tae him, as far as eh ken but sitting around wi' a load o' junkies is nae fun; he used tae draw a lot o' wee pictures o' animals. He never made onything o' himself at school. He never passed an exam but he wiz nae trouble till he started playin hookie. Then he never had a job. Bairns deserve a better start than that. At first, eh thought Kenny wiz good fir him cos he was daeing things like the Wullie Wallies but eh couldnae be mair wrang. It seemed like it wiz an interest fir him, at last.' She held up her hands in despair. 'It's nae excuse but growing up on Bannockbrae is no' whit ye'd wish on yir worst enemy. There wiz plenty o' stuff here fir him tae get involved in like the campaigns about schools or housing or health but eh suppose none o' that wiz cool and young laddies need to be cool.'

Lakshmi nodded her head. 'It's probably easier to feel cool about a mythical Scotland than it is about sorting out the damp in your granny's flat. But I still find it hard to understand what all this Scots purity thing is about. Nationalism I can understand but the idea that you can create some kind of pure Scotland if only you can just get rid of the Pakis, the queers, the stroppy women...'

'Sounds like maist o' meh pals,' said Dolly.

'It's just a fantasy. We have to try to get on with our neighbours, whoever they are and whether we like them or not.'

'Even if they do play the bloody drums!' sighed Dolly. 'This mythical Scotland is jist a daft fantasy. Eh know that but eh nivver thought they'd be mad enough to pull a stunt like they did wi' the bus. Eh thought Radio Dighty would keep them happy.'

'Seems to have given them some more ideas! Radio Dighty is back pedalling now. Saying that they and Scotland First are law-abiding organisations that would never promote any forms of violence.' Lakshmi was beginning to sound more like the journalist she was.

They both scoffed and shook their heads. The electric drill resumed briefly.

'And you will speak to his granny about him needing to get a lawyer?' Lakshmi was persisting with her advice.

Dolly nodded her head but she seemed to be miles away. 'Whit a bloody mess. And there's nae easy way oot. Eh wish eh could dae mair but eh need tae be thinking aboot Pablo, first and foremost.'

Lakshmi leaned over and touched Dolly's belly; she stroked it for a few minutes. 'That's right, he's the one you need to be concentrating on.'

Dolly drew breath, a bit embarrassed at herself for welling up. 'But eh could dae without that fuckin drumming, driving me fuckin mad. He's no' even any good. Still, it was a Christmas present and maybe he'll forget aboot it when things get back tae normal, if ehv no' killed him first.' She stood up with a start and paced over to the window, where she could see another of her neighbours revving up his motorbike.

'Euan said he'd like to come round soon,' said Lakshmi.

'He phoned me last night. He wants me tae get back on the access course wi' him but wi' aw this going on, ehm no' sure.'

'The course tutors will understand if things are a bit slow at first and they'll probably encourage folk to talk about the whole bus hijack thing. Everybody's been affected by it, in some way or other.'

'Eh, you're right but eh feel that torn; Euan's meh pal and so is Haris but Kyle's meh cousin. Fowk wull be sayin aw kinds o' shite aboot Kyle, and maybe they're right, but it's hard tae sit there wi' your moo shut tight if somebody that ye ken is bein slagged aff.' She looked very sad.

'Dolly, ye're a strong woman. You've been through lots o' things, Timex, all the problems at Bannockbrae, your surgery and, of course, Craig. You'll find a way to deal with this and you have pals there like Euan that'll back you up. You'll no' be on your own.'

Dolly didn't look convinced.

'Here, Lakshmi,' she said, changing the subject completely. Her face began to look more relaxed. 'You'll ken the answer tae this better than onybody else. Is there something goin on atween Euan and Haris, something romantic like?' She paused. 'Or even something like a regular fuck?'

Lakshmi laughed. 'I don't know for sure but I think there could be. Euan was real wound up about Haris during the hijack. I mean, I was as well but there seemed to be an extra edge with him. They've become very close over the last few months and I wouldn't be surprised but neither of them has said anything to me about it.'

'Euan's no' said anything to me either but they seem a bit closer than they were at first. Maybe it's jist meh imagination but eh have got a bit o' a nose fir thae kind of things.'

'Women's intuition?' Lakshmi suggested with a smile.

'Something like that. Eh wouldnae mind a go wi' Haris masel, eh hear he's hung like a horse!'

Lakshmi was laughing now. 'And where do you hear information like that? I thought your access course was for serious study. Anyway, I'd heard you were a carrot and two peas girl.'

'Carrot and twa peas! That's nae way tae talk aboot the faither o' meh bairn.'

Their raucous laughter drowned out the sound of the doorbell; the midwife was left standing on the doorstep for some time.

32

It was still dark when Euan woke up. This single bed had never been intended for two and although he felt crowded, he didn't mind one little bit. Haris was still asleep and seemed to have taken possession of the duvet; Euan stroked his back gently as he thought about the events that had brought him to this place, where he had wanted to be for so long.

He had felt so fiercely passionate about Haris during the hijack that it had made him rethink their whole relationship. One thing he knew was that he wanted to be with Haris more than he wanted anything else in the whole world. All the ifs and buts that had seemed so important last month fell away in comparison with his desire for Haris and for a relationship with him. It was a few days after the hijack before they got a chance to meet up and to be together. Stephen had, tactfully, gone out and they had the flat to themselves. He thought that they might spend time talking about the hijack but neither of them seemed to want that.

He felt absolutely alive just being with Haris and he needed to express that physically; words, really, were not enough. He wanted to explore every inch of Haris's body and that was what he did with his hands, with his tongue, with his cock. It was a voyage of discovery, almost as if he had never seen a man's body before, and every part of Haris had seemed wondrous. It was sex and it was good sex but it was more than sex; it was a mutual act of loving. Haris seemed as joyful about the long, slow, wonderful business of making love as he did. Euan had felt content with his life since his return into the waking world but that contentment faded in comparison with the glory of their love making. He felt that he had never really been close to anyone before this time. Loneliness disappeared as their two bodies connected and flowed into each other. How could he be so lucky as to find a lover who loved him as much as he loved the lover? He wouldn't say that it made him forget about the fact that he had lost twenty years of his life but it helped to put it into a different perspective; in time, he felt it could become a distant perspective.

Haris was still asleep. He was still exhausted after his experience on the bus but he looked at peace. He was lying on his back and breathing smoothly and steadily. Euan was perched recklessly on the edge of the bed. The pleasure of watching the loved one was so great that he almost wished that Haris would never wake up, but then, he thought, that was a particularly cruel thing for him, of all people, to wish on anyone else. The thought must have become physical for, shortly afterwards, Haris woke up with a start as though something external had disrupted his sleep.

'You are here?' he said to Euan.

'I'm here and you're here too, Mister Jakupovic. And I'm rather pleased about that.' Euan kissed Haris's neck. 'Are you pleased too?'

'Very pleased,' he replied.

Euan was now able to move down into the body of the bed and snuggle up closely to Haris, like two inseparable creatures. Two matching S-shapes. Lying very still together, they simply let time slip by them. No longer asleep, neither of them seemed interested in getting out of bed or making love again. Being next to each other seemed enough for the day.

It was Haris who broke the silence. 'Shall I make some coffee?' After some thought, Euan confessed that he'd rather have a fruit tea. Without a word, Haris got up and, for inexplicable reasons of decorousness, put on his jeans while he wandered off into the kitchen in search of a kettle. Some minutes later, he returned with two mugs of hot liquid in his hands.

'I hope that peppermint is ok.'

'Perfect. Are you coming back into bed?'

'Your bed is too small. It would have been better to go to my place, where there is a real bed – a bed for making love. Your bed is more like a bed in a prison.'

'Well,' said Euan. 'I'll tell my landlord that I need a real bed. You could have asked me back to your bed if you had thought about it.'

'I was not thinking very clearly last night. I knew what I wanted to do but it was not a matter of thought, or planning in advance.'

'We waited long enough before we made it happen.' Euan thought back on the previous night. 'Perhaps, if it hadn't been for the hijack, we would still be waiting.'

Haris gave him a withering look.

'Do you want to talk about the hijack?' asked Euan. 'I'm sure you'll be talking about it to counsellors and psychiatrists but I'd be happy for us to make a start with it.'

'I will talk about it with you sometime. But what is puzzling me today is the way the whole hijack came to an end very suddenly. Kenny was shouting into the loudspeaker and Kyle was watching us carefully, as though we might escape, even although we were tied together. Then there was a loud bang and the bus filled up with tear gas and policemen were setting us free and taking us off the bus. But it was all so fast and I do not really understand that.' He tensed his shoulders and then relaxed them again.

Euan was keeping some of his thoughts to himself. This was not the time to mention John Knox. Maybe it had all been clever police work anyway. Any discussion about the hijack had to focus on Haris and whatever he wanted to say about it. One of the things he liked about the last twelve hours they'd been together was just that – they'd been together. Haris was not taking care of him in any way that was reminiscent of his psychologist's role. It was months since that had come to an end but Euan had often felt that the vestiges of that role had been difficult for Haris to shake off. The end of the hijack had seemed like a new beginning; a new millennium was what he'd been looking forward to and they were in a completely different place together.

'This all means a lot to me, Haris.' Euan was lying on his back, looking up into some faraway place. 'Last night was not a one-night stand. I want us to make the most of the time that we have. I want us to see what we sort out for ourselves together. But I know that it's best to take our time about whatever we decide to do. I'm new to all the business of making a life for myself and you have just come out of a hijack. I know that there will be all kinds of pressures on you, what with legal stuff and just getting your head together. I don't want us to rush at things and then spoil it all. Or maybe I'm getting ahead of myself just saying all this.'

'No, no, you are not getting ahead of yourself – which is a very strange English phrase, by the way,' Haris said, as he stroked Euan's hair. 'But there is something that is going to happen that may slow down your plans, I mean, our plans. My sister Maya, who lives in Montreal, is flying over to Scotland this week. She read all about the hijack and she wants to come and see her little brother.'

'That makes sense,' said Euan. 'When is she coming?' He was a tiny bit nervous about this figure from Haris's past coming into their midst but he understood, intellectually at least, why it was important. He bit his lip.

'Do you know that you bite your lip in exactly the same way as Gregor does when he is nervous about something?'

Euan didn't really want to have a discussion about the origins of shared family traits and so he avoided that remark. He looked at Haris and laughed. 'Well, when's she coming?'

'She is flying to Glasgow on Thursday. I will drive over to meet her and then we will decide what to do from there.'

Euan was finding this difficult. He wanted to appear cool and relaxed about the unexpected arrival of Haris's sister. He wanted to ask if he could come along too but while he was swithering about what to do, Haris answered the unasked question for him.

'We'll spend some time alone, just catching up and speaking Serbo-Croat to each other. I am a bit out of practice and I will give you a daily update on what we are doing until we come back to Dundee. You can meet her then. I know that you will like each other and, of course, if you can't think of anything to say to each other, you can always talk about me.'

'Good and bad?' Euan asked, all innocence.

Haris laughed. He was still very stressed after his experience on the bus but that day he seemed relaxed. Euan could hear him humming as he went down the stair.

33

'Good evening, Scotland. You are listening tonight to Radio Dighty, the radio station where you can always be sure of hearing Scots voices. Tonight your programme is brought to you by Millar Gibb. We have a special programme for Burns Night and I'm afraid to tell you that this is also my farewell broadcast. I don't want to take up too much time with my personal business but I thought that I owed it to all you good people to let you know that I am leaving to take up a post as a manager of a golf club in New Zealand. This will maybe come as a surprise to some of my regular listeners but I wanted you to hear the news from the horse's mouth, so to speak.

'New Zealand is sometimes known as the Caledonia of the Southern Hemisphere and I have visited my family members there many times. When my cousin, Finlay, told me that there was a chance to become manager of the Purple Thistle Golf Club in Wookawara, I leapt at it. I have always been a keen golfer and golf is, of course, the great traditional Scottish sport, even more naturally Scots than football. From what I hear of this golf club, I can expect to hear more real proud Scots voices than I can some days in the Overgate. Membership is open only to those who have at least two Scots grandparents and there are compulsory Scots accent classes for all new members. So, as you can imagine, it will be a home from home for an ardent patriot like myself. I will endeavour to send you reports of life at the Purple Thistle Golf Club. I hope you'll no' forget me and I'll certainly never forget you, the salt o' the earth.

'So, without wishing to detract too much from the great

Rabbie, I am going to hand over the first part of the programme, before the commercial break, to you listeners. I have invited some of my regular callers to phone in and share their thoughts with us all as we enter the year 2000. My first caller is Donald from Dunnichen. 'Tell us what's on your mind tonight, Donald?'

'Well, Millar, it's a privilege to be here on your final programme like this. Many's the hour that I've spent listening to your thoughts on Scottish Heroes. Sometimes, when I've had to go away on business, I've telt the wife to make sure that she listens to your programme. She's a braw obedient woman is my wife and without fail, she does that and reports back to me when I get home to Dunnichen again.'

'Sounds like a braw Scots wife you've got there for yourself, Donald. And what was it you particularly wanted to speak about on this final programme?'

'Well, Millar, it's the thing that's been on awbody's mind these last three weeks and that's the hijackin o' the bus tae Carrot Hill. It beats me how they couldna find their way tae Dunnichen Hill which would hae been a much more historic place for tae mak a Declaration like they did.'

'That's a fair point, Donald. We both know what an important battle took place at Nectan's Mere at Dunnichen but I wonder if these two laddies would ever have heard of it. The pair o' them sound a bit confused about Scots history and I'll guarantee you that they only ever got to study unionist history at school.'

'Aye, I'd agree wi' you there, Millar. Maybe if these laddies had been better educated about Scotland, they might have found a better way o' protesting about what was on their minds.'

'I think a lot o' folk are saying that very thing, Donald. They were fair away wi' their ideas about what's wrong wi' Scotland, and all credit to them for that, but to hijack a bus is an awful un-Scottish way o' doing things.'

'Aye, ye're right there, Millar. A lot o' fowk will be embarrassed about being Scottish now, in case anybody mistakes them for a terrorist.'

'Well, thanks very much, Donald, for sharing your point o' view with us and a lot o' folk will, I'm sure, agree with what you've got to say. And now I'd like to invite our next caller, Angus from Auchterhouse. What's on your mind, Angus?'

'Well, Millar, it's the same thing as the previous caller was talking about, that's the hijack o' the bus. I just wonder if these laddies might have got a bit carried away wi' some o' the ideas that they've heard on this programme....'

'Aye, steady on there, Angus, that's a pretty serious point you're makin there. I'm sure it's no' an accusation from a regular caller like yourself but it gives me the chance to explain the difference between what Radio Dighty, and our friends at Scotland First, say and what these two misguided laddies say.

'We're all agreed that Scotland is in danger from alien forces, both outwith our country and inside it. There's all kinds of folk that want to make our country an imitation of other places; they want to drive the very special Scottish essence out of the life of our country. They want us to forget the things that have made us great in the past and the great things that Scots have done for the world. They want to make us bow the knee to folk and to countries that think they are better than we are. Once I get started on this, there's no stopping me and I see our producer is waving a yellow card at me. So, I'd better get on with explaining things. It used to be that invaders came into countries in armies and you knew who was your enemy and who was your friend by things like their uniform or the language they spoke. Nowadays, things are different, much more insidious than ever they used to be.

'Some of the folk in our midst are willing to act on behalf of alien interests. I can give you an example. You'll mind that we warned folk at the recent election in Dundee about Craig Baxter and his clever, clever plans to transform Dundee and make it just like Brussels or one of these other daft places in the European Union. Well, I can reveal to you tonight that Craig Baxter is trying to take Radio Dighty off the air. He knows full well that we are the only station that speaks the language of the people of Dundee and Angus and he wants rid of us. He got your votes with his smiley, smiley campaign and all his talk of understanding football and then, give him some power, and he's out to silence his enemies.'

'Aye, I've heard rumours like that too,' said Angus, 'but that could be an argument for doing more things like hijacking buses. I'm just saying, like, I'm no' actually arguing for hijacks.'

'No, Angus, fair enough. I get your point, you're trying to be a devil's advocate. The thing is that when folk try things like bus hijacks, they give Craig Baxter and all his alien pals the chance to smash us to bits. First, they close down our radio station and then, they move on to something else and smash it to bits. You mark my words, they'll be trying to outlaw Scotland First; they'll say it's a terrorist organisation.'

'I've heard that they're after our food as well. Our lassie has been telt that she cannae use the microwave at her office to heat up some chips for her dinner. She has to eat salad and stuff like that; they call it health promotion but it seems to me this is just another attack on our way of life. I mean, chips are a traditional Scots dish. Give them half a chance and they'll be closing down the pubs next.'

'Aye, well, Angus. There's a lot in what you say but we need to go to our next caller, Freda from Wellbank. Freda, tell us what's on your mind? Freda! Freda! Are you there, Freda? It's no' like a woman to miss the chance to speak up. But I see what time it is and maybe she's had to go and cook her man's tea.

'But before we go on to our scheduled programme on Burns, I have a breaking news story for you. Our newsdesk has just informed me that Kyle Fullerton, one o' the hijackers, has escaped from police custody while he was being transferred from one prison to another. It seems that the other two criminals that he was travelling with had arranged for the police transport to be halted on the Kingsway. They fled into cars that were waiting for them and young Fullerton took the chance to make a break for it. It is not known where he is heading for but police are focusing their attentions on Bannockbrae where he is known to have family connections.

'We will keep you informed of developments as we hear of them but we would give a word of advice to young Kyle, should he be listening to Radio Dighty. It's time for you to give yourself up and face justice like a real Scotsman. Radio Dighty is a law-abiding radio station and we do not condone violence and illegality in any form. What you did on Carrot Hill was illegal; what you are doing now is illegal. It's time to turn your back on illegality and face up to the truth. It is time for you to start behaving like a Black Watch soldier, disciplined and loyal, rather than Billy the Kid. This is not a storybook. I would also say to our friends in the William Wallace Youth League: do not be tricked into helping this runaway. By so doing, you will do great damage to the cause of this great nation of ours. If you know where he is, then you should tell the police. Scotland is being damaged badly by the antics of ill-disciplined folk like Kyle Fullerton.'

34

Spring cleaning had come early to the *Pilot* this year. The fact that Lakshmi wanted a clear out and a lick of paint might have been due to the neglected state of the office but it also reflected a desire for a fresh start after the trauma of the hijacking. Whatever the motive, the idea was not up for discussion and Lakshmi put out a three-line whip to her nearest and dearest to be at the office at 9am on Sunday. It hadn't been a very effective whipping process because only Fergus, Euan and Lakshmi herself were there at the appointed hour. Haris and Stephen were expected to make an appearance but no one was holding their breath about this. There were those who might have claimed that there was something profoundly un-Scottish about cleaning an office at nine o'clock on a Sunday morning in January but no such view was expressed there that day. An unacknowledged graffito on a wall near the office read: **Dundee is not Sharpeville.**

The filing cabinets were pulled away from the walls to reveal decades' worth of dirt and damp; mice scuttled around, perplexed by the disturbance to their ancestral homes; the solitary hoover was in danger of choking to a halt with all the stoor that it was trying to absorb. Walls were washed and windows were opened to let the cold fresh air into the foustie interior. By ten o'clock there had been little in the way of conversation but over a dozen bin bags had been packed full of unwanted and totally forgettable junk.

When they stopped to have a cup of tea, Kyle was the only topic of conversation. It was five days since he had escaped and the police appeared to have no idea where he was hiding. Somehow or other, he had turned into a folk hero and dozens of people had began to glorify him as soon as he became a fugitive. The website of the William Wallace Youth League was given over entirely to chat about Kyle; the stories about his generous behaviour on the bus had proliferated to such an extent that you could be forgiven for thinking that there had been no hijack at all. There were suggestions that folk were providing him with food but once the police cottoned on to that, they began tracking the mobile phone calls of his admirers in the hope that might lead them to him.

'It's a bloody cold time of the year to be a runaway,' remarked Fergus. 'Seriously, if he's no' got shelter, he could freeze to death.'

'Unless he gives himself up,' said Euan. He shrugged as if he didn't quite believe that was a real possibility.

'We've got no idea if he's likely to give himself up or fight on to the death,' said Lakshmi. 'In fact, we don't know much about him or his ideas, except that he had a shite start in life.'

'You're surely no' gonna say that he was as much a victim as the passengers on the bus?' asked Fergus.

'No, he's no' a victim of the hijacking,' said Lakshmi, quite sharply. 'He is responsible for the part he played in all that but he is a bit of a victim of the circumstances of his life, no father, mother died of AIDS, life in a damp flat in Bannockbrae, no qualifications and so on. He did not have a lot going for him and that must have been one of the reasons why he got involved in all this Scotland First stuff. There was a bit of a buzz about that in a way that there wasn't anywhere else in his life.'

'What does Haris say about that theory?' asked Euan, looking into the middle distance.

'Well, right enough, it's easier for me to be dispassionate about it because I was not on the bus.' She paused for a moment. 'But he does say that Kyle did not come out with any of the rabid stuff that you heard from Kenny or like you hear from Radio Dighty. He says that he felt Kyle believed that the bus hijacking would help to bring about a better Scotland, just one part of a bigger picture. He wants to make sure that if he's called to give evidence in a trial he's able to distinguish between the behaviour of Kenny and the behaviour of Kyle. If Kenny was the officer, Kyle was the subaltern.'

Euan warmed his hands on his mug and nodded his head, thinking as much about Haris as about Kyle and his motives.

'If there is going to be a trial,' said Lakshmi, 'I'd like to see Millar Gibb in the dock along with these two. That stuff he spews out on his programme is like fertiliser for hatred, the man is a disgrace.' She wrapped her jacket closer around her.

'He may well be a disgrace but he's probably out of the country by now,' said Euan.

'What are you talking about?' asked Fergus, who felt as if he couldn't quite keep up with this conversation.

'He announced a couple of days ago, on Burns Night, in fact, that he's off to New Zealand to manage a golf club there. Apparently, golf is the most Scottish of sports.'

Fergus knocked over his mug of tea. 'Jesus Christ! What a fucking toad of a man! Anyway, knowing him, he could be anywhere. Just because he says he's going to New Zealand, that doesn't mean that's what he's gonna do. He could be heading for...' He was struggling to think of unlikely places where he might have gone, as well as trying to find a rag to wipe up his spilled tea.

'Brazil?' said Euan, trying to be helpful.

'Aye, well, poor bloody Brazilians!' said Fergus.

'Or, if he really has gone to New Zealand,' said Lakshmi, 'poor bloody Maoris.'

Just at that moment, the bell rang and Lakshmi went over to the intercom to press the entry bell. 'It's Haris,' she said. 'Better late than never!'

He came in well wrapped in scarves and jumpers and a woolly hat, like someone who was setting off to cross the Antarctic. There were hugs and kisses all round.

'Fergus, we need to get some more paint,' said Lakshmi.

'No, no, we're fine; I checked that yesterday. I just want to catch up with the stranger here...'

'Fergus!' said Lakshmi, in a tone of voice that would brook no opposition. 'The car!' Fergus went off meekly enough but squawks of protest could be heard through the open window.

Euan and Haris hugged each other again, more closely and personally than they had done moments before.

'It seems so long,' said Haris, stepping back from Euan. 'Let me look at you. I have missed you, you know.'

'Me too,' said Euan. 'I do hope we can see a bit more of each other now that things are getting a bit calmer. Well, I know they're no' very calm as far as Kyle is concerned but for you, and for me, they are less stressed than they were. I got your messages about going off on a trip around Perthshire with your sister.'

'She read some publicity about it being the Heart of Scotland and so she decided that she wanted to go there. I had hardly ever been myself, I am ashamed to say. I seem to have adhered to the more urban bits of Scotland such as Dundee, Edinburgh and Glasgow. So, it was as new for me as it was for her. And it was very beautiful; it reminded us of some of the more up-country parts of Bosnia, all these beautiful mountains and so much greenery.' Haris continued with his eulogy to Perthshire, the glens, the rivers, the views, the pubs and on and on it went.

Euan was beginning to wonder how long this traveller's tale

was going to continue. They hadn't seen each other for two weeks and the Heart of Scotland was not really what had been on his mind. He was feeling impatient. 'Haris, is there something on your mind? Something maybe that you want to tell me?'

Haris looked a tiny bit startled. 'Yes, there is, in fact. That was the main reason why I wanted to speak to you today.' He cleared his throat. 'My sister and I have been talking and we have decided to go back to Sarajevo. We both want to see our family and, of course, we want to see what has happened to our country since the war...'

'You want to go back to Bosnia!' Euan felt as though he had been hit across the face with something wet, not exactly in pain but definitely shocked. He walked over to the window and stood looking out of it, although he was seeing nothing; he had his back to Haris and they couldn't see each other's faces while they talked.

'I have often felt guilty about never being around during the war and, talking to my sister, I discovered that she felt the same way. We had been concentrating on building new lives for ourselves and the past had been pushed into the background. It was impossible to avoid talking about those feelings when we were together and eventually we agreed that we would benefit from going back to where we had come from. Of course, it will not be the same for us as it was for everyone there who lived through these terrible experiences; our knowledge can only be second hand. I thought a lot about these things too while I was sitting on the bus on Carrot Hill. I wondered why people were so obsessed with the idea of the purity of their nation? I wondered why that would make them hijack a bus and put so many lives at risk because of a vision of Scotland? Why would people in Sarajevo kill their neighbours because of a vision of Bosnia?

'There are all kinds of good reasons,' he continued, 'why I

did not go back to Bosnia but it is also the case that I have been in some kind of denial about the civil war there. I need to discover why my brother killed himself, why my sister took to wearing a Muslim headscarf, why my father stopped believing he could be a psychiatrist and why my mother stopped writing letters to her children. There is so much.'

He paused, as if he might have been hoping for some response from Euan, but none was forthcoming. Euan stood where he was, tense and disappointed; this was not the news he had been hoping for when he had embraced Haris. But he felt guilty too for thinking only of his relationship with him when Haris had so many other things on his mind.

'I do not think,' Haris continued, 'that I could have gone on my own; I know that I am a coward about this part of my life. The fact that Maya wants to go there too makes the project much more feasible. We will have each other to talk to when we want to explore our feelings. That will be less of an imposition on the other members of our family.'

Euan turned round. 'When will you be going?'

'Tuesday.'

Euan shook his head. 'I suppose I can understand why you want to go to explore your past and find out what's happened since you left. You've been away nearly as long as I was in my coma.'

'Ten years,' he said, clinically, almost as if Euan would not have known that.

'Ok, a bit less than my time away but I can understand about the need to go back and I can understand that you might want to do it with someone with a similar kind of history. What I don't understand is that you didn't make the time to tell me on my own. You come down here, when you know that there'll be a crowd o' folk hanging around. I thought that you and I were going to try to make something together for ourselves but right now, it feels like I might have got that wrong.' Euan's shoulders were hunched together, like some kind of useless protection from attack.

Haris began to move towards him. 'I am so sorry, Euan. The last thing I wanted to do was to hurt you.'

'A hug will not make this all right, Haris. I need to know more.' He was facing Haris directly now, not very close but looking right into his face.

'We are going to make something together, I promise you. But it will be after I come back from Bosnia. I have arranged some time off work and I will start again on the 1st of April, just after the end of the financial year.'

'And you make it all sound so reasonable, so well planned, apart from the bit about me. How come you can find time to arrange time off work but you can't find time to meet me on my own and tell me all this face to face? Are you scared of me or something?' Euan was shaking his head, as if he wanted to get rid of his sense of disbelief.

Haris was sweating now. 'I am not scared of you but I am scared of relationships. I always have been. I thought Lakshmi might have told you that.'

'Lakshmi might have thought that was something you would tell me yourself. What's the problem?' Euan was cutting to the quick.

'I had two relationships when I was a student where I was eaten up, I almost felt destroyed by the experience. Since then I have been very afraid of close involvement with a lover. It may go deeper than that as well, something historical about the development of my identity. But it is not because I am scared of you; you are not the problem.'

Euan was thinking to himself that his health meant that he

couldn't wait around forever; he knew that his medication might cease to be effective; he knew that Haris was more aware of that than anyone else; it was so obvious that it remained unsaid. He didn't feel that words were very helpful to this situation where so many forces beyond their control were at work. He loved Haris and he so badly wanted them to be able to create a life for themselves. But while he knew what it felt like to want someone, he had no notion of how to care for someone other than himself. Setting aside his fears, he moved towards Haris and embraced him. As soon as he did this, Haris broke down and began to sob. It was a sob that seemed beyond consolation; it was a sob full of fears unspoken and grief untouched.

Euan was surprised at this physical outpouring of grief; this was something he had never known in Haris before. He held him tight for several minutes.

'I am so glad that you are here, Euan. I know that we can be strong together. I know that we will be,' said Haris. 'We will be.' His customary self-control was reasserting itself. They held each other's hands for a few minutes; the silence was palpable; some boys on the street kicked a football against the window but they seemed not to hear it. A single tear ran down Haris's cheek and after a few minutes, he headed off into the cold winter's day.

Euan felt bereft. He was no longer sure whether to allow himself to feel hope any more. They had seemed ready for a future but their pasts were still tugging away at them, demanding attention. Would there ever be an escape from the past? When would he ever be allowed to live in the present? When would he ever have a future?

His reverie was interrupted by the sound of voices in the building. He recognised Fergus and Lakshmi but wasn't sure who the third person was. Fergus, with a nobody-tells-me-anything face, came into the room in search of Haris.

'Gone?' he said.

Euan nodded. 'Gone.'

'He'll be back,' said Fergus kindly.

Euan was desperate to change the topic of conversation. 'Who's that with Lakshmi?' he asked, with absolutely no interest in the answer.

'It's Craig, with a scoop, he says, for the *Pilot*.'

'But you're no' sure?'

'The editor's no' sure. She doesn't want her paper to turn into a mouthpiece for the Lord Provost's office and so, she's interrogating him – vigorously.' The thought of that tickled them both. They were smiling when they went through to the main office.

'Hi, guys,' said an ebullient looking Craig. 'I've just been sharing some good news with Lakshmi here. I'm sure you're all aware that Radio Dighty has been funded for some time now by an American multi-millionaire by the name of Logan J. Tree. Well, I've been in touch with him since the hijacking and he's agreed to end his funding for Radio Dighty and make a major investment into a youth sports scheme here in Dundee. He said that he felt embarrassed to be associated with the hijack and it wasn't difficult to encourage him to support something more obviously beneficial to the people of Dundee. I persuaded him to set up a trust called the Tree Foundation so that his name will always be associated with good works. It will make folk think about him in the same breath as Andrew Carnegie, massaging his ego a bit as well as easing his conscience. His resources will give a kick start to this youth scheme and that, in turn, will make it easier to access funding from the European Union. They like projects that are supported by the private sector as well as themselves.'

Fergus laughed. 'You sound a bit like Daphne Pattullo now.'

'A politician nowadays has to be pragmatic.' He nodded his head, undaunted. 'I'm just being pragmatic enough to borrow ideas from someone else to breathe some new life into Dundee and some hope into the lives of young Dundonians. Obvious, really!'

'And none of us is gonna disagree with that, Craig,' said Fergus. 'Nor are we gonna accuse you of being slow off the mark. I take off my hat to you or I would do, in the event of me wearing one.'

'Thanks, Fergus. That means a lot to me. Anyway, I must be off. No rest for the wicked, as they say.' He shook everyone's hand and almost floated out of the office, high on a cloud of self-regard.

'So, that's your scoop?' asked Fergus.

'It is indeed,' replied Lakshmi. 'It's no' all done and dusted yet. I'm gonna report it as a rumoured story in this week's edition and then he'll issue a press release to confirm that talks are under way. I'm no' sure about his motives or his way of working but it is good news for young folk in Dundee. It is a response to the hijacking that acknowledges some of the underlying problems without rewarding the hijackers. His withdrawal of funding takes Radio Dighty off the air without anyone having to try and close it down legally. Craig is one clever bastard, that's for sure.'

Euan was sitting quietly. His mind was really on the conversation that he'd just had with Haris but he was trying to make himself focus on where he was at that moment, in the *Pilot* office with Fergus and Lakshmi, two of his best friends. He tried to be thankful for that and to concentrate on the day, on the present.

He was disturbed from this reverie by the sound of a car door banging. Fergus went over to the window and called out, 'There is a god.'

Lakshmi and Euan looked at each other, more than a little surprised.

'It's Dolly. A minute earlier and she'd have bumped into Craig. What an encounter that might have been! Blood on the carpet for sure.' He laughed rather manically.

Dolly rushed in like a dervish, with Stephen struggling to keep up. She never appeared in public ungroomed or without her make-up and today was no exception. But while she was wearing a smart leather jacket, tight-fitting jeans and a green woollen top, unlike everyone else in Dundee, she was wearing nothing for the cold weather, no hat, no scarf, no gloves, nothing at all to protect her from the elements.

'It's Kyle,' she cried. 'He's hanged himself at Carrot Hill. Eh'm just goin to the mortuary and Stephen said you'd all be here. Fucking hanged himself, the stupid wee bastard!' She broke down.

Euan went over and took her in his arms. 'Tell us what happened, start at the beginning and take us through it.' He tried to usher her towards a chair but she was too agitated to sit down, preferring to pace back and forwards. She breathed deeply.

'Weel, it's five days now since he escaped and at first naebody hid ony idea where he wiz. Some o' the young fowk frae the Wully Wallies thought that he might want tae go back tae the scene o' the crime, ye ken, Carrot Hill. And that's where they found him. They gave him some food and he telt them which direction he wiz headin in so that they knew where tae look for him the next day. But he never strayed far frae Carrot Hill. One o' the lassies that took him food cam tae see me and she telt me that he wiz proud o' the hijack; he said it showed that Scots could dae things if they set their minds tae it. The whole notion o' the dependency culture wiz nae mair than English propaganda.' She punched her clenched fist on the desk.

'Apparently, he kept on saying that they never killed any o' their hostages and they never wanted to. They just wanted to let the world ken aboot Scotland's problems and Scotland's solutions.

They wanted to get politicians tae tak them seriously and they were real scunnered that none o' them cam up tae Carrot Hill tae speak tae them. Him and Kenny hid spoken beforehand aboot whit they would do if things went wrong wi' the hijack. They had talked aboot how they might hae tae kill one o' the hostages; it hid nivver been their plan but it had crossed their minds and they hid discussed it. They thought that it should be a random choice, like puttin aw the names in a hat and then killin the first name they took out. Him and Kenny hid not spoken aboot it on the bus but he knew that Kenny would be thinking aboot it as well. But, like he said, they nivver went that far.' A tiny part of her sounded relieved, as if acknowledging that it could all have turned out a lot worse.

'The lassie that telt me aw this said that he wouldnae say any mair; she thought that he felt he'd maybe said too much. And, tae be truthful, ehv never heard him say that much aw the years ehv kent him. She felt scared fir hirself. What if the police tried tae mak her gie evidence at a trial? She wiz also worried that one o' the Wully Wallies might be an undercover cop but even if he wiznae, they kent the police would try to track their mobile phones. She began tae feel paranoid aboot whit was goin on and they knew they were bein followed when they went tae look for Kyle. So, they hid tae decide whether tae tak him food and risk him being discovered or drive awa somewhere else, which would maybe leave him safe frae the police but withoot food. They decided tae lead the police car following them on a wild goose chase, up country roads and then down into Forfar. It went on fir hours but, by the time they thought they'd shaken off the police car, they couldnae find Kyle. And although they'd lost the police car, the police hid got wind o' the area where Kyle might be and they sent oot a helicopter tae search fir him. So, Kyle had nae food, he thought he had nae pals and there's a helicopter lookin fir him and, on top o' that, it wiz bloody cauld. That's when he hanged himself. He wiz found the next morning hangin frae a tree. The polis said that if he hadnae been sae underweight the branch that he hanged himself on might have snapped. Fuckin bad luck, right up till the end.'

Dolly had a frightening nervous energy and she never stopped moving. All the others were sitting down taking in the details of her story. Lakshmi had stopped fidgeting, Stephen had crossed his arms and was looking out of the window, Fergus was holding his head in his hands and Euan was trying to decide whether to go over to her and comfort her. But still she paced back and forwards, as though she were a caged animal.

'Eh should hiv been able tae dae mair. Eh should hiv found mair time tae be wi' him. Naebody kent whit was going oan in his mind coz naebody wiz makin the time tae listen. He must hiv felt like he hid nae voice; it wiz like we were aw deaf. When he wisnae in ony trouble we thoght that a'thing wiz fine, but it wiznae fine. He must hiv been that lonely that he jist got mixed up wi' the Wully Wallies and Radio Dighty coz there wiz nothing else. Eh ken how dangerous boredom can be for some fowk and eh should hiv… '

'You're being too hard on yourself, Dolly,' said Euan.

'But, tae be truthful, it wiznae jist me, wiz it? Whaur wiz his mum and dad? Whaur wiz his granny? Whaur wiz his school? Whaur wiz social services? They're aw supposed tae be there tae help fowk. But he wiz overlooked, aye, that's it, he wiz overlooked. If he hid got involved in petty crime, like stealin cars or something, then somebody else wid hiv noticed him. He might hiv got a probation officer and that wid hiv been somebody tae listen tae him. Eh mind tellin you, Euan, that it wiz fine when he got involved wi Kenny and aw this stuff cos it would keep him busy, it would be company fir him. Aw thae schemes that we have in

Bannockbrae fir young folk and none o' them wiz ony good fir him. Aw thae plans that fowk hiv tae mak Dundee a better place tae live in and they didnae begin tae touch him. The trouble wiz that there wiz naebody tae look oot fir him. His granny wiz ower auld and wiz struggling herself; it wid hiv been better if he'd gone intae care or been fostered. Then there wid hiv been somebody tae look oot fir him.'

Her pain was raw. She was inconsolable with grief and anger about her cousin. But she had stopped pacing around the room.

Her voice became much quieter. 'Ehv got tae mak sure that ehm there aw the time fir Pablo; he's gotta ken that ehm here fir him. He must nivver ever feel forgotten and overlooked like Kyle did.' She stroked her belly, almost as if to check that Pablo was listening, and tears began to run slowly down her cheeks. She visibly pulled herself together. 'Can eh use the toilet, Lakshmi?'

Lakshmi went out to the back of the building and stayed there with her.

It was Stephen who broke the silence. 'This might seem a bit weird but I think I saw Kyle at the Planet Scotland Festival. I didn't know it was him at the time but, having seen all these pictures of him in the last few days, I'm beginning to think that he was loitering around in the City Square. I was running around like a bit of a headless chicken and so I'm no' one hundred percent sure but what I remember was that he was on his own. It was strange because guys of that age usually hang around in groups. I'm sure that he wasn't with the Wully Wallies because they came early on to sneer at us but they didn't hang around for long.'

'You could be right,' said Fergus. 'He was at the football hustings in the Caird Hall and he was on his own there too. It was a pretty stressful night for me, if you remember, but I mind thinking it was strange that he was there on his own. Every other time I saw him, he was with Kenny, and Kenny was the one doing all the talking.'

'And I saw him,' said Euan, 'out of the side of my eye the night I met you in kps', Stephen. I had met him with Dolly when I first visited Bannockbrae but I was a bit wound up that night. Maybe, I should have gone over to speak to him.'

'Maybe lots of things,' said Fergus, shaking his head. 'But he was definitely looking for something; a shame that he thought he'd found it with Kenny Horsburgh and Millar Gibb. We'll never know now what was going on in his head.'

Dolly came back at that point, refreshed and looking very determined. 'Ehm ready now, Stephen, fir tae go tae the mortuary. If you all would like tae come wi' me, I'd like that, no tae come in like, but jist tae be a bit o' company fir me.'

Euan took her arm, Stephen went ahead to open up the car, while Fergus and Lakshmi checked the windows and the doors of the *Pilot* office. It was too late for there to be any company for Kyle but they could all make sure that on this, the worst day of her life, Dolly would not be alone.

35

He needed a shower. It had been a stressful time and Euan was exhausted. He didn't expect the shower to wash away the exhaustion but he hoped to be refreshed enough to enjoy the celebrations for the Chinese New Year. After the unexpected events of the Millennium, the Year of the Dragon had assumed an unusual importance for Dundonians. A fresh start was widely desired and all his friends were going to the Golden Dragon party at the Ashet restaurant. He felt he'd been rather negligent in his role as uncle and he'd offered to take Gregor and Adam along to the festivities. An uneventful good time, with food and music and a few fireworks, was all he wanted.

Relaxed he may have been but he still felt restless; his mind was racing around here and there until, unexpectedly, he found himself thinking about Andy. The good friend from his youth, whose ghost he had previously decided not to meet. That decision had been made at a time, after his conversation with the ghost of his father, when he'd been feeling rather negative about the pursuit of the past; it had seemed more productive then to concentrate on the present and the future. Time and events had moved on and, particularly after his discussions with Haris, he had begun to feel that there was a difference between acknowledging the past and wallowing in it. Summoning the ghost of his father felt like a mistake but perhaps it would be different with Andy; it should be different. While there was no possibility of them renewing their friendship, he began to allow himself to feel curious about what Andy had been doing in the fifteen years before he died. The photograph which Andy's sister had sent him was certainly of a very different person from the schoolboy he remembered from 1979. He convinced himself that it would be easier to summon the ghost of someone who had only been dead for five years than it had been to summon the ghost of John Knox. He was right; it was much easier.

'About time too!' said Andy. His appearance was as it had been on the most recent photo that Euan had seen, dyed blonde hair, an earring and a gym-toned body, all very different from the scrawny lad that Euan remembered. He was a good looking man but it was difficult to know if the expression on his face was an amused world weariness or just the fruits of the ageing process. But, best of all, Andy was pleased to see Euan. If they'd been able to hug each other, they would have done but they couldn't and so they made do with conversation.

'You look really great,' said Euan. He stood up to be on an equal footing because ghosts, of course, can't sit down on material objects.

'Thanks. You'll be aware that we ghosts look like we did at our best; so, the person you're seeing today is not the one who died ravaged by AIDS. That's the cliché that the media used to talk about gay men dying off in their prime but, like lots of clichés, it had some truth in it. I tried all the treatments that were going but, in those days, there was nothing that worked. But, enough o' that. I'll accept your compliment and return it too. You look a lot better than a forty year old really should. How's that for a Scots compliment, with a critical value judgement woven in?'

'I'll accept it with pleasure. I've gone to the gym a lot since I woke up. It's done wonders for me. I wasn't sure about it when Haris first started…'

'Is that the hunky Bosnian number?'

Euan laughed nervously. 'He's my psychologist.'

'Oh, aye. Silly me! But you do fancy him, don't you?'

'Well, we have, you know, talked about getting to know each other a bit better. Actually, he's not really my psychologist any more.'

It was Andy's turn to laugh. 'Get on with it, Euan. I hope you're not holding yourself back because of some deep, lasting love for me. It would never have worked between us, you know. No chance. I never fancied you but I think you might have fancied me, if only you would have admitted it to yourself.'

Euan went bright red.

'Oh, don't go and get all upset on me now. When it comes to sexual chemistry, you were never my type. I went more for rugby player types; mind you, they were a dead loss, a fatal combination of butch and sentimental. No, had you and I been around together a bit longer, we'd have been a bit more like sisters.'

'Sisters!' cried Euan.

'Yeah, you know the sort of thing, sharing secrets of those bastard men that kept building up our hopes and then dashing them.'

'But you used to loathe guys at the Harris who played rugby – rugger buggers, you called them – you said they were beyond the intellectual pale or something like that.'

'I know, I know,' said Andy. 'But I was obviously just suppressing my desires; your psychologist – sorry, your ex-psychologist – can tell you all about the theories of suppression of sexual desire. And I'm sure I wasn't the only one who was suppressing things!'

Euan wasn't altogether comfortable with this talk of sexual suppression and the idea of sisterliness was even more unsettling. So, changing the topic somewhat, he decided to ask Andy about how he had dealt with the onset of his sleeping sickness.

Andy rubbed his chin and breathed deeply. 'Well, I was devastated, to put it mildly. It felt like my life was completely fucked up. I used to spend all my waking hours by your bedside, talking to you, reading to you, playing music, doing anything that might bring you back from the dead. And it seemed like a death to me, a particularly cruel death. When it became obvious that there was to be no speedy recovery, my dad and your mum persuaded me to go back to Glasgow.'

'Glasgow?'

'I was at the School of Art there. Don't you remember? I used to come up to Dundee most weekends to see you and talk to you and hope that I could wake you up. Latterly, it was less regular but after a couple of years, it was only your mum and me that still visited. It was a real scunner when they put you in some bloody institution in the middle of the countryside, beautiful surroundings but bugger all use to patients like yourself. I still went there, although it was awkward getting buses and all that sort of thing. One day your mum asked me, in a particular tone of voice, where I was going to go when I'd finished my degree. She knew I was doing well and she came through to see an exhibition of mine in Glasgow. She told me I should do whatever I could and go wherever I wanted to develop my talent. She was very firm that she would keep an eye on you and would contact me if there was any change in your condition. But, she told me that I must not waste my life; one wasted life was more than enough. I was very upset but I took her advice.

'I was in New York for a couple of years; then I travelled around South America and eventually I came back to London, just in time for the epidemic. I had a great time, maybe not romantically successful but a whole lot of fun. I guess I wasted my artistic talent on freelance commercial design, but it paid very well and it had the advantage that you didn't have to get involved with your workplace or your workmates. I was involved in the gay scene – some would say devoted to the gay scene –

clubbing, cruising, taking all kinds of drugs that you've probably never heard of and, oh yes, lots of sex.'

'Lucky you!' It all sounded like another planet to Euan.

'Yes, I was. I had a great time and I made lots of friends and a few of them turned out to be good friends too. These were the ones that I used to tell about the Sleeping Beauty in the wilds of Scotland. I'm sure some of them thought it was all fantasy. Deirdre has their contact details and they'll be really good to you, once they've picked themselves up off the floor in amazement at your comeback, your return from the dead. They'll be getting on a bit now, of course; unlike your gorgeous self, they'll look like normal forty year olds.'

'You mean they'll have beer bellies.'

'No, darling, that's not what I mean.' Reassurance mixed with sarcasm. 'I'm sure there are some gay men in London with beer bellies but I didn't know any of them! Some of them will be worried about their weight or about their drinking. Some of them might even have problems getting it up but they won't tell you about that; actually, that's not true, if they think they're never going to see you again, they'll tell you all about it. And they might have become a bit more specialised in their tastes, some into younger boyfriends and some seriously into leather. And lots and lots of counselling and therapy. I hope I'm not putting you off going to London?' He paused for a moment. 'I really am going on too much. Sorry.'

'Well, you're not putting me off; I'd really love to go there sometime. We did talk about it, if you remember.' Euan wasn't altogether sure if it really was easier to talk about their shared past, but at least he had something to say in these more familiar parts of the conversation.

'Of course, I remember. I loved the plans we made and I think you did too.'

Euan nodded his head. 'But we barely even got to Edinburgh...'

'Thrown out of a pub in Rose Street for looking under-age, even though we were both 18...'

'As you kept on saying to the barman. And you made it worse by telling him that this kind of thing never happened in Glasgow.' He chuckled at the memory. 'I'm sure we'd have been good drinking buddies, as well as sisters.'

They both went quiet. Talking about their shared past and their plans seemed, in an odd way, to remind them of the situation they were in now, in the year 2000.

'Don't take this the wrong way, Euan. But I hope that you don't want to see me again. We're so far apart that seeing me would really be a distraction for you. Maybe even a deviation. Apart from what you call getting to know your ex-psychologist a bit better, there's all kinds of stuff for you to be doing, like studying. You were gonna go to university and I hope you're gonna do that now.'

Euan nodded. 'I'm hoping to go to university in the autumn. And I agree with what you're saying about meeting up. This was supposed to be a one off. Since I'm lucky enough to be able to summon ghosts, it seemed daft not to summon the ghost of my first real friend and just say hi.'

'And then good-bye.'

'Ok. But we were such a big part of each other's life all those years ago that I was curious to see how you'd turned out.' He seemed a bit scared for a moment. 'I was curious to see what you'd made of all these plans that we used to discuss at such length.'

'Some of them worked out and some of them didn't. But at least I had the chance to give them a go and I guess that's what you'll be doing now.' He looked at Euan in such a way as to encourage him to talk more about his plans.

'That's what I want to do with Haris. I want to see how things turn out between us but I don't know what to expect. I've learned a lot about sex in the last few months but I want more than that, really.' He felt very hesitant as he tried to put his desires for this relationship into words that someone other than he or Haris might understand. 'I want someone to hold, someone who will hold me too; a life without someone to hold would be a lonely life.' He fell silent again. 'And talking is important too, I want someone that I can talk to; I know I can talk to Haris and some of the time I think he can talk to me.' He nodded his head. 'Talking and holding, that's what I want, but we've got a long way to go.'

'Well, it's certainly good to know what you want.' Andy grinned. 'Just don't count on getting exactly what you want; it may not work out that way.' He held out his hand as if he wanted to touch Euan reassuringly. 'All you can do is take a chance and see what happens. And, at the risk of sounding cynical, if it doesn't work with Haris, it's not the end of the world. You can learn from it and try again. I'm really pleased for you.'

Euan stood absorbing his friend's advice; Andy had an inscrutable but attentive look on his face and it was difficult to know what to make of it but it was definitely attentive. Soon, Andy began to fidget, perhaps that was his way of saying he was ready to go. Euan wanted to round off the conversation before he sent him on his way; it was just a bit of old-fashioned hospitality. 'Some of my ghosts like a sniff o' whisky; can I tempt you with that?'

'The perfect hostess! No, I don't go for whisky but if you had some gin, that would be great.'

Euan knew where Stephen kept some gin and he went to fetch it for Andy.

'Don't bother with the tonic. I'll just have it straight, so to speak.' Andy breathed deeply and savoured the smell. 'You could buy your pal some decent gin for his birthday. This is ok but it's definitely some cheap supermarket brand.' He breathed out. 'And now it's time.' He blew a kiss to Euan.

Euan could feel the tears rising up at the prospect of never seeing his oldest friend again. It might have been easier if he had never summoned him but, however painful it felt, it had been better to do the more difficult thing. 'Thanks, Andy, for everything.' He blinked and Andy was gone.

He sat down, reflecting on the conversation they'd just had. It struck him that he hadn't mentioned the summoning of John Knox to Andy; it hadn't been a conscious decision but he knew then that if he was ever going to talk about that with anyone, it would be with Haris. But the biggest thing from the conversation was the realisation that Andy had lived another life in his absence; he was not just a person with dreams; he had developed into a real person who had made mistakes and knew that he had made mistakes. At least, if he was going to get sentimental about Andy in the future, he would be able to focus on the person he had become or part of the person he had become. That was better than dreaming about a schoolboy frozen in time. The doorbell rang; there would be no chance of time being frozen once Gregor and Adam were here.

They were very excited about the Chinese New Year. Their overnight rucksacks looked full enough for a month's holiday. Gregor was itching to take part in the dragon dance, while Adam was fascinated by the prospect of having his head massaged. They chattered away and told Euan that they'd like to go to China sometime, when they were big. It was all noise and bustle. The evening seemed set to be as enjoyable as Euan had been hoping for.

'When will Uncle Haris be back from Bosnia?' asked Gregor out of the blue.

'I don't know,' said Euan. 'He's going to stay there for a few weeks with his mum and dad and then he'll decide when to come back here.'

Gregor went straight to the core of the issue. 'Will you be sad if he doesn't come back?'

Euan was struggling now. 'I would be very sad if he didn't come back but I wouldn't always be sad. I want to make the most of my life and being permanently sad would make that very difficult.' He walked across the room to move a bowl of fruit from one side of the table to the other. His mind was racing away and he almost forgot where he was.

Gregor and Adam were staring at him, not quite sure what to do next with their distracted host.

Euan pulled himself together and cleared his throat. 'But I have lots of friends who could stop me being sad. Maybe they could tell me jokes to cheer me up.' He had come back into the present.

The boys were relieved. They hadn't upset Euan too badly and they always had jokes to cheer up adults.

'Adam has a new joke. Would you like to hear it now, Uncle Euan?' Uncle Euan nodded.

Adam blushed with the excitement of being pushed centre stage and Gregor had literally pushed him into the middle of the living room. 'There were four boys who went along to a fairground to see a juggler. One of the boys was Scottish, one was French, one was Spanish and one was German. They were all wee...'

'Just like Adam and me,' explained Gregor, who was bursting with pride at his friend's performance.

'Yes,' said Adam. 'They were all wee and because of that they could hardly see the juggler. The people in the crowd were all big and were blocking their view. But the juggler saw that the boys were having problems...'

'He was a very nice juggler,' explained Gregor.

'Yes,' said Adam patiently. 'He was a very nice juggler. So, he jumped up on to a table and said to the boys: "Can you see me now?" And they replied: "Aye! Oui! Si! Yah!" He and Gregor dissolved on the floor in laughter.

'Aye, we see you?' said Euan, trying to join in but aware that he was missing something.

Gregor and Adam called out in unison. 'Aye! Oui! Si! Yah!'

The penny dropped for Euan. 'Aye! Oui! Si! Yah!' He could laugh now and perhaps his laugh was louder than was really necessary, but it delighted his young visitors. He began to get his act together. He had learned a lot about friendship in the last year. It was important to remember absent friends but it felt even more important to connect with the ones you were with at any given time.

'Come on, you two comedians. I can see that there will be no time for me to be sad with you two around. But now we have to get off to Ashet to get stuck into the Year of the Dragon. Who knows, there might be some nice friendly jugglers waiting there for us.'

They walked down the tenement stairs together, laughing and anticipating an exciting New Year celebration with their friends. When they reached street level, they all gasped at the sight of a prominent graffito opposite them.

Dundee is....